What People Are S

Freebourn

This races off in top gear from the start and the pace never slackens. A true page-turner.
Nick Ferrari

Definitely a thinking reader's thriller. I was delighted to find that this wasn't a run-of-the-mill procedural, but rather a rich and complex story with such a shocking twist at the end that I was genuinely unprepared for it. It's the sort of revelation that makes the reader want to read the book again from start to finish, to look for any subtle hints or signs that the author may have seeded throughout. It's such a clever and intelligent narrative, especially the way the big secret is revealed. I also admired the way Salman Shaheen embeds politics, philosophy, religion and science into such a fast-paced story. It reminded me in its complexity of the novels of Barbara Vine (Ruth Rendell): grisly, shocking, darkly funny, with more twists and turns than Snake Pass.
Trezza Azzopardi, Booker-shortlisted author of *The Hiding Place*

Freebourne is a stunning debut from Salman Shaheen. Compelling, propulsive and endlessly surprising, it might just be the thriller of the year.
Charles Elton, bestselling author of Richard and Judy Book Club pick *Mr Toppit*

This is an edgy, fast-paced excursion into the near future, with a series of murders set against a background of artificial intelligence and opportunistic populist politics. It raises big questions about individual free will and whether moral codes can be overwritten by computer code.

Sean Coughlan, *BBC News*

Shaheen creates a recognisable universe before upending expectations with a series of violent twists and a denouement that had me gasping aloud. Midsomer Murders meets The Matrix. A riveting read.

Judith Woods, *The Telegraph*

A gripping murder mystery with a sci-fi flavour and an utterly original twist that keeps you guessing at every turn. Playing out in a convincing near-future setting, this riveting thriller grapples with the implications of unrelenting technological advancement and its impact on the human experience. One for the AI age.

Aristos Georgiou, *Newsweek*

Freebourne by Salman Shaheen is a standout debut. Shaheen explores the intersection of technology, morality, and justice with incredible nuance. The story grips you with its suspense while also offering a profound commentary on the human condition. With unforgettable characters, *Freebourne* is a thought-provoking and exhilarating read that keeps you hooked from start to finish. A truly compelling read from an extraordinary new voice.

Lord Bilimoria, CBE DL

Freebourne is a gripping thriller that blends suspense, science, and human nature into a compelling narrative that will keep you on the edge of your seat.

Channi Singh OBE, lead singer of Alaap and the 'godfather' of Bhangra in the West

Harry arrives in a new town and makes a horrific discovery — the body of a young woman in the snow. He is the witness to a murder. In an opening reminiscent of a film noir, the witness suddenly becomes a suspect. Salman Shaheen's writing style is lean and fast-paced, laced with brief, telling poetic descriptions. In this novel set in the immediate future, he sets up all the elements of a thriller, an incident that sets a life on a new, dangerous track, a secret lurking in the past. You will be hooked. I was.

Alan Gibbons, bestselling author of Blue Peter Book Award-winning *Shadow of the Minotaur*

A twisty debut thriller set in a near future that is both reassuringly familiar and frighteningly not. Nothing in *Freebourne* is quite as it seems, least of all the meaning of friendship, or what it means to be free.

Andrew Cowan, author of Sunday Times Young Writer of the Year Award-winning *Pig*

Freebourne raises timely questions about the future use of AI, for both good and bad, as well as social debates around free will that reminded me of one of my favourite novels of all time, *A Clockwork Orange*.

Attila the Stockbroker

Freebourne is a gripping, mind-bending thriller that will have you questioning reality at every turn. Prepare for a tension-filled ride where nothing is as it seems.

Andy Fryers, Sustainability Director, Hay Festival

An outstanding novel, full of suspense. Salman Shaheen's mind-bending, speculative thriller, with its richly drawn world and characters, will have you racing to the denouement and a twist that will knock you sideways. You won't be able to put it down.

Seema Malhotra MP, Parliamentary Under-Secretary of State in the Home Office

Freebourne is a brilliant novel from a great writer. Its beautiful setting and compelling characters draw you into an ever-deepening mystery where the stakes are at the same time highly personal and of huge national and political importance. The ending will take your breath away.

Ruth Cadbury MP

Beneath the picturesque façade of Freebourne's rural idyll lies something much darker. A cautionary tale about human freedom and the excesses of technology amid a page-turning hunt for a killer. *Freebourne* is a masterpiece and absolutely thrilling right up to its final moments. And then. Wow. The twist blew my mind.

Jaz Delorean, lead singer of Tankus the Henge

Salman Shaheen has crafted a classic thriller with a very modern twist for our AI age. It's like Black Mirror meets Broadchurch! The opening scenes are filled with horror and intrigue, giving way to a deepening sense of claustrophobia as we explore the town of *Freebourne* through Harry's eyes for the first time and uncover the secrets it holds.

Andria Zafirakou MBE, author of *Those Who Can, Teach* and *Lessons in Life*

A riveting and original read full of twists and turns that held my attention from beginning to end. Definitely one you won't want to miss.

James Bloodworth, author of *Hired* and *Lost Boys*

From the moment Harry steps off the train to discover her dead body, to the gut-punch of an ending that is both terrifying and ingenious and has you questioning everything that came before, *Freebourne* takes hold of you and it never lets go. It is an assured debut, brilliantly written and fiendishly plotted.

Vikas Pota, author of *India Inc* and Founder and CEO of T4 Education

Totally gripping! It had me hooked from the first line to the final, shocking conclusion. You'll never see it coming.

Jen Offord, author of *Sunday Times*-shortlisted *The Year of the Robin*

A masterpiece. Beautifully written and utterly compelling, *Freebourne* is one of those thrillers that just simmers, long after you've finished reading it. The twist is completely original and mind-blowing. *Freebourne* is one of the best thrillers I've ever read.

Karim Theilgaard, award-winning actor

What begins as a small-town murder mystery in the not-too-distant future turns into something wholly original that left me guessing throughout all its twists and turns until the final revelation.

Cllr Shantanu Rajawat, Leader of the London Borough of Hounslow

Freebourne

A novel

Salman Shaheen

Freebourne

A novel

Salman Shaheen

ROUNDFIRE
BOOKS

London, UK
Washington, DC, USA

CollectiveInk

First published by Roundfire Books, 2025
Roundfire Books is an imprint of Collective Ink Ltd.,
Unit 11, Shepperton House, 89 Shepperton Road, London, N1 3DF
office@collectiveinkbooks.com
www.collectiveinkbooks.com
www.roundfire-books.com

For distributor details and how to order please visit the 'Ordering' section on our website.

Text copyright: Salman Shaheen 2024

ISBN: 978 1 80341 925 1
978 1 80341 958 9 (ebook)
Library of Congress Control Number: 2024945942

A CIP catalogue record for this book is available from the British Library.

Design: Lapiz Digital Services

UK: Printed and bound by CPI Group (UK) Ltd, Croydon, CR0 4YY
Printed in North America by CPI GPS partners

We operate a distinctive and ethical publishing philosophy in all areas of our business, from our global network of authors to production and worldwide distribution.

For Alexander

Contents

Contents

Chapter One:

The Fault in Our Stars

Harry didn't know how long he'd been staring at her body lying lifeless on the verge, but he knew the moment when it came. When her blood finally surrendered its fight to melt the fresh snow falling on the blankness of her face. When the last trace of her humanity passed its event horizon and slipped out into a world cold enough to do something like this.

He couldn't move. He couldn't look away. Frozen in shock, the horror gripped him, tearing at every part of him till the chill air caught in his burning lungs and the tears welled in his eyes and at last he forced his face away. And still he could see her. Lying there, thick fur coat buttoned to her chin, an easy nothingness in her icy-blue eyes. And in them an inevitable conclusion. Someone had done this to her. Worse. Someone could do this to her. Even before he'd scrabbled for her frigid hand in search of a pulse, the sheer quantity of blood that had seeped onto the snow from the open wound at her temple told him it was futile. In that instant, he felt so small, so utterly powerless. He didn't even know her name. But there were people here in this town who must do. A mother and father waiting for her to come home. A boyfriend or maybe a girlfriend who'd expected to meet her that evening. People whose universes — still cushioned for a few more precious minutes of ignorance — he was about to shatter with the press of a button and a single word.

"Police."

Harry stayed by her side as the first stars pricked the night and the sodium-amber glow of the town at the bottom of the hill rose up to silhouette the pine copse, where the road wound its way down. He could feel his hands shaking and he knew it wasn't just the cold, but he cupped them anyway, blew on them, and pulled his long, black coat tighter about him. This was not how he imagined starting his new life. He'd barely stepped off the train from London and begun making his way down the hill towards the town when he'd spotted her lying there by the side of the road. If he'd arrived just a little earlier, was there something he could have done? There was no one else about. Freebourne was not the kind of place many people stopped at this time of year. Even so, whoever had done this had made no effort to conceal her body. It was almost as if they'd left her there for him to find.

A siren whooped once and the frozen penumbra was transformed into a bowl of swirling blue. Harry looked up to see two police officers stepping out of their car — a short woman and a wiry young man who couldn't have been more than a few years out of school. The policewoman wasted no time in hurrying over to inspect the body, but Harry could tell from her expression how quickly she'd given up any hope that this wouldn't be a murder investigation. As for the policeman — the way his eyes darted in quick succession from the body to his colleague to the ground and finally to Harry told him the young man had never seen anything like this in his life.

"Good evening, umm, sir. My name is PC Atkins. You're the person who called us?"

"Yes, it's Harry. Harry Coulson."

"Thank you, Mr, umm, Mr Coulson. I hope you won't mind coming, err, I mean, the thing is we'll need you to come down the station and give a statement."

Harry blinked back at the officer. The man's lips were moving but they were no longer making any sound. He knew he was still in shock. No one should have to see what he'd just seen. A person dead. Murdered. Even saying it to himself in his head sounded wrong. And yet something about this seemed all too familiar. Like another headline in another newspaper about another tragic waste of life. She'd be in the news soon. And all he could think about was her family. Every thread fraying out from the rip left in their lives now she was gone. He tried to close his eyes, but the afterimage of her was still there and it hurt. It hurt so much. Like nothing he'd ever felt before. Harry scrunched his face tight, gripping his temples and bending double as a lancing pain shot through him and stabbed at the back of his eyes.

"Sir?" PC Atkins said.

Everything seemed to be spinning.

"Are you alright?"

Harry pulled off his glasses and pinched the bridge of his nose as he tried frantically to dam an agony unlike anything he'd experienced.

"Sir, are you ok?"

"Yeah," Harry said at last, blinking away the pain, receding as quickly as it had come. "I don't know what... Yeah. Migraine."

"Did you hear what I said?"

"You want me to come down to the station."

"There's nothing to worry about sir, it's just routine. You're not under any suspicion."

The way both officers were looking at him now, Harry couldn't help but feel he was very much under suspicion. This wasn't how he'd intended to arrive in Freebourne, riding in the back of a police car, its rear lights illuminating the cordon disappearing from view behind them. But he wouldn't walk away. He couldn't. Somewhere in the haze, he could still recall the night of the accident. All those vehicles streaming past as he counted the drops of blood dripping from his head onto the roof of his upturned car to keep himself awake and he tried to mouth to his then-wife that it would all be ok and someone would come to help them as she screamed.

Maybe if a stranger had stopped sooner, they might not have lost everything they did. And he wouldn't be here, staring out of the window as they wound their way down the hill along the line of frost-bare trees raking the darkened firmament, over the low stone bridge where the little river marked the edge of town, through streets of Georgian and Tudor houses, past the medieval church by the green, dimly lit by heritage lanterns, past the brighter lights of the high street still packed with people who all turned to stare, and on to the police station on the corner by the sycamore tree.

The station was deserted except for the man yawning behind the front desk. It was hot in there and the LED lights were uncomfortably bright. Harry unbuttoned his coat, pulled off his bobble hat and ruffled his mess of black, grey-streaked hair. They ushered him into the interview room, sat him down and made him a cup of tea with too much milk. He'd finished it long before the two plainclothes officers — a squat, middle-aged Asian woman in a hijab and a slightly younger man with a pinched face and a receding hairline — entered the room and sat opposite him.

"I'm sorry to keep you waiting, Mr Coulson," the woman said. "My name is DCI Khan. This is DI Manning."

"Hi," Harry said, a little more nervously than he felt he should as a person who had done nothing wrong. He didn't feel now was the appropriate time to tell her it was actually Dr Coulson.

"You are here because you discovered the body of the victim in what we are now treating as a murder investigation. We are interviewing you as a witness. Do you understand?"

Harry nodded. He didn't need any advanced knowledge of criminology to know what he'd seen spattered in crimson across the white.

"Mr Coulson, if you nod or shake your head, I will explain for the record that you have done so. And for the record, I am explaining that Mr Coulson has just nodded his head. DI Manning will be taking notes of this interview."

"Sure."

"During this interview, we will talk to you about the crime scene you witnessed and confirm your movements immediately prior to your discovery of the victim's body. I will also ask you about anything else which may become relevant during the interview in order to properly establish the facts."

"Ok."

"I'd like to start by asking you to describe the events leading up to your discovery of the body."

"Ok, I, err... I'd just arrived, on the, umm, the train from London. I came out of the platform and I started walking down the hill into town. That's when I saw her lying by the roadside. I thought she must have been drunk at first. You'd have to be to want to lie down in that cold. I went over to see if she needed any help. But when I got closer, I saw the blood. There was so much blood. She must... She..." Harry closed his eyes. Her face was still there. He could feel the words choking in his throat. He opened his eyes again. "She must have been hit on the head, really hard. I don't know who could do something like this. Why."

"And that's when you called the police?"

"Yes."

"Straight away?"

"Well, sort of."

"Sort of?"

"I was in shock." Harry looked down at his hands and saw they were still shaking. "I am. I am in shock. I didn't know what to do at first. Maybe it took me a few minutes. A bit longer. But yes, I called the police and I waited there until your officers arrived."

DI Manning looked up from the tablet he'd been tapping notes into. "Can I just clarify — you said you were walking down the hill?"

"Yes," Harry replied.

"With that?" DI Manning nodded to the enormous suitcase sitting in the corner of the room that contained all that was left of Harry's old life.

"Have you ever been in one of those driverless taxis? No thanks."

"One of those Anthropros, are you?"

"No, as a matter of fact, I've spent the last two decades designing AIs."

"You've spent 20 years designing artificial intelligence and you wouldn't get in a driverless taxi?"

"Listen, I once worked on a computer that could emulate and exceed brain function to such a degree it could play simultaneous chess matches with a hundred grandmasters and win every single time. All the while giving such a perfect facsimile of human trial and error not one of those champions would ever guess they'd been beaten by a line of code. Why? Because it's a matter of logic. But would I ever get in a car being driven 60 miles per hour down the road by that computer? What happens when a child steps into the road and it is left to your AI to decide whether to run them over or swerve and send you into oncoming traffic? You can't programme ethics or moral philosophy. There's no algorithm yet invented that I would trust with that decision."

"We still have human bus drivers here."

"Honestly, I think I just fancied a walk to clear my head. It's been a long day. It's been a long few months, to tell the truth."

Harry thought about mentioning the divorce. But how would it help them to know that his ex-wife, having conducted a lengthy and by all accounts heartfelt and quite passionate affair with his old friend and erstwhile business partner, had forced him out of his house and his company? How would it help that poor girl's parents to know that he'd come to Freebourne in search of tabula rasa having tired of picking through the intricacies of his story in the courts and by the watercooler, only to find himself thrust into a story far more tragic? How would it help anyone to know what he'd lost, what he'd thrown away, when there was still the breath in his lungs to recount a night she never could? For Harry lived his life by seven simple rules. Seven guiding principles, which he had to admit he'd mostly stolen from the decades-old geek culture of his childhood but he knew made him a good person, and this was Rule 1: The Needs of the Many Outweigh the Needs of the Few or in This Case the One.

"Did you see anyone else in the area?" DCI Khan asked.

"No. There was no one."

"So to your knowledge, you were the only person in the vicinity at the time the victim's body was discovered?"

Harry nodded and swallowed the uncomfortable lump that was beginning to rise up in his throat.

"For the record, Mr Coulson nodded his head. Mr Coulson, was the victim known to you?"

Harry shook his head and then thought better of letting someone else put words on his body. "No. I've never seen her before. I'm new in town."

"Yeah, I'd say!" DI Manning almost-snorted in a way Harry couldn't help but find wholly unsympathetic. In fact, everything about the man was beginning to appal him for the reasons of Rule 2: The Day Will Come When You Won't Be. Harry didn't like to judge people, but when he did, he liked to imagine them in the kind of ruined, zombie-infested, post-apocalyptic wasteland that featured heavily in the TV programmes and computer games he once enjoyed. What would they be after the rule of law had broken down and all societal customs and conventions had been stripped away? That's the only way you could really know a person's character, in that state of nature guided only by one's own moral compass. And in humanity's bleak twilight, DI Manning would find himself the enthusiastic enforcer of some brutal warlord, maintaining the bloodthirsty new order every bit as judiciously and as joyfully as the old.

DCI Khan cleared her throat. "We've identified the victim as Serena Brandreth, the youngest daughter of Guy and Rosemary Brandreth. Have you heard of them?"

"No," Harry replied. Then he thought again. "Wait, not the property developers?"

"They own half of Freebourne. Probably one of the wealthiest families in Sussex."

"So you think there might be some sort of financial motivation?"

"We're investigating all possibilities, Mr Coulson. As you say, you're new in town. So I expect you won't know there's not been a murder in Freebourne since 1945."

Harry didn't know, but he could tell from the way DCI Khan explained that she'd told the story many times before. Probably everyone in this town had. The story of a farmer's son who went to war like a hundred other Freebourne farmers' sons believing he would be every bit as adept at shooting fascists as he was rabbits. Unlike most of those other sons, he returned, but the horrors of war came with him. They didn't have a name for his condition back then. Those were more barbaric times, when a nation's leaders could still turn a generation of innocent boys too young to vote for them into killers. He spattered his brains across the barn wall with a shotgun some months later, but not before he'd blown away his old headmaster outside the school gates, screaming something about authority. Freebourne had never seen anything like it before and it would never see anything like it again until today. And though Harry knew the police were not accusing him of anything, he couldn't help but feel they had far from dissuaded themselves from the coincidence that he had arrived as a stranger in town the same night it had witnessed its first murder in over a century.

DCI Khan smiled. "So what brings you to Freebourne, Mr Coulson?"

"I'm trying to set up this new MindTech company..."

"In Freebourne?" said DI Manning. "It's not exactly Silicon Valley, is it?"

"Things have been difficult. I wanted the space to think and be inspired. No distractions. I mean, it's a different mindset here. Everyone I've ever worked with back in London, they all talked about how they wanted to revolutionise this or harness that for the good of humanity, but all they ever really wanted to do was make a lot of money. Most were narcissists or Machiavellians if not outright psychopaths, and you wouldn't trust any of them to have your back when it came to it."

"But not you?"

"All I've ever wanted to do is help people."

"And how does your work help people?"

"I'm modelling a device that allows you to see into your memories and..."

"Seriously?"

"Yes, seriously. Well, if my calculations are correct. It's a wearable device that you can use to visualise your memories, identify traumatic experiences, and overcome them. Heal pain. Move on."

"That's some pretty advanced tech."

"Think of it like a guide. Lighting the way through the darkest parts of your brain. I call it Polaris. It will use an external neuro-linked AI which ... is not at all interesting for you, is it? Sorry. Is there anything else I can help you with?"

DCI Khan nodded. "Mr Coulson, I hope you won't mind us taking a DNA sample, just to eliminate you from our enquiries."

"Of course, if that will help."

"You didn't move or touch the body in any way, did you?" DI Manning said without pausing his tapping.

"No. I mean, I did check for her pulse."

"So we might expect to find your cells around the victim's wrist."

Harry nodded. "And her neck. Obviously, as when I couldn't find her..."

"Obviously."

"Thank you, Mr Coulson," DCI Khan said. "I believe we have everything we need for now."

DI Manning's face fell in a way that was impossible to conceal. "Ma'am?"

"We've prepared a witness statement which we'll need you to check and sign," DCI Khan continued without looking at her junior colleague.

"Ma'am, come on, seriously, you know that..."

DCI Khan's otherwise composed demeanour cracked as she shot her subordinate a warning glance. "DI Manning if you say one more word in front of the interviewee it'll be the last you utter this side of the table."

Harry eyed them warily. The police were holding something back, he was certain of it, but it didn't matter. All he wanted to do was conclude his civic duty and get out of there as quickly as possible.

"Is everything ok?" Harry said.

"Yes," DCI Khan said, turning her gaze back to him. "We're finished here. Of course, we may need to ask you some further questions. You're not planning on leaving town, are you?"

Harry shook his head. That was recorded too. DI Manning concluded his furious tapping and then passed Harry the tablet over the table and a digital pen. He looked over the statement they'd typed up for him. Everything he'd said had been accurately recorded, but to read it back it sounded so detached. Behind the lines of clinical description there was a life that wasn't because chance, or worse, design, saw her lying bloodied in the snow on Station Road, Freebourne at 5:18 p.m. on Friday 24 February. The machines into which he programmed artificial life could make decisions that seemed real and random, but everything was ultimately written, fated, they could be no more than intended. She had so much more in her. Fifty, maybe sixty years of learning, loving, living — a young woman's potential stolen from her and reduced to a few paragraphs and a space to sign a name. Harry signed it.

He allowed the police to usher him out of the door, into the corridor and into another room that contained a large metal refrigerator where he let them swab his cheek for DNA. When they'd finished and stepped back into the corridor he saw PC Atkins, half a dozen other officers, and an assortment of journalists and photographers crowded around a tall, black man in a navy suit as well cut as his cheekbones. Elliott Nwosu, MP for Freebourne and Battle, looked even more imposing than he did on the television and with good reason. His place in the zombie apocalypse was already assured. The vast melting pot that was society was like any kind of stew with that slick, unpalatable layer of oil that, no matter how vigorously the pot was stirred, would always end up back at the top. Once a junior minister and rising star in the former PM's administration, Nwosu had swiftly found himself out of favour when she was ousted by her own party over leaked documents that revealed she was negotiating to bring Britain back into the EU. There were some who suspected Nwosu himself of the leak, but in politics those who wield the knife, no matter how well they buried it and where, rarely get to wear the crown. After a failed leadership bid, he found himself on the backbenches with a far better view of the new Prime Minister's back. He'd since reinvented himself as the fiercest defender of the people of Freebourne and its surrounding towns and it was hardly surprising to find him here, like a fly drawn to the opportunity of a carcass, inserting himself into the story of a community's collective heartbreak.

"I want to thank you, all of you, our fine policemen and women for everything you do every day to keep our community safe," Nwosu was saying to the officers gathered around him without ever taking his eyes off the cameras. "A great and terrible tragedy has befallen our town, one that will touch us all. I have every confidence that you will bring the person responsible for this reprehensible crime to justice. Know that you have my full support. Thank you."

Harry caught Nwosu's eye as he pulled his suitcase past him down the corridor. Everything about the man's face was hitting all the right notes of solemnity and earnest empathy. But where were career politicians like him when his mother, who'd run a small charity helping the homeless, was crying herself to sleep every night as government after government cut their funding and she had to watch what numbers on a balance sheet cost in human terms? He'd hear her talk about the battered and abused women running for their lives only to freeze on the streets with needles in their arms, years of hurt hollowed out by narcotic stares, and it would break his heart to see her collapse into tears when she didn't know he was watching, because for all their talk no one in charge would do anything to help. Politicians like Nwosu didn't come out for those women on those streets.

Someone was screaming. A pained howl growing louder and louder with every step as DCI Khan and DI Manning led Harry down the corridor until he pushed his way through the double doors into reception and he saw her. A woman standing wailing, her head of curly, grey hair burrowed into the lapels of the thin, bald man holding onto her, tears in his eyes too. Serena's parents were here. Harry wished there was something he could say, anything, to ease their suffering. He would always remember how he felt when he lost his mother so young to the last wave of the pandemic all those years ago, and his father far more recently to cancer. But even then, that was the natural order of things. It wasn't meant to work the other way. And he longed to tell them how sorry he was. To find their precious daughter like that. Alone. But there were no words. And all he could do was avert his gaze as the man looked up at him, but not quick enough.

"What is it?" Mr Brandreth said, dabbing his eyes with his handkerchief.

"I just..." Harry began.

"Out with it."

"I'm sorry. I was the one who..."

Suddenly Mrs Brandreth looked up, her eyes puffy and red and flashing from grief to an inconsolable rage as she caught sight of Harry looking terrified and flanked by two high-ranking detectives. "You!" she howled, launching herself towards Harry. "It was you, wasn't it?"

"Please Mrs Brandreth," Harry cried, taking two steps back as she lunged for him only to find he'd just backed into a wall of reporters, every camera aimed at his face.

"You killed my baby girl!"

Chapter Two:

It's About How Hard You Can Get Hit and Keep Moving Forward

"Mrs Brandreth, no..." Harry began but he didn't get far.

"You did it!" Mrs Brandreth shrieked. "I know you did!"

"Darling, please!" Mr Brandreth was straining to hold back his wife. "We don't know..."

"It had to be! It had to be!"

"Madam please, I'm going to have to ask you to step back," DCI Khan was saying but even her commanding voice was drowned by Mrs Brandreth's pained screaming as her arms flailed wildly for Harry's throat or eyes to tear at them.

A dictaphone appeared in Harry's face. "Aakesh Lal, Freebourne Herald," the young Asian man with the ponytail holding it was saying. "Sir, do you have anything to say in response to these allegations?"

A TV camera came at Harry from the other side, the red-haired woman with thick black glasses in front of it brandishing a microphone at him. "Harper Sloane, BBC South East. Please, tell us your side of the story."

"I didn't kill anyone, I just found her," Harry was trying to shout back but he too found his voice lost.

"Mr Coulson has been assisting us with our enquiries," DCI Khan was insisting but absolutely no one was listening until the sonorous tones of Elliott Nwosu's voice broke through the febrile atmosphere like rain on a hot day.

"Ladies and gentlemen, please," Nwosu said and everyone fell silent as he stepped forward, hands clasped. "I know we all have so many questions in the face of this evil act that has ripped our community apart and robbed the two most loving parents anyone could ever imagine, my good friends Guy and Rosemary, of their precious daughter. I know we are all afraid. But we will find who did this, Rosemary, I promise you that. I promise everyone here that we will see justice served. Our tireless police officers will see to it that no stone goes unturned. I urge everyone to do everything they can to assist them. If you can think of anything, any little detail, no matter how insignificant it may seem to you, then I urge you to come forward. Anything at all out of the ordinary."

Harry didn't like the way the MP turned to look at him as he said that last part. Nwosu might have saved him from being strung up there and then for a crime he did not and could never commit, but Harry understood all too well that he was the unordinary in this town, the variable no one could account for. He wouldn't wait for the cameras and the dictaphones to turn back in his direction, or for the barrage of questions to come. He just slipped as quietly as he could out of the door and into the cold night.

A crowd had already gathered outside the police station. Thirty, maybe forty people clustered under the sycamore tree. Some of them were young, late twenties at most, no older than Serena, hugging and holding onto one another, exchanging tearful glances. But there were others in the crowd with drier eyes and smartphones held aloft, jostling to the front, circling as they caught sight of Harry heaving his suitcase down the steps. The cameras on their phones and glasses flashed at him as he pushed his way past and the anger in his face flashed back. It would be all over the metaverse soon. Fear and outrage traded for clicks, views, shares, likes, influence, vanity. A young woman was dead and all these people cared about was collecting experiences. Tourists in the misery of others.

Harry kept on walking until they were out of sight. He stopped on the corner by an old Tudor house sliding out above him into the street. There was a smell of woodsmoke in the air. He breathed it in and he breathed deeply, for the first time allowing his mind to comprehend the enormity of everything he'd just witnessed. A girl murdered. And for what? He'd seen the look in her parents' eyes. He'd seen her friends there in the crowd. Serena was loved. Why would anyone do this? Was it for money? Or was it something even baser? Even more despicable. Had they done something to her first? Something he couldn't even say to himself in his head. Or had she got herself into some kind of trouble with someone? Someone out there. Harry glanced around. The night was quiet and still. Except. What was that? For a moment, he thought he heard a noise behind him. He turned to see a shadow move. He strained to look but it was gone. Was there someone there? Were they following him? No. No. Shaking the uncomfortable feeling away, he tapped the button on the side of his glasses.

"Time," he said. The time flashed up in red numbers in front of his eyes. It was 9:46 p.m. Far too late to pick up the keys from the estate agent today and he was close to collapsing. He'd have to find somewhere else to stay tonight.

"Room to rent," he said and the options appeared on his glasses' display. He scrolled through them with his eyes, swiftly eliminating the Penrose, Freebourne's exorbitantly priced five-star hotel, and the dingy motel on the main road out of town. Half the pubs seemed to have rooms above them that had probably sat empty since the summer influx of tourists and the nearest was The 319.

"Directions," he said and a set of blue augmented reality footprints sprang up on the snow-covered cobbled street in front of him and he followed them until he arrived at the old red brick fire station with the pink neon sign that had been converted into The 319.

Pushing his way in to a waft of stale booze, he found himself surrounded by exposed brick and industrial metal, dimly lit by filament bulbs and adorned with bicycles, record sleeves and electric guitars, American memorabilia from another age, and framed colourful squiggles that someone probably thought of as art. A crowd of young Metaheads, dressed in the same cartoonish clothes these people tended to use for their digital avatars to blur the lines between the worlds they walked, was gathered around an old VR arcade machine on one side of the room, laughing and drinking. There was a middle-aged man with big glasses sitting and chatting with a younger woman on the vintage sofa in the corner. An ageing hipster with a bushy grey beard and a faded tattoo creeping up his neck was standing behind a bar made of what looked like reclaimed driftwood, pouring a pint of beer and handing it to a heavy-set man in a pinstripe suit with a face hewn like an Easter Island head. The man in the suit was on the phone and clearly engaged in a heated discussion and he took the glass without ever glancing up at the barman.

"Thank you," the big man in the suit was saying. "No, I wasn't talking to you. Why would I thank you? What could I possibly have to fucking thank you for? I don't care what he's paying me, it's nowhere near enough. This is the biggest fucking fuck up I've ever fucking seen in my entire fucking career and who the fuck has to clean up this fucking mess? Fuckins over here!"

Harry tried to catch the barman's attention as he walked up to the bar. "Hi there," he said. "Excuse me," he said louder this time, raising his voice to be heard over the swearing man verbally eviscerating the unfortunate individual on the other end of the line and the sound of Rupert Holmes blasting out his timeless desire for a woman who liked pina coladas from the flashing jukebox in the corner.

"Yes mate," the barman said, turning to Harry. "What'll it be?"

"Err..."

"Don't have any Err."

"Umm..."

"Don't have any Umm neither. Got rum. Kind of stuff that'll put hairs on your chest, then set them on fire. Then spray you with a fire extinguisher. Only someone replaced the water in it with hydrochloric acid. You look like you could do with one of them."

"Just a beer please," Harry said, though he had to admit to himself the rum sounded tempting after the day he'd had. "One of those IPAs. What do you recommend?"

"Satan's Asshole."

"Ok."

"Coming right up," the barman replied, grabbing a pint glass, chucking it in the air like he was a mixologist in a much better establishment, catching it and bringing it to the tap in front of him.

"I saw you have rooms to rent here."

"Yes, we do. We do indeed. Right you are."

"Great, well could I rent one please."

The barman handed Harry his pint and a little white digital pad displaying its price. "Eleven eighty, please. Sure, let me check with the owner."

Harry tapped the button on the side of his glasses and looked down at the pad. "Pay," he said and then looked back up at the barman. "You're not the owner?"

"Oh what, you see a guy with a big beard and sailor tats who's been wearing flannel shirts before and long after they were cool and you automatically go and assume he owns a bar like this? That's discrimination man."

"Sorry, I..."

The barman laughed. "I'm just yanking your chain mate. Yeah, I'm the owner. Name's Chris."

Harry took a large gulp of beer and forced a polite but insincere laugh out of his mouth. "I'll take that room then."

Chris winked. "Like I said, gotta check with the owner. My owner. Y'know, the wife."

"Right," Harry said into his glass as Chris walked off into the back room singing to himself. He was in no mood for jokes and certainly not misogynistic ones about marriage. All he wanted was to finish his pint, put his head down for the night and, in the morning, pick up the keys to his new place and the pieces of his life as quietly as possible. A few feet away the man in the suit was still swearing into his phone.

"Yes, don't worry, I'm here in fucking Fuckbourne. Yes I have. Yes he is. Yes she fucking is. Hopefully fucking doing her fucking job like I should be doing. Oh just fucking bye ok." The man hung up the phone and slammed it down on the bar. "Prick."

"Rough day?" Harry said, glancing over at the swearing man who had fixed the big black tyre tracks of his eyebrows into a vengeful scowl at his nearly empty beer like he was going to attack it. "You and me both. Can I get you another one?"

The man looked up at Harry, regarded him for a moment, and, without another word, turned and walked out of the bar. Harry shook his head in disbelief. When he'd picked up that glossy magazine in his solicitor's office — a double page spread of bucolic images and purple prose on Freebourne's rural idyll — it was all a 42-year-old unemployed divorcee needed to believe this was the perfect place to start again. It never warned him about this. But these were strange times. People were afraid and Harry couldn't blame them for that. He was afraid too. Terrified to close his eyes for fear her face would still be there staring back at him in the dark. Even more so that someone out there had killed Serena and they were still out there because the police didn't have the first idea who they were. He glanced anxiously around him. The crowd by the arcade machine had already begun to stare at him. They were speaking in hushed tones, but by the way they were almost all checking their phones or tapping their glasses and then looking back at him, he could imagine what they were saying. The stocky, middle-aged man with the beard and the oversized glasses sitting on the sofa with a woman young enough to be his daughter, but who was evidently not his daughter by the hand he had on her knee, had yet to clock Harry; the pair were too engrossed in their devices, but he could hear them talking about him.

"He did it, he's the one, it was him," the man was saying, pointing his finger at his phone.

"You really think so, David?" said the young woman.

"Just look at those eyes."

"He's pissed off some dick shoved a camera in his face. Wouldn't you be?"

"This was a safe town before that man arrived. I can't believe she's gone."

"I know what she meant to you David, I know you're hurting, but don't kid yourself. If you knew what it's like being a woman, how it feels walking home alone at night, even in Freebourne, you wouldn't think it's safe."

"Look here," David said, thrusting his phone in the young woman's face. "The Freebourne Herald is saying he's the one who found her body."

"Yes, it says he's the one who called the police."

"Then why is Serena's mother accusing him?"

"She's just lost her daughter. She's not thinking straight. Grief does crazy things to you."

"It was him! I know it was!"

Harry felt that flash of anger return and he slammed his glass down on the bar. "Are you all having a good look?" he cried and the room fell silent. "Are you? Well? This isn't gossip. A girl's dead! Just think about that. Her parents, her friends, they'll never see her again. She's dead and I didn't fucking kill her, ok? I didn't. You don't know what it's like, finding someone like that. It's horrible. It's really fucking horrible."

"You'd say anything!" David cried, leaping to his feet and pointing his finger at Harry.

"I tried to help her!"

"Let's see if the DNA agrees."

"I didn't do this!"

"Because if you're lying, well..."

Harry gripped his throbbing temples. "Please, just shut up. Shut up!"

"Alright mate," Chris said, re-appearing behind the bar. "I think it's time for you to go."

Harry wiped away a tear from his eye. He felt like he'd been punched in the gut. "What about the room?"

"Sorry mate, got nothing."

Harry slapped his glasses. "It says you have two rooms available."

"Yeah, but not for you."

The place detonated into noise again as Harry grabbed his suitcase and fled the bar, past David glowering at him through his big glasses and every other pair of eyes that followed him as he went. The tears were flowing freely now and he didn't know why. Were they for her? The life of a young woman with so much ahead of her stolen by some monster for reasons he did not know and would never be able to understand. Or were they for his life? Everything he'd lost these last few months — his wife, his best friend Ben, a business he'd loved and nurtured from its infancy — and everything he'd hoped to find worth living for again in Freebourne now falling apart under the harsh gaze and harsher words of some frightened people. It was then that he decided to call her.

"Call... umm..." Harry paused. "Call ahhh..." he stopped again, alarmed to realise that for less than a second amid everything that had happened his ex-wife's name had momentarily left his head before it came rushing back again and with it the deluge of memories, beautiful and painful — that first kiss in the nightclub at Old Street after they'd tired of shouting in each other's ears on the dancefloor, their first date walking along the river down South Bank to the smell of caramelised nuts, the sunshine and smiles on their wedding day, the morning she woke him up to tell him he was going to be a father, the car crash that ended it all, waking up from surgery only to learn about the miscarriage, the long hours throwing himself into his work while she threw herself into a bottle, the longer, slow drift that ended the day he found her like that with him and it almost wasn't a surprise but it took his world apart all the same and with it the one person he'd always had to talk to when there was no one else. "Call Melanie."

She didn't answer.

Harry closed his eyes and repeated to himself Rule 3: It Ain't About How Hard Ya Hit, It's About How Hard You Can Get Hit and Keep Moving Forward. This was for the best. It was. It was for the best. What would he have said to her if she'd picked up? He didn't know. That was the truth. But he knew the days of burdening her with his problems were over. He was going to sort his own life out. That's what his father would have told him to do if he were still here. For all his kindness and his wisdom, Harry's dad had been a tough man — he had to be growing up partially sighted and in poverty on a Hackney council estate. He never let that stand in the way of forging a successful career as a doctor through hard work and an iron resolve he'd instilled in his only son. Harry could still picture his face. Hear his voice telling him what he needed to do. That he had to let it go. Just like they'd let his mother go. That lives divide, just as our cells divide, making imperfect copies of us all, and we are changed, and we may barely recognise who we once were, but as the inheritors of ourselves it is our duty to go on. He would go on. He would move into his new home, he would start his new tech business, he would get to work on Polaris, on his great dream, and it would make everything better. Just as soon as he could get some sleep.

The nearest place now with a room to rent was The Barley Mow. It was a fifteenth-century coaching inn nestled on the corner of the green opposite the church, its exposed black timber and white plaster covered in ivy and the skeletal tendrils of wisteria and illuminated by the warm amber glow of the heritage lanterns. Heaving open the heavy wooden door, Harry's face was greeted by a wall of heat crackling out from the blazing log fire in the old stone hearth. A spindly, golden-haired vicar with a moustache and a dog collar that added years to his otherwise very young face was enjoying a drink in front of it. The priest, whose name appeared to be Reverend Vinicombe if the little chalk table reservation sign was anything to go by, wasn't wearing any technology. He was just sitting there dabbing something off his black cassock with his handkerchief and he barely glanced twice at Harry as he wheeled his suitcase past, stepping over a black cat preening itself on the flagstones and stooping to avoid hitting his head on the low hops-draped wooden beams as he made his way to the bar. There was no one behind it, but there was a little brass reception bell sitting on top. Harry slapped it and pulled up a stool to wait. It wasn't long before someone appeared — a little lady in a baggy green fleece with short grey hair and grey eyes that exploded into beaming crow's feet as she greeted him with a big smile.

"Well hello there sweetie," she said clapping her hands together. "I've not seen you around before, which means either you're lost or you've come in search of the best bloody pub in all of Freebourne in which case you're very much found. I'll give you the usual spiel. My name's Grace Parry, I'm 29 years old and have been for the last two decades, I run this place with my six cats — Chico, Harpo, Groucho, Gummo, Zeppo and Karl — we serve 14 types of ale and they're all fricking lush, the wi-fi code is on the back of your beer mat but I wouldn't bloody bother because it's never working anyway, in the event of a fire please prepare to burn to death cause there aren't any fire exits. Any questions? No, good. What can I get you?"

Harry couldn't help but smile back. "Actually, I was wondering if I could rent a room for the night?"

"Certainly you can, sweetie. It's just you, right? One night? No problem. Let me go fetch you a key."

Grace bounced off as quickly as she'd been speaking. Harry was glad at least one person in Freebourne still didn't know who he was. She'd find out soon enough. The television on the far side of the room had the news on and that BBC reporter who'd shoved a microphone at him earlier, Harper Sloane, was speaking to the camera outside the police station.

"And though there appears to be no evidence that the 28-year-old victim was sexually assaulted, the police are treating this as a murder investigation," the reporter was saying. Harry saw his face pop up on screen. "Serena Brandreth's body was found earlier this evening by a man named Harry Coulson. His statement could prove vital in the hours and days ahead as police continue their hunt for a killer whose crime has shaken this town to its core."

Harry pinched his temples; he could feel the first pangs of his headache returning.

"You're him, aren't you?" a voice came from his left and he glanced over to see a tall, blonde woman in an expensive-looking red coat sitting at the bar next to him holding a pint. Harry observed her for a second, but only a second. She had streaks of green running through the waves of her bob cut and she was wearing a silver Ankh pendant around her neck. Her eyes were keen and dark and for some reason they were smiling at him. If today had turned out differently, he might have smiled awkwardly back at someone as attractive as her sparking up a conversation with him, but he just looked away, shaking his head.

"Please, just leave me alone," he said.

The woman raised her thick, dark eyebrows. "Sorry, I... I didn't mean anything by it."

"Anything by what? That you think I did it, like everyone else in this town, just because I was the one to find her lying there on the ground covered in blood and I had to stand there and watch, just watch, all that time waiting for the police because it was the right thing to do but those images, they don't go away. They won't. I can still see it. Her face..."

"Actually, I think what you did took so much courage. If only there were more people in the world like you. You shouldn't listen to all that stuff online. I think..."

Harry wasn't interested in what she thought. He wasn't interested in what anyone thought anymore. He was tired and his head hurt and the room was beginning to spin and all he wanted was to lie down and forget, but the television was still blaring and on screen there flashed an image of the police cordon and the place where he found her and the vision of her blank and bloodied face staring up at the stars came flooding back, her mousy-brown hair caked in crimson, the picture etched behind his eyes and with it the pain, the lancing, stabbing pain and he tried to blink it away again but it was growing worse and the room was getting darker and he was trying to stand but it was all too much.

Harry took two steps forward and then everything went black.

Chapter Three:

St Jude's

"Good morning, it's Harry isn't it?"

Harry opened his eyes to find himself lying on a bed surrounded by blue curtains. He was in his t-shirt and there was a plaster over the vein on the inside of his left elbow. There was a bitter smell of antiseptic in the air. Squinting without his glasses, the cardiac monitor slowly loomed into view and just the sight of it sent his heart rate leaping. A short, East Asian woman in teal scrubs was standing over him holding a clipboard.

"Dr Coulson?" she said.

"Yeah?" he replied groggily, rubbing his eyes.

"I'm Dr Chang. Do you know where you are?"

Harry forced himself to give a withered smile. "Well, I've just been in a police station and a fire station, so I'm guessing I've gone for the hat trick."

Dr Chang didn't laugh at his attempt to mask the rising anxiety he was feeling with gallows humour. He'd always remember his mum lying on a bed like this, joking with the nurses and doctors until — intubated and connected to a mechanical ventilator — she was no longer able to speak. He didn't know if she could hear him at the end, but he told her anyway: how much he loved her, the memories of childhood he'd never forget, her values of kindness and compassion he'd always keep with him, his hopes for the future — all those years she was meant to see distilled into one last teary soliloquy and a kiss on her forehead.

"You're in St Jude's Hospital," Dr Chang said. "You arrived unconscious last night. How are you feeling?"

Harry thought about it for a moment. The pain was gone. The room wasn't spinning. The strip lights above his head were a little too bright but objectively so. "Fine, I think. I'm fine. Yes, fine."

He said it again and again trying to convince himself it was the truth, but he was anything but fine. What was he doing in hospital? How had he even got there? Had he really been passed out for hours? Was that normal? That wasn't normal, was it? He'd never felt anything like that before. Something was wrong. Was he ok? Was he sick? Was he dying? He could feel the sweat on his palms. He tried to slow his breathing.

"Please try to stay calm," Dr Chang said in a reassuring voice. "I'm pleased to say your bloods have come back clear. We've run an MRI scan and there don't appear to be any physical brain abnormalities."

Harry breathed in deeply, trying to process everything he was hearing. "That's good, isn't it?"

"Yes. There's no indication of any tumour. I can see that you've had some surgery in the past."

Harry felt the scar at his temple. "I was in a car accident, it was bad, but that was years ago. It can't be that, can it? The doctors said I made a full recovery. I have, haven't I?"

Dr Chang nodded. "I can only concur with my learned colleagues. I don't believe we are seeing any complications from the surgery."

"Then what's wrong with me, doctor? Please tell me. Because I've never felt anything like that before. The pain it... and then I was just... it all went blank."

"The EEG, which we use to monitor brain waves, showed a slight decrease in low-frequency oscillations in the right temporoparietal region of your brain. Have you experienced anything traumatic recently?"

"Yes. I was the one who discovered Serena Brandreth's body. What's that got to do with anything?"

Dr Chang scribbled a note on her clipboard. "That must have been terrible. I can only imagine what you've been through.

Have you had any other symptoms besides the pain and the blackout? Concentration problems? Memory loss?"

"I forgot my ex-wife's name for a second. Oh god. What does that mean?"

"It's likely you're suffering from post-traumatic stress disorder."

Harry saw his heart reading spike again. "PTSD? You mean like that soldier who came back and shot his headmaster?"

Dr Chang smiled warmly. "In my professional opinion, I don't think you're a danger to anyone, Dr Coulson."

"You must be the only person in Freebourne who thinks that." Harry sighed. "So what now? Is it therapy? Is that what I need? Am I going to be ok?"

"Two out of three people who develop these sorts of problems after a traumatic experience find they get better on their own within a few weeks. I'm going to recommend we monitor your symptoms for now and see whether they improve. You should book an appointment with a GP in a month's time. If you experience any more headaches, take some paracetamol. In the meantime, try to avoid stressful situations."

Harry inhaled and exhaled deeply again. He could hear someone moaning in agony a few beds away. "They seem to be finding me at the moment."

"Just try and get some rest, ok?"

"Ok."

Dr Chang turned to go and then stopped and turned back. "Oh, there's someone here to see you. Lauren, she said her name was."

Harry frowned. "I don't know a Lauren."

"She was the one who called the ambulance when you collapsed. She waited with you till the paramedics arrived. She was very helpful, I'm told. Just over there." Dr Chang looked behind her and waved. "You can come in now."

Harry propped himself up and reached for his glasses on top of his suitcase by the bed to see the tall blonde woman in the red coat from the pub the night before emerging from behind Dr Chang. She was smiling at him and it was spreading dimples across her face. It was infectious. Harry couldn't help but smile back until he felt self-conscious and guilty and stopped. He noticed his heart rate increase again and he hoped she hadn't.

"I'm so glad to see you're looking better," Lauren said. "Not that you could have looked much worse."

Dr Chang scribbled on her clipboard, tore off a sheet of yellow paper and handed it to Harry. "I'm discharging you now." She turned to Lauren and added: "You make sure he gets some rest."

"Sure," Lauren said as Dr Chang walked off down the ward. "You heard the doctor, Harry."

Harry looked up at Lauren and all of a sudden, he felt irritated. Why was she still here? What was she even doing there? Looking at him like that in this undignified moment. He didn't want her pity. All he wanted, all he'd ever wanted since coming to this town, was to be left alone.

"You can go now," he snapped. "It's not your job to look after me."

Lauren stroked her chin unfazed. "Yeah, well, I'm still going to give you a lift home all the same."

He blinked slowly and opened his eyes again. He felt bad and said, "I'm sorry."

"What for?" she grinned disarmingly. "Being a prick last night or being a prick today?"

Harry burst out laughing and almost didn't realise it was the first time he'd laughed in seven months. "Both. I was rude. And you didn't deserve that. I'd probably still be passed out on that pub floor if the rest of this town had their way."

"In your defence, you'd had a pretty shitty day. I should have known better than to poke my nose into it."

29

"You were only trying to be kind. Which is more than I can say for everyone else in Freebourne."

"You'll get used to them. Come on. I'm going to grab a coffee while you get dressed. Then I'll give you a lift. You want a coffee?"

"I'm fine, thanks."

"You sure? Don't want you falling asleep on me again!"

Harry rolled his eyes. "Har har! Go."

His gaze lingered on her for a moment as she walked off and then he shook the thought away. Too soon. Way too soon. Harry unhooked himself from the cardiac monitor, climbed out of bed, pulled on his woolly jumper and his coat, quickly called the estate agent, then grabbed his suitcase and wheeled it out of the ward and into the corridor past beds of pale people looking a lot sicker than he did and he met her by the vending machine where she was fitting a bioplastic lid on top of her cup.

"What did you get?" he asked, trying and failing to make conversation as they headed into the lift. He wished he was better at small talk.

"Flat white, obvs." Lauren pressed the button for the basement.

"Oat milk?" he tried and failed again. "I like oat milk."

"Fuck that. You're not vegan, are you?"

"Not quite. Tried it for a bit."

Lauren wrinkled her nose. "Me too. What was it for you?"

"Cheese. All the cheese."

"Eggs for me. And bacon. And sausages. Black pudding. Basically, there's a universe where Lauren Fontaine loves animals and the planet and being healthy and there's a universe where she loves English breakfasts and we're in that one."

"Ha! How's the coffee?"

Lauren took a sip. "Great, actually. Better than half the places on the high street. I really only came here for the coffee."

"Is it too late to say I want one now?"

Lauren cuffed him playfully around the back of the head and handed him the rest of her coffee as the lift dinged and the doors opened. Was she flirting with him? Harry couldn't be sure. And was he flirting back? Again, he couldn't tell; it had been so long since he'd allowed himself to do so. But whatever it was it felt good. Why should he feel guilty? He'd been blamed long enough. She walked out into the car park and he followed her to her car — a sleek black Tesla in a wireless charging bay along the back wall.

"Nice car," he said, heaving his suitcase into the boot as she popped it open.

"Thanks," she replied, opening the door and climbing into the driver's seat. "You drive?"

"No." Harry got into the passenger seat next to her. He hadn't driven since the accident. He could still remember the little girl's wide eyes in his headlights as she stepped out into the road. It was raining. Melanie was screaming. There was a car coming at them fast the other way, but Harry knew he had to swerve. He wasn't going to kill a child. In the end, it was his unborn child that died and, in time, his marriage.

"Where are we going?" Lauren asked as she pulled out of the bay.

It was Saturday and the estate agent was closed, but the young man who'd sold him the house had agreed to meet him at the door to his new place with the keys. Harry told Lauren the address and she drove them out of the car park into the crisp, bright morning sun. St Jude's was up in the hills surrounding Freebourne, just outside of town. Harry gazed out the window at the fields and hedgerows rolling past as they wound their way down. Most of the snow had melted now, leaving little pools of blackened slush and clumps of ice like coal by the roadside. The news was playing on the radio.

"Pressure is mounting on the UK government to meet its quota of climate refugees after Germany announced it would be taking in an additional 500,000 people forced to flee their countries due to widespread droughts and crop failures across Sub-Saharan Africa," the anchorman was saying. "Protests outside Downing Street turned violent last night after Anthropros called on the government to ban experimental research on human brain editing. Nine people were arrested and a police officer was injured after clashes lasting almost two hours."

"Not that lot again," Harry groaned.

"Who?" Lauren said as they reached the foot of the hills and she turned them onto a country lane.

"Those Anthropros."

"I don't know, maybe they've got a point. Not the way they make it, obviously, that's too much but... Listen I'm a scientist and even I think sometimes science and technology go too far."

"Maybe, but where's the line?"

"When it changes what it means to be human even if that means being flawed? When it takes away the freedoms nature gave us? Man is born free, Jean-Jacques Rousseau said, but everywhere he is in chains."

"I suppose," Harry replied but he wasn't really listening as the newsreader had moved on to a story much closer to home and much more painful to hear.

"Tributes continue to pour in for Freebourne murder victim Serena Brandreth," the newsreader said. "Friends described her as 'loyal', 'intelligent', 'loving', 'the life and soul of every party'. David Castle, Serena's former science teacher, called her 'the most gifted student he had ever taught'."

Lauren reached over to change the station. "You probably don't want to listen to that."

"No, leave it, please," Harry said.

"I'm pretty sure your doctor wouldn't recommend it."

"I want to listen."

"Police have been analysing forensic evidence at the scene, but so far, according to Serena's mother, Rosemary, it seems the only DNA they have recovered from the victim's body belongs to Harry Coulson," the newsreader said. "For more on this, I'm joined by our correspondent Harper Sloane. Harper, what does…"

Lauren switched the radio off. "Stop it."

"Stop what?" Harry said through clenched teeth.

"What you're doing to yourself. Or I'll have to turn around and drive you right back to hospital and I can't drink any more coffee today."

"You heard what they just said."

"It doesn't mean anything. They know you were at the scene; you were trying to help. All this means is whoever did this was someone clever enough not to leave any trace."

"I guess." Harry exhaled deeply. Somehow, whether it was her words or simply her presence, she was making him feel calmer, happier. Safer. He could see a township of frightened survivors banding together behind her in the zombie apocalypse.

"Now, are you going to behave yourself or am I going to have to take another St Jude's flat white for the team?" Lauren punched him gently on the arm and that had to be flirtatious, didn't it? Surely, he almost caught himself hoping, but then it was too soon.

Harry smiled. "I'm going to behave myself."

"Good, because we're here," Lauren said pulling up the car. "Wow, look at that. You bought this?"

It looked just as beautiful as in the brochure. The old, grey stone house standing tall and alone by the river on the edge of town was once a watermill, its great wooden wheel, though long since jammed, still jutting out and down towards the water shimmering in the sunlight below. There was a little bridge outside by the weeping willow bending its bough to the river.

On the far bank, the woods stretched back up the hill as far as the eye could see. A set of weathered stone steps led up to the house's elevated oak front door, battered by the wind and the rain and time. A young, impeccably dressed Asian man with short, curly hair and thick black-rimmed glasses was standing on the bottom step. Catching sight of the car pulling up in front of the gate, the man bounded down the path to greet them.

"Hi, it's Sachin," the man said, extending his hand as Harry got out of the car and pulled his suitcase from the boot. "Sachin Roy. We spoke on the phone. I've got the keys here for you."

Harry took his hand. "Thank you for coming down here." He turned back to Lauren who had wound the car window down to say goodbye. "And thank you, Lauren. I really appreciate everything you've done for me."

She smiled up at him. "It was nothing. I wouldn't say anyone would have done the same because the world's full of selfish pricks and I'm pretty awesome, but hey, it was nice meeting you. I'll see you around hopefully."

"Not if I see you first," Harry replied and instantly regretted it as he watched her wind up the window and drive off up the tree-lined country lane. "That was stupid," he muttered to himself. "Why did I say that?"

"Yeah, that was literally the dumbest thing I've ever heard," Sachin laughed.

"I sounded like a stalking weirdo."

"You got her number though, right?"

"Just shut up and give me the keys."

Sachin pulled out a set of keys from the inside pocket of his immaculately pressed three-piece suit. "There's a knack to it. Let me show you."

The estate agent ushered Harry through the low wooden gate in the fence and up the path through the spacious front garden, where snowdrops and crocuses were already flowering in the grass. Sachin climbed the steps and showed Harry how to wedge his knee against the door and push up as he turned the key in the lock. They stepped into a high-ceilinged hallway with stone walls and rustic wooden beams brightly lit by a shaft of light streaming onto the floorboards through the window above the door. At the end of the hallway was a far more modern kitchen-diner in which, just for a moment, Harry entertained the idea of cooking dinner for Lauren if he ever saw her again, just as a thank you, because it was still too soon of course. To the right, the original wooden staircase, excellently preserved, led up to what would be the study and his bedroom once he'd bought himself a desk and a bed. To the left was a big bare room with a brick fireplace and wood burner that with some decent furniture and art would make a perfect sitting room. It was warm inside, cosy despite the age of the building, and the place had been renovated throughout with the latest voice-activated appliances and AR enhancements. Just as he'd been promised.

"It's a great place you've got here," Sachin said.

"So a great salesman's been telling me," Harry replied, casting an approving eye around his new home.

"Please tell that to my boss. I've been Knight & King's top salesman three years running, and you know what? Mr King literally still thinks my name's Sanjay."

"Seriously? Man, that's so wrong."

"I even came up with their slogan for all the thanks I got. 'Make your next move count!' It's chess, get it?"

"I think you deserve a lot better." Harry reached into his coat pocket and handed Sachin a glossy business card with the word Polaris embossed on it, which was at present the only thing that existed of his new company. "Listen, I'm founding a start-up. If you're bored of selling houses and fancy selling MindTech, then let's talk. Just as soon as I can get some funding."

"Dr Harry Coulson," Sachin said reading aloud from his business card. "I thought I recognised your name when I saw it online." He closed his eyes and let out a long sigh through his nose. "You found Rena."

"Rena?"

"Serena. That's what I called her."

Harry knew that if he was still hooked up to the cardiac monitor the machine would have spiked. "You knew her?"

Sachin looked sad. "We went out for a bit, but, well, I suppose it didn't work out. I think she meant more to me than I did to her. Her parents never really approved. Turns out she left me for her drug dealer, so who knows what they thought of that. Bastard called Ryan Miller. Works as a mechanic at the garage. Only last week, I heard he beat up some poor bloke outside The 319 who owed him money. Nasty piece of work. If you ask me, that's who the police should be talking to, not bothering you and me."

Harry shook his head. He felt for the young man, he really did, but this was the last thing he needed. "I don't like to speculate. I just hope they find whoever did this. I'm so sorry for your loss." He tapped the top of his suitcase. "Listen, I've got a lot of unpacking to do and..."

"Of course," Sachin said, backing out of the door. "Enjoy your new home, Dr Coulson."

This place was all he'd longed for these last few tumultuous months. His solicitor once tried to subtly hint that, after selling his half of their house in London to his wife and his half of his tech business to his philandering best friend and business partner in the name of a clean break, ploughing most of his not inconsiderable proceeds into an old mill in the middle of nowhere constituted something of a midlife crisis. But his idea was sound. He was sure of it. He'd staked everything on this new life because there was nothing left to go back to in his old one. He'd find the funding for his new venture somehow. What this place offered, what he needed more than anything, was privacy and seclusion and the peace and quiet to think undisturbed.

There was a knock at the door.

Harry opened it and his heart shot off again when he saw Harper Sloane standing there with a microphone in her hand and two cameramen at her back. The crews of at least three other channels were setting up behind her down the path and another car was already pulling up outside his gate and then another. He could hear the sound of drones buzzing in the air. An army was preparing to lay siege in his garden with booms for banners.

"Mr Coulson," Harper cried, thrusting her microphone at him. "Rosemary Brandreth repeated her public allegations against you today. Did you know yours was the only DNA found at the crime scene? What do you have to say in response? Mr Coulson? Harry? Harry! Did you kill Serena Brandreth?"

He slammed the door in her face.

Chapter Four:

Serena's Law

Harry looked down from the battlements of his bedroom window to see two dozen journalists had set up camp in his garden below. At the centre of them all was Harper Sloane, vaping like the destruction of his life was just another day in the office. A cursory online search told Harry everything he needed to know about her. Harper's first job after graduating from Cardiff was on *The Sun* where she'd made a name for herself, several in fact, and none of them good — The Grim Writer, The Fourth Horseman of the Fourth Estate, The One Who Knocks — for the tenacity and effectiveness with which she extracted teary statements from grieving parents on the worst day of their lives. Watching the world burn wasn't enough for people like her; she had to record it, document it, exploit it. He pictured her grabbing the camera and keeping it rolling even as a zombie ate the brains of her cameraman and knew she wasn't going anywhere and that was a problem. Harry's empty house and empty cupboards were ill-prepared for a protracted siege. He hadn't eaten since the flaccid cheese toastie he'd woken up to and winced his way through on the train and he could hear the whir of rotors outside. A delivery drone was descending to drop off a large package in his garden. The bed he'd ordered online yesterday, perhaps. Or the armchair. He'd never know as long as it was surrounded by reporters ready to jump on him the moment he opened the door. Sooner or later, he would have to face them. He would have to tell his story or they would continue to tell it for him.

Making his way downstairs, Harry took a deep breath and then another, bit by bit forcing the anxiety back down. Then he opened the door to a hailstorm of questions.

"Mr Coulson, what do you have to say about Rosemary Brandreth's allegations?"

"What were you doing on Station Road last night, Mr Coulson?"

"Why did you come to Freebourne, Mr Coulson?"

"Mr Coulson, did you know the victim?"

"Please!"

"Do you have any comment?"

"Enough!" Harry cried and the reporters fell silent, waiting to capture his next word. "If you would just let me speak, for a moment, please. Do you really want to hear my side?"

"Yes," Harper Sloane said, pushing her way to the front of the pack, BBC-branded microphone at the ready. "Yes, I do."

"Ok. But not here. I'm not having you lot hounding me outside my house, following me everywhere I go. I'm a human being for god's sake!"

Harper gave a rapid series of encouraging nods. "Then come to the studio Monday, 6 p.m. We'll give you the lead interview slot. All the time you need to tell your story. Tell us anything you want. Give us the exclusive and you won't need to speak to anyone else."

Harry reluctantly agreed on the condition they left him in peace and he spent the next two days regretting it. The TV crews and reporters decamped from his lawn, but he barely left the house except to sneak out to the high street after dark to shop for food and cooking utensils and tools to assemble his bed and desk and office chair and hang the Frida Kahlo and Andy Warhol prints when they arrived box by box by drone in his garden. He'd never given an interview to the media before and the prospect terrified him. His peers starting out in London's startup scene — the founders and CEOs of an alphabet soup of tech companies proclaiming to change the world from the broom cupboard co-working space they once shared with him — would all fall over each other and their own indefatigable egos for a few inches in a tiny trade mag only they read, or a motivational speech to a crowd of people who only cared when the canapes were coming. But not Harry. He preferred to let his work speak for itself. He never wanted to be famous. He certainly never wanted to be infamous. And what he had to say now for the cameras would be infinitely harder.

Monday evening came around all too quickly and Harry, freshly shaven and wearing his best jacket and shirt, was walking up the lane into town listening to the old songs he loved as a kid. They always seemed to comfort him. The sun had dipped beneath the tree-lined crest of the hills, brushing red dusk across the bruising sky, but it was warm for February. The air smelled of jasmine. Harry had just crossed the green, where three young teenagers were programming a robot dog to perform complex tricks, and turned left onto the high street by the vintage red telephone box when he heard raised voices. Pausing Arcade Fire's *Everything Now* and removing the nanopods from his ears, he looked up to see Sachin standing outside the door of the estate agent and he wasn't alone. A gaunt, skin-headed young man in dirty Adidas trainers and a black hoodie with black studs in both ears and a scowl etched onto his pale face was jabbing a finger at Sachin's chest and he was shouting.

"You better watch your fucking mouth!" the young man in the hoodie cried.

"Haven't you done enough, Ryan?" Sachin was saying.

"I heard what you've been saying, bruv. Telling everyone I killed her."

"I loved her!"

"That why you kept calling her five times a day, like?"

"I loved her so much!"

"All them messages. I saw them you little creep."

"I loved her and you took her away from me!"

Ryan grabbed Sachin by the lapels of his suit and slammed him hard against the window of the estate agent. "Wasteman! You shut your fucking mouth! I should tell the feds. See what they gotta say, innit."

"Please, Ryan," Sachin was gasping wide-eyed, but Ryan only tightened his grip.

"It was you, wasn't it? You or her nonce science teacher. I'm gonna find out who killed her and when I do, swear down, they're fucking dead."

A crowd had gathered in the street to observe the spectacle from a safe distance, but no one seemed the least bit inclined to intervene. No one except Harry who had heard enough to know that he was witnessing the breach of Rule 4: All We Have to Decide is What to Do With the Time That is Given to Us.

"Hey!" he cried, bounding over to them. "Hey, get off him. Let him go!"

Ryan released his grip on Sachin with a shove and turned to Harry, eyed him for a moment, then hocked up a load of phlegm and spat at his feet. "Then again maybe it was you."

"What?"

"You heard me."

Harry narrowed his eyes at Ryan like he was a leather-clad raider terrorising the last settlements of the wasteland to come. "I think it would be best if you walked on now."

Ryan didn't say anything else. He simply raised his right hand and extended two fingers to make a gun gesture at Harry's head, then shoulder-barged past him and slouched off down the street.

Watching him go, Harry couldn't help but remember the bullies at high school. He was never particularly popular back then, but he was smart enough to know which football team to support and which bands to listen to and what clothes to wear to avoid the stigma of coming bottom of the classroom's harsh pecking order. The same could not be said for Simon Bovington, brave enough to be different and the first kid in the year to come out as gay. Harry had always tried to keep his head down, but when he saw Simon surrounded in the boys' toilets by five of the school's most notorious bullies, something snapped in him. He took a black eye and a lengthy spell of social isolation for his troubles, but he wore both with pride. Because when it came to it, he'd stood up for what was right, and that was the birth of Rule 4. When, years later as a student at Imperial, he'd spotted half a dozen drunk young men in white tie who knew enough about etiquette to start with the knife and fork on the outside but not enough to refrain from burning a fifty-pound note in front of a homeless man, it was Harry who sent them on their way and found the man a hostel for the night. When, as a middle manager in a company that designed AIs to help blind people, three junior female colleagues complained to him about the COO's inappropriate conduct, Harry blew the whistle at the cost of his own job. And when he found the body of a young woman lying bloodied by the roadside, he was never going to walk on by.

Harry turned to Sachin. "Are you ok?"

"Yeah, I'm fine," Sachin replied, though his voice was shaky and he sounded out of breath. "I think I managed to fire off a few pretty brutal quips before he had me against the wall. Enough to cause lasting damage to his fragile ego. But thanks. I owe you one."

"Do you really think he did it? That Ryan guy?"

Sachin straightened his dislodged tie. "I thought you didn't want to speculate?"

Harry glanced over at the crowd in the street who were still staring, but now straight at him. "Everyone else seems to be doing it. Most of them in my direction. Why haven't they pulled Ryan in yet?"

"They did. They questioned him. They've questioned half the town from what I've heard — you, me, an ex-friend of

Rena's who was posting horrible stuff about her online, this weird science teacher at our old school — but Ryan, well, Rena was going to meet him that night. You know the police found cocaine in her system, right? Who else could have given it to her? But what do they do? They let him go. Not enough evidence, they said."

"Really?"

Sachin looked vengeful. "That's Ryan Miller. Bastard always gets away with it. He breaks my nose at school and says it was an accident and the teacher believes him. He gets caught shoplifting and he gets off because the CCTV wasn't working. He sleeps with Rena after giving her god knows what and he knows I've loved her since sixth form, but he does it anyway, and he..." Sachin paused to wipe a tear from his eye with the palm of his hand. "He killed her, I know he did. I kept trying to warn her about him, but she wouldn't listen. And now she's dead."

Harry placed a gentle hand on Sachin's arm. "I'm so sorry."

Sachin sniffed. "I just miss her so much. I'm sorry, I don't know why I'm telling you all this. I just..."

Harry pulled Sachin into a hug. He barely knew the young man, but he knew the grief that was there when love wasn't. Melanie hadn't died, but he'd grieved her, nonetheless. Mourned the happiness they once had together when everything was perfect and unblemished by loss and the grind of carrying on when life didn't seem so carefree anymore. Happiness they might still have if she hadn't been in the car with him that night. If he'd taken a different route. If he'd chosen to let someone die.

Harry patted Sachin's back and released him from the hug. "I'm sorry, I've got to go, but if you need anyone to talk to, I'm always around for a pint."

Sachin wiped another tear from his eye. "Thanks, but you don't need to worry about me."

"No, honestly, I could do with a mate in town. It's not as friendly as my estate agent had me believe!"

Sachin laughed and he looked a little better as Harry left him locking up Knight & King and made his way down the high street, past the shuttering shops and cosily lit restaurants and pubs already heaving with the after-work crowd. And maybe Harry felt a little better too. Knowing there was someone in this town who understood. He stopped by the brightly coloured Rainbow Café at the end of the high street, waited as a driverless taxi glided silently by, and then crossed the road and took the path round the back of the library where he found the BBC's studio in a large Georgian townhouse by a tall palm tree.

Harry buzzed on the door and gave his name. There was a pause and then he heard the click and he pushed his way in. He walked up to the receptionist's desk and spoke to the woman behind it who tried her best to look professional as he gave his name again, but the second glance she gave him told him she was thinking the same thing as everyone else. She took his coat and showed him into the empty green room, offered him a glass of water and then sat him down on the sofa to wait in front of a large TV showing the news being broadcast live from the studio next door. They were playing a clip of Elliott Nwosu from a press conference earlier that day. The MP was standing on the steps of his constituency office next to Guy and Rosemary Brandreth speaking to a row of microphones.

"And I know so many women in our community and across the country who say the same thing," Nwosu was saying. "Who walk home with their keys between their fingers after dark. Who look twice at every shadow because we have not made the night safe. I am ashamed to say that we live in a country where women still have to fear for their lives when they leave the house and we have the temerity to still call it Great Britain. And I am ashamed to say that our government, my government, has not yet acted decisively to stem the alarming rise in violence against women. It stops here. Serena Brandreth will not be another statistic. That is why I am joining her parents, Guy and Rosemary, to call on the Prime Minister to introduce a new law that would see an automatic full-life sentence with no chance of parole handed down to all those convicted of murdering a woman. When a woman dies on our streets, her killer must die in jail. Prime Minister, I urge you, act now. Give us Serena's Law."

Harry couldn't help feeling intensely uneasy as he heard the MP say her name, but it was a clever move. In one string of empty vowels and consonants, Nwosu had not only captured the public mood but cornered the man whose back he'd stared at too long and from too far away. The overgrown schoolboy of a Prime Minister was a fiscal conservative who would sooner cut taxes for the 1% who'd attended Eton and Oxford with him than cut the queues at the foodbanks, but he was a classic social liberal and for all the PM's talk of much-needed reform to rehabilitate criminals and alleviate the country's overflowing prisons, a crime that united the nation in horror would always leave him looking weak. Nwosu surely knew that, just as he knew half of his colleagues in Parliament plus one and 52% of the country agreed.

The door opened and a short, young black man in a floral shirt walked in holding a makeup kit and a miniature wireless microphone.

"Dr Coulson, hi, my name's Marcus, I'm just here to get you ready for your interview," the man said. He had a kindly voice, American, Californian, soft and slightly effeminate. He clipped the wireless mic to the lapel of Harry's jacket. "There we go. Please make sure your glasses are in flight mode so we don't get any feedback." Marcus took out a makeup brush and selected a medium light colour from his palette that matched Harry's skin tone and started dusting his face. It tickled a bit. "Just close your eyes for me for a moment.

Perfect. We'll get you on in a couple of minutes, just after this item. So sad, isn't it?" Marcus glanced up at the TV where Rosemary Brandreth was speaking now, reading from a sheet of paper with a shaking hand and struggling hard to hold back the tears.

"Serena, our beautiful baby girl, was taken from the world far too soon," Mrs Brandreth was saying. "She was so talented, so clever, she loved life and she had so much of it to look forward to. That life was stolen from her and now she is with God. The man who murdered our precious girl should never be free to walk our streets again. To prey on young women walking alone at night. No parent should have to feel our pain. A pain that will be with us for as long as we live. So please, I pray, write to your MP, tell them to stand with Elliott Nwosu. I beg you, for all our daughters, support Serena's Law."

Harry's mouth felt dry. He took a sip of water and then a gulp and another one. What was he thinking agreeing to this? How could he go on after that? Tell everyone watching his truth when theirs was something much worse. He could feel his fists clenching by his sides. His leg was tapping up and down uncontrollably.

The TV programme cut back to the studio where Harper Sloane, sitting in front of a bright background screen with an image of Freebourne's church and green on a cloudless clear blue day, was looking solemnly at the camera.

"Ok, that's our cue, let's go," Marcus said.

"I don't think I can do this," Harry replied.

"Of course you can, Dr Coulson, just relax, keep calm. Maybe I shouldn't be saying this, but if it helps, I believe you. Now come on. You got this!"

Marcus led Harry through the far door and into the studio and sat him down on a high stool at a tall glass table opposite Harper Sloane who was reading autocue from the camera in front of her.

"That was Rosemary Brandreth, speaking earlier today in support of Elliott Nwosu, MP for Freebourne and Battle, as he broke ranks with the leader of his own party to call for what is now being termed Serena's Law," Harper said to camera. "The move comes following a massive outpouring of grief over the shocking murder of Serena Brandreth. Police have yet to make any arrests since the victim's body was discovered on Station Road last Friday. Officers were first alerted to the scene by a man named Harry Coulson who is here with me in the studio." Harper turned from the autocue to Harry. "Dr Coulson, thank you for joining us."

"Umm, thanks," Harry said. He didn't feel like they'd given him much of a choice and he couldn't imagine anywhere he'd rather be less.

"Dr Coulson, the police interviewed you as a witness the night Serena was killed, is that right?"

"That's right," Harry said, though here he was, once again, being interviewed as a suspect.

"But there are some people who think maybe you know more than you're telling the police, don't they Dr Coulson? How did you feel when the victim's mother said what she did about you?"

"I've told the police everything I know. Honestly, I wish there was more I could do to help them catch whoever killed Serena. I don't know if it would help ease her parents' pain, I suppose nothing ever will. But I didn't do this. I didn't. I couldn't."

"But you can see why some people find it odd that you were the only person known to be in the area at the time Serena was killed, and that yours was the only DNA found on her body, can't you?"

Harry closed his eyes and felt the first throb of pain behind them again. He could still see her face. Her icy blue stare fixed on the vast infinity above. "I tried to help her. I thought maybe I could save her. When I saw her lying there, I ran to her, and then I saw the wound and all that blood in the snow and she wasn't breathing and I realised what must have happened and I looked for a pulse, but she was already gone. She was already gone."

Harper gave a couple of her quickfire nods as if trying to coax something more out of him. "So your cells were found on her wrist and neck because you checked her pulse?"

"Yes. I mean what would you do?"

"It doesn't sound like everyone is satisfied with that explanation, though, does it?"

"I can only imagine what Mrs Brandreth is going through. How hurt and angry she must..."

"I'm not just talking about Rosemary Brandreth. Are you aware of the comments posted online this morning by David Castle?"

"Who?"

"He's a science teacher at Freebourne High School."

"Not the one the police questioned?"

"Dr Castle wrote: 'The presence of DNA in those places on Serena's body could equally indicate a struggle had taken place, that she might have been grabbed by her arm or by the throat. Such speculation will not bring Serena back, or take away the hole she has left in all our hearts, but in the absence of any other DNA evidence I hope police will not be too quick to accept Harry Coulson's version of events'."

"But that's ridiculous!"

"You disagree with Dr Castle?"

Harry pinched the bridge of his nose. "I tried to help her."

"Then there was Reverend Vinicombe who told us you looked highly agitated when he saw you in The Barley Mow that night."

"Did he also tell you that I was taken to hospital? I'm suffering from PTSD for god's sake and you're not helping."

"Ok, Dr Coulson, let's move on to the other question I think a lot of people are struggling with. This is a close-knit community. There hadn't been a murder here in over a hundred years until the night you arrived."

"Come on!"

Harper leaned back in her chair. "I'm not saying it's not a coincidence. But this is what I'm hearing from people. Why did you come to Freebourne, Dr Coulson?"

Harry reached for the glass of water they'd placed in front of him and took a big gulp. "I came here to start a new life. There wasn't much left of my old one."

"Go on."

"And I want to set up a new company here."

"What kind of company?"

"MindTech."

"MindTech? What's that when it's at home?"

"Erm, well, I don't really like talking about my work publicly."

"I think people would want to know what it is you've come to Freebourne to work on."

Harry shifted uncomfortably in his seat. "Ok, well, I'm working on this device, you see."

Harper nodded pneumatically again. "Go on."

"It's, uhhm, a wearable AI. You strap it to the side of your head and it can detect when you're experiencing harmful, negative emotions brought about by painful memories and when it does, well, it can remove them from your focus."

"That sounds a lot like brain editing."

Harry shook his head. "No, not like brain editing. That's a theoretical procedure, no one's ever even perfected it on animals let alone successfully trialled it in humans and if they did it would involve highly invasive surgery. That's not what I'm talking about at all. My device doesn't remove traumatic memories or replace them. It just sends electrical signals, stimuli that help the mind process these feelings and events it's dwelling on and move on. They say time is the greatest healer. Well, Polaris just guides you there a bit faster. And if you're not ready, you can switch it off any time you like."

"And it works, does it?"

"I'm still trying to get the funding I need to build a prototype, but if my modelling is correct, I am confident it will work."

Harper shuffled her notes in front of her. "This all sounds fascinating. But forgive me for asking, who's going to fund someone with your track record?"

"What track record?"

"Well, exactly. I tried to look you up and, ok, you have social media profiles and a metaverse account and, yes, they say you've been working in tech for over two decades, but you don't seem to have posted anything much, if at all. I've not heard of these start-ups you've worked for, you don't say anything about what you've done for them and nor does anyone else — there are no articles about Harry Coulson anywhere."

"Like I said, I don't really like talking about my work. I hope maybe one day the things I'm doing will help a lot of people. And that will speak for itself."

Harper smiled. "Ok, let's move on, we're almost out of time. One last question if I may. Earlier today we heard Elliott Nwosu announce his campaign for Serena's Law. Two hundred thousand people all over the country have already signed his petition. Will you be joining them?"

"Erm, well, I'd need to take a look at it and…"

"Yes or no. Do you support Serena's Law?"

Harry felt a flash of heat in his face. "Well, it's not as simple as that, is it?"

"It's very simple. Either you agree people who murder women should be imprisoned for life, or you don't."

"I think that murderers should face justice and, yes, that means jail, but for the rest of their lives? I'm just not sure. Prisons shouldn't just be a place to keep dangerous people away from the rest of society, or even a form of punishment, should they? That sounds to me like giving up. Like admitting we don't have any chance of reforming people. Making them better than they were born to be or society made them. That's what I think prison should be for and there's no hope of that if we just lock people up and throw away the key."

Harper gave another series of nods like a song thrush about to take apart a snail. "So you don't think the person who killed Serena Brandreth should face life in jail?"

Harry's heart jumped as he realised too late the trap he'd just walked into. "I, erm…"

"Ok, that's all we've got time for."

"No, wait," Harry protested.

"Thank you for joining us, Dr Coulson." Harper turned away from him and back to the camera's autocue feed. "In other news, Anthropro protests have spread nationwide triggering violent incidents around the country. Here in Sussex, we've seen…"

Harry ripped the microphone off his lapel, dumped it in Marcus' waiting hands without a word, grabbed his coat and ran from the studio and out of the building. How could he have been so stupid? Harper Sloane had never wanted to hear his side of the story. She had already made up her mind just like everyone else in this town. He was nothing to her but a line in her CV. No one would ever believe him after today. Shaking now, close to tears and feeling weaker than he ever had, he tapped his glasses and rasped the words: "Call Melanie."

She didn't answer. She never did. She was gone and all their mutual friends had gone with her. There was no one he could turn to. No one from school, no one from university, none of his old colleagues. So consumed with his work, he'd let them believe, just like he'd let Melanie believe, that he cared more about machines than he did the people who loved him. In reality, he was simply less afraid of losing a line of code. And there was only one person besides Melanie who he'd ever really let in, who'd ever truly understood him.

"Call Ben," he gasped, but Ben didn't answer either. And how could he? They were moving on with their lives while he was stuck here all alone. So desperately alone. He felt the tear rolling down his cheek and he was reaching to wipe it away when something stopped him. A voice. It was coming from the alleyway by the studio. Someone was speaking in hushed tones into a phone and Harry was sure he heard them say Serena's name or one that sounded a lot like it. And then he heard the swearing and he knew he recognised that voice. It was the angry man he'd seen in The 319 the night she was killed.

"I'm outside the studio," the swearing man was saying as quietly as someone with his voice could manage. "He'll be finished soon. I'll be fucking finished soon if this carries on. There's been far too much fucking publicity already. No. No. No. Look, this could derail everything. The MP's been asking questions again, hasn't he? Don't you dare fucking tell him anything. Listen, DCI Khan, you and that fucking weasel of a DI are privy to privileged fucking information. It's need to know and Elliott Nwosu doesn't fucking need to know. Look, we need to wrap this up quickly. You know what this means to my employers. Yes of course we know he didn't do it. You know that and I know that, but do the fucking public? Someone needs to swing for this and fast."

Chapter Five:

This Too Shall Pass

Rule 5: Take the Blue Pill. Questions and curiosity were antithetical to a quiet life and in Harry's experience rarely led anywhere good. He found out the hard way the consequences of breaking that rule the day he came home early to find the client Ben had been meeting was in fact his wife and the only thing on the agenda was an oral presentation. He'd had his suspicions about her — all the signs were there and he'd been studiously ignoring them long enough — but he had no reason to imagine it would be with his best friend and business partner. His world wasn't exactly happy before that moment, but it existed. And now he knew where the trail ended. Here in Freebourne, his life and his name in tatters, and more questions.

Who was this swearing man? Why was he talking to DCI Khan? This had something to do with the murder, didn't it? What did they know? That Harry didn't do it? Why did they care what the press had to say? Who was this man's employer? Surely it was someone very powerful if they thought they could keep it from Elliott Nwosu? But what were they trying to hide? Was there something bigger going on here? Every instinct, every fibre of his being, told him not to look, told him not to step out into that alley and prick his world again, but if that man knew something, if he knew Harry was innocent and could prove it then maybe, just maybe, he'd get his life back after all.

Harry strode out into the alley and sure enough, there was the swearing man and he had his back to him as he walked away, heading round the side of the library and back towards the high street. Before he could think to stop himself or even realise what he was doing, Harry found he was following him. He hurried to the end of the path just in time to see the man cross the road and disappear through the brightly painted doors of the Rainbow Café. Harry still wasn't thinking as he ran across the road, sending a hyperbike swerving to avoid him, and straight into the café after the swearing man.

He was nowhere to be seen. The café, which smelt of cumin and coriander and incense and was decorated every inch in Persian wall hangings and psychedelic art and statues of Buddhas and Hindu gods, was empty except for the shaven-headed young woman in blue denim dungarees and Doc Martens stacking the last chair on top of a table.

"I'm sorry, we're just closing," the woman said.

"Did you see a man come in here?" Harry said somewhat breathlessly.

"No, no one's been in for the last half an hour."

"He just walked in here. Big guy, pinstripe suit, looks like he's made out of stone. Like a golem."

"Unless he's wearing a +1 Cloak of Invisibility, I'm afraid I'm going to have to refer you to my previous answer."

"But I just saw him!"

Catching sight of Harry's face as it fell, the woman offered him a reassuring grin. "Listen, I haven't seen anyone, I'm sorry. But maybe you could come back tomorrow and see if your man turns up?"

"I guess," Harry replied despondently.

"I'll do you a turmeric latte on the house, you look like you need it."

"That's kind of you. Considering." Harry looked at patterns on the Turkish rug beneath his feet. "I assume you know…"

"I don't know anything. No one does and we're all the wiser for it. Listen, mister, this is a safe space and Zero Judgement Zone. At least it is between the hours of 8 a.m. and 6:30 p.m. After that, it's time for my gin and tonic. So if you don't mind coming back tomorrow. My name's River and it'll still be

River tomorrow and it was a pleasure meeting you and all the obligatory niceties, but please shoo."

Harry did as he was told and left. There was no sign of the swearing man on the street either. How a man as large as that could have completely escaped him was a mystery, but it wasn't one Harry was going to solve today and the people on the high street were already beginning to stare. He headed home, prepared himself a quick dinner which he barely touched, and went to bed and looked at the ceiling for three hours as his mind whirred like an overclocked computer until at last it shut down and he slept a dreamless sleep.

The next day he decided to follow River's advice and return to the Rainbow Café on the slightest chance he might spot the swearing man again. Harry wasn't exactly surprised to find the stranger wasn't there, but River was with a grin on her face and a cup of turmeric latte for him and he took it on the yin-yang painted table in the corner under the dream catchers. He stayed there half the morning, reading the news on his glasses and occasionally swapping anecdotes with River from their favourite Dungeons & Dragons campaigns, until a policeman walked in and Harry caught sight of that uniform and a shot of adrenaline crackled through his heart. Suddenly the questions were back. Were they here for him? Had they seen him on TV last night? Had they made up their minds like everyone else in this town? Was he about to be arrested in front of everyone in this lovely little place for a crime he'd never committed? Is that what the swearing man meant? Who was going to swing for it? Was it going to be him? Was he being set up? Why?

The police officer walked straight past him and up to the counter and ordered two cups of matcha. It was then that Harry saw it was the young lad, PC Atkins, and he wasn't alone. He was with Marcus, the makeup artist from the BBC studio across the street, and they were holding hands. Neither of them was paying him any mind and nor was anyone else in the café and Harry remembered that he was in a Zero Judgement Zone and he smiled.

Harry came back the next day for a falafel and a masala chai and again no one seemed to pay him any attention except River, when she got a quiet moment to debate Buddhist ethics or who would win in a fight between Drizzt Do'Urden and Elminster. This was the one place in town where the eyes and the accusations didn't follow him. So he came back the next day and the next. He began to bring his laptop with him and he started to work in the quiet calm he'd craved all this time. The fog that had descended on his mind ever since he found himself staring at the horror of her bloodied body seemed to lift at least for a little bit and he found himself able to think at last. Ideas were flowing freely now. Lines of code wrote themselves in his brain and he typed out the last few details of the model for his prototype. He was even able to draft a business plan and a funding proposal and Sachin was kind enough to swing by for a coffee to help him with his messaging.

By the end of the week, Harry was almost a fixture in the corner of the Rainbow Café. His was the first chair River took down in the morning and the last she stacked up in the evening when everyone else had gone home. He got to know the other regulars through conversations here and there and plenty of people-watching but never judging. Grace, the landlady from The Barley Mow, popped in from time to time and always stopped to ask Harry how he was after his stay in hospital. It turned out she was River's aunt, which explained a lot about the young café owner's eccentricities. Grace had taken care of River since her mum, Grace's sister, died of a brain haemorrhage when River was only 12 and her father, a soldier River said, was stationed abroad. It was Grace who had first brought River to India for her 18th birthday where she'd taken in a lot of cannabis and religion. River didn't smoke these days, but she still baked hash cookies,

Harry learned, a rare guilty exception she allowed herself from the Five Precepts, and sold them under the counter to her most trusted customers of which it appeared PC Atkins was one.

Another of those trusted customers, Harry observed, was a Brazilian trans woman named Carla. Harry learned that while most of the country had settled the question of trans rights over a decade ago, with a productive peace breaking out over the definition of a woman, the entente cordiale had not yet reached Freebourne where their MP, then an ambitious young council leader, had first taken his seat on a culture war to block unisex public toilets in front of the supermarket. The Battle of Waitrose Loo they called it and the fact anyone was still waging it was enough to make Carla feel at home more than anywhere else in the Rainbow Café where prejudices were left like coats and umbrellas by the door.

The regular clientele was on average younger than Freebourne's wider population and all manner of youth subcultures from the Metaheads to the Augments with their oversized AR visors and armbands and of course the Hippy 2.0s and plenty of others Harry had long ago stopped keeping track of were represented here. One of the few older customers was Farhad, the owner of the Halal butcher on the other side of the street. They called him a butcher back in Tehran too, some said, but for different reasons. He would never talk about what he did for the regime, and River never put stock in such rumours, but those eyes had seen things. He and his surviving family had fled to Freebourne after the Second Revolution and he often came in with his son Darius, a reserved but bright-eyed and well-built young man who would usually sit coding apps on the table next to Harry, only ever occasionally glancing up. The only patron older than Farhad didn't have a name that anyone knew and never spoke but River called him The Last Survivor. It was said that the man, who could frequently be seen hobbling in wearing a pair of baggy jeans and a baggy jumper and a dirty old bucket hat emblazoned with yellow smiling faces, was all that physically if not mentally remained of the 90s rave scene, a living reminder that not everything that went up back then ever came down. Seemingly unwilling or unable to do so, The Last Survivor would take five hash cookies from River every morning at 8:33 a.m. and five more in the afternoon at 4:56 p.m. and leave without saying a word.

"Sure I can't tempt you, mister?" River said to Harry one morning as she clocked him observing The Last Survivor stacking the cookies into his Tupperware.

Harry glanced at her over the rim of his laptop. "No, thank you."

"Ah, Dr Harry Coulson, don't you ever get bored playing Lawful Good?"

"I like to stay on the right side of the law. That and the last time I tried one of those things I ended up talking to a tree for three hours."

"Trees are famously great conversationalists."

"If it's all the same to you, I think I've nearly cracked this," Harry said, tapping the top of his computer. "I'd rather keep a clear head and…"

River frowned. "And what?"

"Shhh!" Harry said, gesturing to the battered old radio sitting on the bookshelf. "Could you turn that up?"

River turned the volume up and Harper Sloane's voice filled the room. Grace and Carla and Farhad and everyone in the Rainbow Café was silent now and listening in, but no one more intently than Harry.

"News just in," Harper was saying and Harry took a deep breath. "Police investigating the murder of Serena Brandreth arrested a 52-year-old man yesterday evening. Reports suggest officers recovered a necklace the victim was thought to be wearing the night she died from the man's house. The man, believed to be a science teacher at Freebourne High

School named David Castle, has been held overnight for questioning."

Harry felt all the air escape his lungs. As if all the horror and darkness and pain and sadness and fear and confusion and anger that had welled up in him day by day in this town came pouring out of him in one ecstatic release.The light in the room seemed brighter all of a sudden. The feeling of intense unease he'd carried around in the pit of his stomach ever since the police had sat him down in that interview room loosened. The café erupted into chatter.

"Thank god," Carla was saying. "Is that it? Are we safe now?"

"That poor girl, her family," Farhad said. "Inshallah, they will find justice now."

"Hey sweetie," Grace called over to Harry. "I knew you didn't do it! I always said it. Wasn't I always saying it, Carla?"

"You were always saying it, Grace."

Harry caught himself grinning and then he remembered Rule 1 and he felt bad. This wasn't about him. He never wanted it to be about him. This was about a young woman robbed of her life by that monster for no reason he could understand. It was about a grieving family, an empty seat at their table and an empty bed in their house and an empty nothingness in their lives that would never be filled again. Harry only wished he had seen something that night, anything that might have helped the police catch her killer sooner. But the truth is he'd seen no one. And this science teacher, if it was him, knew enough about forensics to hide any evidence. But now the police had found something.

"Figures," River murmured, staring into the dust motes caught suspended in the sunlight pouring through the window. She seemed unusually quiet.

"Are you ok?" Harry asked.

"I always wondered..."

"What?"

"I heard the rumours about her and Dr Castle. Serena was in the year above me at school, and several grades above me in terms of social capital. I didn't know her that well, but people talked. I never believed them. Not until Sixth Form when I was in his Biology class." River paused as a tear rolled down her cheek. "Let's just say I found out first-hand what a creep that man is."

"I'm so sorry."

"Don't be. I don't know why I'm telling you this. I've never said that out loud before. Maybe I should have. Maybe Serena would still be alive if I had. Listen, you seem like a good guy. I hope everyone else in this narrow-minded little backwater will get a chance to see that now." She sniffed. "I think I need to be alone now, sorry."

Harry could only begin to imagine what must be going through River's head. The scars that don't heal from a trauma left unspoken all this time, suddenly real again, tangible, with a name and a face and a motive for an act of incomparable evil. He felt a lance of pain behind his eyes again and he blinked it away. This wasn't over. He was in the clear, but it didn't end there. Not for him, not for River, not for Serena's parents or her friends or Sachin or Ryan, not till David Castle was in the dock and confessing for all the meaningless hurt he'd inflicted on their lives.

An incoming call notification flashed up in the corner of his eye. He tapped the button on the side of his glasses and said "Decline". He was in no mood to talk to anyone. The notification popped up again. He glanced at it and the telephone number jumped out onto the table in big red augmented reality digits. He didn't recognise it. "Decline," he said again. But no sooner had he done so, the call came again. Harry sighed. "Accept."

The numbers floating in the ether in front of him dissipated and in their place appeared the digitised face of Guy Brandreth.

"Dr Coulson," Serena's father said. "I trust you know who I am."

Harry tried to answer but the words stuck behind the painful lump that had all of a sudden lodged itself in his throat. He just nodded.

"Good, then I'll make this brief."

Harry cleared his throat. "Listen, Mr Brandreth, if this is about what your wife said, then I want you to know it doesn't matter. I know grief can…"

"I am not calling you to apologise. Words don't change anything, do they? But I think you know what does. And I think maybe we can help each other."

"If there's anything I can do to…"

"I am opening an exhibition at the Freebourne Museum tomorrow afternoon. One o'clock. Come. We'll talk then."

Guy Brandreth's digital avatar dissipated, but an afterimage lingered there in Harry's mind, like phosphene in the dark. There was something in those frigid blue eyes, cold even in life, that looked so much like his daughter's. He didn't know what Mr Brandreth had left to say to him or what Harry could possibly say that could make a difference now. But he could hardly refuse. So, when tomorrow afternoon came, he found himself standing outside Freebourne Museum on the far edge of town, by the little boating lake ringed by pine trees.

The museum — a large, three-storey glass cube sparkling in the sunlight — was evidently a new construction. But what it was built upon was far older: the original Roman settlement of Quercus from which the town could proudly trace its origins. You could still see the remnants of ancient streets and mosaics in the rubble several feet beneath the transparent floor when you walked in. And Harry could picture himself — 2000 years ago — a Roman centurion stationed in these rainswept barbarian lands, far from his old life, every bit the feared and mistrusted stranger then as now. The old man in the green cardigan hunched behind the reception desk by a parlour palm did little to make him feel more welcome.

"Hello," Harry said. "I'm looking for Mr Brandreth."

The man regarded Harry over the rim of his spectacles. His name badge said he was called Nigel. "The exhibition doesn't open till one. You're half an hour early."

"I know. I'm looking for Mr Brandreth."

"As our honoured patron, Mr Brandreth will be opening the exhibition."

"Yes, I realise that. That's why I'm here. I want to speak with him."

"I'm afraid there won't be a chance for a Q&A."

Harry felt he'd designed AIs with a better human interface than this. Inflexible no matter the circumstances. He imagined this Nigel fellow as a gatekeeper for humanity's last settlement, greeting some terrified survivor with unwavering bureaucracy even as a horde of zombies lumbered behind to eat their brains.

"No, I have a meeting with him," Harry persisted.

"Mr Brandreth has never held meetings at Freebourne Museum," Nigel replied in the kind of monotone voice that sounded like the drone of a bagpipe.

"It's quite alright, Nigel," Guy Brandreth's voice came from over Harry's shoulder. "Come," he said as Harry turned to greet him. "We'll talk in the café."

Serena's father led Harry up the escalator to the right of the reception desk and into the gloriously bright café a-hum with the chatter of families out for the day. The place looked like a giant greenhouse with vines creeping up the glass walls and palm trees brushing the ceiling. A waitress caught sight of Guy Brandreth as he entered and she hurried over to speak to a middle-aged couple sitting at what was quite clearly the nicest table in the room overlooking the glittering lake below. Harry didn't know what she said, but he could guess when he saw the couple stand up, collect their things and shuffle off. The waitress had already cleared, sprayed, wiped and re-set the table before they reached it to sit down.

"Thank you for coming," Mr Brandreth said in a way that suggested he had never entertained the possibility that Harry might not come because he was accustomed to getting everything he wanted.

"It's no trouble, really," Harry replied. "I'm just sorry there's not really anything more I can tell you. I've already told the police everything."

"And I believe you. I admit, I didn't at first. I dare say my wife is still sceptical. But when the police told me what they had learned about David Castle, well ... I should never have allowed Serena to go to the local comprehensive, but she always had a rebellious streak in her and she did everything she could, and that was a lot, to get herself expelled from Roedean. It turns my stomach to think that he preyed upon her — a young schoolgirl, her teacher, and he had the temerity to tell the police it was a relationship. A relationship! That man had a duty of care to my daughter. I trusted him and he betrayed that trust." Mr Brandreth wasn't looking at Harry as he spoke. His gaze was a thousand lightyears away and clouded by the welling of tears and a seething, quietly spoken rage. "They tell me she broke it off years ago. But I..." He paused and his gaze snapped back to Harry. "You don't have children, do you Dr Coulson?"

"No, I, I wish, nearly..."

"No, I know you don't. I know pretty much everything about your life. I've had you watched. Oh don't look at me like that, I thought you killed my daughter. If only I'd paid as close attention to her. To think, I never knew. Her own father. She was different back then, angry at everything, sad at the same time, I just thought that's what daughters do. I never imagined in my worst nightmares what she was going through. I don't know why she waited all this time. But I think she may have been about to tell the truth about Dr Castle. She's not going to say now, is she? Why else would he..."

Harry smiled as sympathetically as he could at a man who'd just admitted to paying someone — presumably someone very big who swore a lot — to follow him. "I wish I could say. The truth is, I found your daughter's body and I called the police and that's all. I never saw anything else. Anyone..."

"Like I said, I believe you. I did not ask you here to give me closure by telling me something about my daughter's death I don't already know. But you are here to give me closure."

Harry was opening his mouth to ask how when the waitress returned to take their order.

"Nothing for me, Marissa," Mr Brandreth said. "But you should eat, Dr Coulson. Try the quiche Lorraine, it is quite excellent."

"I'm vegetarian," Harry said, glancing down at the menu.

"So is the quiche. The meat was grown in a laboratory, apparently. I'm not sure I understand the world anymore, but there you go."

"Just a flat white, please. Oat milk." Harry turned back to Serena's father as the waitress took their menus and headed for the kitchen. "I'm not sure what more I can say to give you closure, Mr Brandreth."

Mr Brandreth closed his eyes and exhaled deeply through his nose. All the man's mannerisms were measured, calculated, but it was evident that not far beneath the calm exterior a war was raging with an all-consuming darkness. There was someone who'd gazed into the abyss and found it gazing back.

"There was once a great and powerful Eastern king," Mr Brandreth said at last, opening his eyes again. "So the fable goes. So vast was his wealth, he could buy anything his heart desired. Anything except happiness. And so he turned to his sages and he asked them to craft a ring that could make him happy when he was sad. For 40 days and 40 nights, the wise men toiled with their incantations and prayers, but try as they might no magic or faith could imbue a band of metal with the power to change a man's mind. And every day the king would ask them 'Where is my ring'. And every day, the sages would say 'Soon, sire'. At last, one day, the sages came upon their solution and they presented the king with a simple ring inscribed with the words 'This too shall pass'. And looking upon those words the king smiled and knew happiness."

Harry nodded. "I think I understand."

"I somehow doubt that king ever knew the pain of losing a child. If he had, he'd never have been fobbed off by such a cheap trinket. Me, I want a ring that will take away my sadness. And fortunately for me, it would appear we now have something the sages lacked. Science. And your seemingly quite brilliant mind."

"It's still experimental, of course, but..."

"I saw you on the television the other night. I know what you're building. This Polaris. I want to fund your work."

Harry couldn't believe what he was hearing. MindTech was a niche discipline. Still new enough to be unregulated, but widely mistrusted by the public and most VCs with money to burn weren't going to bet on something they didn't think the masses would buy. But Harry wasn't setting up his business to get rich. He just wanted to help people. People like him who were hurting. And Guy Brandreth could already retire one of Britain's richest men without investing in Polaris. Except he'd seen that on this one occasion, maybe money could buy happiness.

Harry grinned. "Mr Brandreth, that's so kind of you. I don't know what to..."

"This is not an act of kindness; it is one of self-preservation. I simply do not see any other way through this for me or my wife. How long will it take you to produce this device of yours?"

"The modelling is complete," Harry replied, pausing to thank the waitress as she returned with his coffee. He took a sip. "With the right setup, I could have a prototype built within a week or two."

"How much do you need?"

"Well, I'd need a workspace, a bank of photonic computers, a 3D printer, and a team. Obviously, I wouldn't expect to pay myself much, just enough to…"

"How much?"

Harry bit his lip. "£1.5 million."

"Very well. My accountant will be in touch in three days to release the funds."

Harry took a nervous glug of his coffee, still unable to process the fact that a man who only days ago believed he'd murdered his daughter was about to help him realise his life's ambition. "Seriously? What kind of equity would we be talking about?"

"You think I need to profit from this? I have all the money in the world and still I don't have Serena. Just this emptiness where her love once was. You did right by my daughter. You did what you could to help even though she was beyond it. A lesser man might not have brought that kind of trouble to his door." Mr Brandreth paused to dab his eye with his handkerchief. "We bury her tomorrow. I'd be honoured if you would come to Serena's funeral."

"Of course, I…"

"Good. Now, if you'll excuse me, I have an exhibition to open. You're welcome to stay for it. You might learn a thing or two about Roman Britain. Jupiter knows, I have."

Harry watched Guy Brandreth stand up, button his jacket and head out of the café. He gulped down the rest of his coffee and followed his new benefactor back to the escalators and up to the third floor where a crowd had gathered in a sunlit atrium surrounded by marble statues of gods and emperors and rows of glass cabinets filled with all the ancient treasures Freebourne's farmers, builders and detectorists had unearthed over the years.

Harry recognised DI Manning among the assembled guests and he was with his wife and two toddlers, identical twin blonde girls tugging on both of his arms and screeching as he hissed and shushed and struggled to maintain order. Freebourne's vicar, Reverend Vinicombe, was also there, and he was speaking with a man with intense green eyes and a wild red beard who turned to stare at Harry the moment he caught sight of him. Over at the far end of the room, standing in front of a banner displaying the columns of a Roman temple that must once have sat here, was Elliott Nwosu and he was clinking a glass of champagne with a spoon.

"Friends, Romans, countrymen, lend me your ears," the MP said, permitting himself a dry chuckle at his own joke as the room fell silent. "It has always been a source of great pride for me that our little town was once the site of one of the earliest Roman settlements in Britain. More learned men than I tell us that they first came here for the oak from which the town took its name back then. There is a certain poetry to think what came from such small acorns. Long after the Roman Empire fell first in the West and then in the East to the Ottomans — whose sultans proclaimed themselves Roman emperors after the conquest of Constantinople — it was the British Empire that rose to become the greatest power this planet had ever known. And it was Britain that finally defeated the Ottomans and in doing so became the true heirs to Rome. That path to Pax Britannica began right here in Freebourne, ladies and gentlemen. That we remember that past, that we cherish it to this day, is all down to one man. The patron of this museum. My good friend, Guy Brandreth."

The crowd applauded as Mr Brandreth took the stage and Nwosu placed a gentle hand on his back. Harry didn't know how the man could do it. What force of inner will allowed him to stand there the day before his daughter's funeral when every atom in his body was tearing itself apart.

"Thank you, Elliott," Mr Brandreth said. "And thank you, ladies and gentlemen, for joining me here for the grand opening of our newest and biggest exhibition: the Temple of Janus. For those of you who know me, you'll know that this museum has been my labour of love for 40 years. I will always remember the day I broke ground on my second-ever housing development and I saw Nero's face glinting back at me. Little did I know that coin was about to cost me £20 million. But the discovery of Quercus on the outskirts of Freebourne put paid to two years of wrangling with the planners and my dreams of giving this town 80 luxury lakeside flats. I couldn't just concrete history, now could I? For those of us who have the privilege of building the future also have the duty to preserve our past. So I built a museum here instead and archaeologists have been visiting Freebourne ever since. I am proud to say that their latest discovery, unearthing the Temple of Janus at the heart of old Quercus, will be preserved here for generations to come. I want to thank our team of volunteers at the museum — all of them, like myself, passionate amateur historians — for taking up that torch. Look for the people wearing purple jackets. If you want to learn more about the ancient history of our town, then they will be only too happy to tell you all about it. I shall leave you in their capable hands. Valete!"

The crowd applauded again and then parted. Mothers and fathers dragged in different directions by their children to this display or that. Harry had never paid much attention to history in school. He was too busy looking forward. But the same man who was funding his vision for a better future had spent a lot of money celebrating a past he loved and Harry felt he owed it to Mr Brandreth to stay for a while, despite the occasional stare he still got from people who really should have read the news and known he was innocent. Doing his best to skirt the throngs of people, he pretended to take interest in some iron swords, read all about the arboreal topography of Sussex in the first century, browsed past more than his fair share of coins and broken pots and was just stopping to look at the two-faced marble bust of Janus in the centre of the room when he heard a familiar and very pleasant voice from over his shoulder.

"Well, I guess I saw you first," she said and Harry turned to see Lauren standing there in a purple jacket.

"Oh, erm, I... hi again!" Harry sputtered, his stomach sending instant jitters to his brain that refused to allow him to in any way act the cool person he'd never been in front of someone he had to admit, if he was being honest with himself, he really did find attractive and to hell with it because it wasn't too soon. "What are you doing here?"

Lauren laughed and pointed at the museum name badge pinned to her volunteer jacket. "Does this give it away?"

"Oh, yeah, of course. I thought you said you were, erm, you said you were a scientist?"

"Neuroscientist by day, local historian by, well, also by day. Sort of."

"You must be very busy!"

"If you must know, my lab's not exactly known for its diversity. I'm the only one there without a Y chromosome or a full head of grey hair. So, I've been volunteering here once a week since I moved to town. Thought maybe it might help me make some friends and I could do something nice for the kids at the same time. Turns out kids ask a *lot* of questions. I've learned to wing more about Roman Britain in the last six months than most people learn in their lifetimes. Ask me anything, go on."

"Ok, well," Harry said, pointing to the bust behind him. "Why does this god have two faces?"

"Janus is the god of transition. Of beginnings and endings. Duality. One face looks to the past and the other to the future. His name literally translates as 'doorway' and he presides over the passage of time beyond."

"Very good. I'm impressed. But, like, why did the Romans come up with all of this?"

"Oh you really want to test me, don't you? Well, the Romans didn't really come up with anything. They nicked most of their gods from the ancient Greeks. Except Janus, curiously enough. They assimilated him from the Etruscan god Culsans."

"To be fair you could be making all this up and I wouldn't know the difference."

Lauren tilted her head and smiled. "Nice to bump into you again. You look well. A lot better than when I last saw you."

"Thanks. Yeah, good to see you too. Listen I'd best..." Harry turned to leave, took two awkward paces, and then gave himself a serious dressing down in his mind and stopped. He turned back to Lauren. "Sorry. Look, I want to thank you. You know, for everything you did for me that day. Maybe I could..."

"Thank me by buying me a drink?"

Harry felt his face flush. "Sorry, I didn't mean to..."

"The 319, tomorrow evening?"

"Erm, ok."

"It's a date."

"Well it's, erm, it's not quite, I mean..."

"Harry?"

"Yes?"

"Learn when to stop speaking."

Chapter Six:

Through a Glass, Darkly

There were many tales told of the Church of St Laurence, each of them more true than the last. It was the site of a monastery once, twice burned to the ground and twice risen. Its first fall from grace came in the thirteenth century at the hands, so it goes, of an unnamed bishop of high standing and low temperament apoplectic upon discovering the state of licentiousness into which the drunken, fornicating monks had devolved. Its second was on the orders of King Henry faced with priests far more resolute in their piety. It's said the ghosts of those put to the sword that day still sing through the vestry when the wind is high. The Tudors salvaged what they could of the monastery's medieval chapel, restoring the blackened stone walls and stained glass windows and wooden beams when they rebuilt the church in 1559 under a new kind of Christianity. The old Devil's door survived the wrath of gods and tyrants and through the centuries that followed it was under this stone arch that thousands of Freebourne's residents passed on their final journeys.

"Please stand," said Reverend Vinicombe, his melodic voice resonating back through the nave to be joined shortly thereafter by the sound of the organ and the slow, soothing sadness of Handel's *Largo from Xerxes* and Harry and all those gathered on the polished pews stood and turned with hands clasped to witness Serena's coffin borne into the church. There must have been 200 black-clad people shivering in that cold and draughty hall. Harry glanced over to Sachin standing beside him, watching as the organ's sombre resonance washed over the young man as he tried his best to suppress the tears.

71

At the front stood Guy and Rosemary Brandreth beside Serena's elder sister and brother, all clinging to each other like driftwood in a tide they could not stem. Behind them was their family friend, Elliott Nwosu. Half of Freebourne seemed to have turned out for her funeral. Serena's boyfriend was there, that thug Ryan Miller, wearing a suit two sizes too big, and he was standing beside a younger girl with Down Syndrome whom Sachin said was his sister. She looked frightened and she was holding onto a robot dog on her lap. Harry spotted Carla among the congregation, and Chris the bore of a barman from The 319 where Harry was apprehensively excited to meet Lauren later on when he'd done his last duties for that poor girl he found. Farhad was there with his son Darius who had been in Serena's year at school. Indeed, two-thirds of those assembled were under the age of 30; over 100 of Serena's dear friends and even just acquaintances who, like River, had come to pay their respects to a young woman whose short life had bisected so many others, or run parallel for a time. At the back was the swearing man in a black suit and tie, silent for once and not watching Harry but standing solemnly as Largo's final elongated note poured over the hall and the pallbearers brought the coffin to rest on the wooden trestles before the altar.

The young vicar with a moustache far beyond his years shuffled his papers at the lectern, adjusted his cassock, and began to speak: "We have come here today to remember our sister Serena; to give thanks for her life, for the time we shared with her; to commend her to Jesus Christ our Lord and to God, our almighty and most merciful judge. Serena Constance Olivia Brandreth, beloved daughter to Guy and Rosemary, sister to Hugo and Annabelle, treasured friend to so many whose lives she touched, will be dearly missed."

The words settled upon the congregation like the snow in which she died.

"Serena was taken from us before her time, but may God welcome her into His arms and into Heaven as we welcomed Serena into our hearts. Let us pray."

Heads bowed in unison. Whispers shadowed prayer — 200 mouths moving in a disjointed murmur to the lead of the vicar.

"Our Father, who art in Heaven, hallowed be thy name. Thy kingdom come. Thy will be done, on Earth as it is in Heaven. Give us this day our daily bread. And forgive us our trespasses, as we forgive those that trespass against us. And lead us not into temptation; but deliver us from evil. For thine is the kingdom, the power and the glory. For ever and ever. Amen."

Harry mouthed a respectful amen though he didn't know if anyone was up there to hear it. His parents had been churchgoers, and not just to get him into a decent school, and he'd been brought up questioning his way through countless hours of assemblies and religious studies. That he found his teachers' answers to suffering and morality and existence itself unsatisfactory even then probably shaped the man of science he would become. But for some years he still entertained the possibility of some greater purpose, some higher truth and justice arbitrated by some force beyond his comprehension for reasons that were unknowable but ultimately right. At least until his mother — a woman who had given everything to help others because there was nothing in her but pureness — was taken so young. What omnipotent creator could there be who would possibly include that in their grand designs and not have it deemed a shitty plan? And, like Serena's — so senseless a death. And in the end, all he could see was that the only order in this chaos was that which we made for ourselves. The only judge of right and wrong was the face staring back at us with pride or revulsion when we looked in the mirror and asked the only question that really mattered. Am I a good person? At the end of the day, that was why he lived his life by so many rules. He wished he was wrong. That there was something more.

That Serena's family would be reunited with her in everlasting peace. But even as he watched her father rise to speak, Harry knew that this was their last goodbye.

"A man who gazed at stars once said: 'To live in the hearts of others is to never die in those we leave behind'," Mr Brandreth began, the paper shaking in his hand and his once deep and imperious voice with it. "I don't know why the stars chose to take you from us so soon. But Serena, my precious girl, I do know that every moment of your life will live on in the memories of so many who loved you as dearly as your mother and me. I remember the day we first met in St Jude's. You were early. You always were early. Always the first to run around the house rousing the troops for Christmas Day. Always the first to speak your mind when something wasn't right with the world. Always the first to step forward — whether it was raising money for climate orphans and refugees or feeding the homeless here in Freebourne. And now you are gone from..." Guy Brandreth's voice cracked and broke. "And now..." He stopped again, trying to wipe the tears from his eyes with the back of his hand but they kept on coming and he was sobbing now; the tears and with them that all-consuming darkness in open flow from his puffy red eyes so that no more words could come and he just stood there paralysed by pain until his wife took him by the arm and took the paper from his hand and she read for them both.

"And now you are gone from us early," Mrs Brandreth read. "But I will still remember that day we first met in St Jude's. That tiny, beautiful little thing in my arms. And you never cried because you knew you were loved. Now you know God's love in Heaven. Until we meet again."

Rosemary Brandreth managed to force those last words from her lips with every ounce of will left in her shattered and trembling body before she too collapsed into tears and husband and wife clung onto each other as step by torturous step they

74

helped each other back to their pew as they would have to help each other through every one of their remaining days.

It was Elliott Nwosu's turn to speak: "It has been the greatest honour and the greatest privilege of my life to have known Serena Brandreth since she was a little girl. Not that she ever cared one jot that I counted her parents among my closest friends — ever the rebel that she was. There's one day I will always remember, when I was still just a young county councillor, on a visit to her primary school to talk about — I don't know what I was there to talk about — but I do recall the little girl who stood up to berate me about the lack of electric vehicle charging points in Freebourne. I'm pleased to say that when I became leader of the council the next year, I made it my mission to act on Serena's words and now you won't see a single fossil fuel vehicle on our streets. But she was always one step ahead of the rest of us, even then. I watched her grow and mature into a young woman who would make her parents — who would make us all — proud. Today we remember Serena and we celebrate her life. And we strive every day for everything that she believed in. For she was the very best of us."

When the MP had finished speaking, Reverend Vinicombe returned to his lectern. Opening his Bible, the priest turned to the correct page, scanned it for a moment to select the appropriate passage, and began to read: "Love does not delight in evil but rejoices with the truth. It always protects, always trusts, always hopes, always perseveres. Love never fails."

"I can't believe he's officiating Rena's funeral," Sachin whispered in Harry's ear with a nod to Reverend Vinicombe.

"Why?" Harry hissed back.

"She hated him. Ever since that lovely old Welsh lady, Reverend Jones, passed away last year and Vinicombe was posted here to replace her. He has some pretty extreme views, apparently. Proper hell fire and brimstone fundamentalist."

Harry shrugged. "You wouldn't think it to look at him."

"But where there are prophecies, they will cease; where there are tongues, they will be stilled; where there is knowledge, it will pass away," Reverend Vinicombe continued. "For we know in part and we prophesy in part, but when perfection comes, the imperfect disappears. When I was a child, I talked like a child, I thought like a child, I reasoned like a child. When I became a man, I put childish ways behind me. For now we see through a glass, darkly; but then face to face: now I know in part; but then shall I know even as also I am known. And now these three remain: faith, hope and love. But the greatest of..."

The vicar stopped dead as a murmur rippled through the congregation and soon the murmur became gasps and then there were screams for the Devil's door was open and under the arch in a patch of sunlight stood a stocky, bearded man with oversized glasses and if Harry hadn't recognised that face from The 319 the night of her murder he would know it from the news: it was David Castle.

"Please," Dr Castle began, "I just want..."

"What the hell do you think you're doing here?" Mr Brandreth roared, shaking to his feet, his finger quivering with rage and pointed across the hall to the man who'd murdered his daughter.

"Who let that man out?" Mrs Brandreth shrieked.

"I just want to pay my respects," Dr Castle said. "Please I..."

"You're fucking dead, mate!" Ryan cried, jumping to his feet, scrambling across the pew and tearing full pelt down the central passageway towards Serena's old teacher.

"The police let me go. They let me go! Please! I didn't..."

Ryan was upon him, a right hook and then a left; blood and teeth sprayed the church door as David Castle reeled and stumbled. Before he could pick himself up, Ryan was charging forward again fists swinging wildly, but someone pulled him back. It was Farhad, with a force that belied his age, and then his son Darius, and then Sachin was in there too, all straining with all their strength to hold Ryan from surging forwards and committing another murder there in cold blood on the cold stone floor.

"I'll kill you!" Ryan screamed, frothing at the mouth. "I'll fucking kill you!"

Harry watched aghast and in abject horror as the commotion unfolded. What was David Castle doing here? Why had the police let him go? Was this not the man who'd ripped a hole in the worlds of everyone inside this church? A man who'd brought so much suffering, so much pain and anguish to so many, Harry included? He watched as the teacher staggered to his feet and stumbled out of the church almost unseen among the maelstrom swirling about a spitting, howling, thrashing Ryan. And Harry recited Rule 5 over and over. Take the Blue Pill. Take the Blue Pill. Don't go out there. Don't go after him. Don't go asking questions you don't want to know the answers to. But it was too late. Harry was slipping as quickly and as quietly as he could out of the church, running out into the sunlit graveyard where somewhere in the trees a woodpigeon was cooing a concluding death march, and down the dirt path along the row of headstones and angels until he caught up to Dr Castle.

"Hey!" Harry cried. "Hey you, stop!"

David Castle turned to face him, his nose and his mouth streaming with blood, his eyes with tears. "I know you," Dr Castle gasped. "You killed Serena!"

Harry felt a flash of anger and indignation. "You killed Serena!"

"I would never, ever do anything to her."

"You killed her and you said all those things about me online, you made everyone in this fucking town think it was me. Just to what ... just to cover your tracks?"

"I loved her!"

"You sick bastard! She was your student!"

"Nothing happened between us. Not until after she left school."

"And then she left you and she was going to tell everyone about you and you murdered her!"

"No, I loved her. And she loved me. I don't expect you to understand."

Harry's fists were clenched by his sides now. "No, I don't understand. I don't understand how you could groom a girl half your age who was in your care. I don't understand how you could kill an innocent young woman who by everything I've seen back there meant the world to everyone in this town. I don't understand how you could make them believe that I did it. And I don't understand how the police could let you go when they found her necklace in..."

"That necklace was planted! It was a fake!"

"I don't believe you. And nor does anyone else in..."

"Maybe it was you who planted it."

"How dare you! How fucking dare you!" Harry lunged forward, grabbing the teacher's lapel with one hand, his other a fist and raised, but he didn't need anyone to pull him back. No matter who this man was, what he'd done, Harry was never going to hit him. He'd never hit anyone in his life, not even the bullies piling upon him for standing up for what was right in school, not even Ben. He was incapable of hurting another human being and that was Rule 6: We Come in Peace.

Ashamed that anyone might see him like this, he released David Castle's jacket and glanced behind him to check if they had been followed and sure enough, standing in the doorway, watching them without a word, was the swearing man.

"What are you looking at?" Harry rounded furiously on the big, black-suited form under the arch. "Why are you still following me? Didn't you get the memo? Your boss and I are working together. That's right, Guy Brandreth is funding my research and probably paying me a damn sight more than you. He knows I didn't kill his daughter. If you want to follow the killer go and follow that man over..." Pain flashed across Harry's face and he screwed up his eyes, trying to calm his breathing, trying to settle his mind even as it went back to that roadside the night he arrived and Serena's bloodied body and all the trauma came rushing back. Harry breathed. In and out. In. And out. In. And. Out.

At last, the pain subsided and he opened his eyes to find the swearing man was gone. He looked around and David Castle was nowhere to be seen either. But Sachin was, and River too, a look of concern in both their eyes.

"Come on, mate," Sachin said, placing a gentle hand on Harry's right shoulder. "Let's get you out of here."

"Yes, mister," River added, her hand on Harry's left shoulder. "I don't really think this is what your doctor would advise."

And so Sachin and River — probably the only two people besides Lauren who'd showed him any genuine kindness in this place, the two people in his whole lonely world he could come closest to calling friends — took him arm-in-arm and led him up the daffodil-lined path and through the shadowed gate, by which rested in no glory at the going down of the sun the gravestone of Lance Corporal Arthur Thomas VC: a young man honoured for killing before he was vilified for it. The last man to commit murder in Freebourne until David Castle.

Sachin and River led a still shaking Harry back across the green, where kids were throwing Frisbees and dogs, both robotic and real, ran here and there, past The Barley Mow down the street of large Georgian houses and then the next of smaller Victorian terraces until they came to the edge of town and the verdant lane leading up to Harry's house. They walked him up to his door and into his house and into his big sitting room and sat him down on the sofa by the fireplace under the enormous Jackson Pollock print and looked at him like they understood what he was going through, like they recognised a man on the edge of a PTSD-induced breakdown, and they made him tea and they talked and they listened until at last Harry felt he could breathe again.

"Thank you," Harry said when he felt calm enough. "Both of you, I mean it."

"Whatever," River replied. "You'd have done the same for me."

"You literally did do the same for me," Sachin said. "You picked me up when I was at my lowest."

Harry smiled. For all the pain of this last fortnight, for all the pain of the last few months, he knew he had his new friends to be thankful for. Friends whom he knew, after today, he could trust far more than Ben, or any of those other fairweathers who'd all abandoned him when he broke from his marriage and his business. And the worst was behind him, he had to tell himself that. Melanie was in the past. And for the first time since he'd left her, he'd met someone who truly excited and interested him and maybe it was a fool's hope, maybe he was reading far more into a simple drink and a few words and gestures than they deserved, but the fact he was even entertaining the possibility was progress. And the richest man in Sussex was backing his start-up and soon he'd go out and get a workspace and a team together and start building a future where no one needed to feel what he was feeling again. But he needed people he could count on. The sort of people with whom he'd actively choose to band together to rebuild civilisation after the zombie outbreak, or take on the no less daunting challenge of launching a revolutionary new business predicated on pioneering technology in an untested market and an uncertain economy.

"Sachin," he said, "I want to offer you that job I promised."

Sachin laughed. "Seriously? I thought you were kidding?"

"Blustering, maybe, but now I've got the funding... That messaging you gave me. Brilliant. I've never been good at talking about my work, but I know you would be. Come and be my new head of marketing."

"I don't know. I've got my job at Knight & King to think about. Hold on." Sachin tapped the side of his glasses. "Call Mr King ... Hey, Mr King. It's Sachin. Sachin. You know, Sachin. No there's no Sanjay. There never has been. And to be honest, boss, there's no Sachin anymore either. I quit. Fuckyouverymuch." Sachin tapped the side of his glasses again. "Right, I've thought about it. When do I start?"

River burst out laughing and Harry turned to her. "I would really love you to come and work for me too," he said.

"Thanks, but I couldn't leave the Rainbow Café. The Last Survivor would never cope."

"Part-time then, we can make it work."

"Your idea sounds pretty gnarly and all that, but I don't know the first thing about tech. I'm still a digital girl in a meta world."

"But you do know more than anyone about ethics."

"A bit of Buddhism. A touch of Marxism. A lot of D & D character alignment. So what?"

"Every MindTech company needs an ethics adviser. To keep the mad scientists in check."

"And what if I come into the office one day and conclude you've enslaved the human will to the cold and brutal logic of a machine dystopia?"

"That's what I'm going to pay you to tell me."

"Erm, Harry," said Sachin. "Don't we need someone who can actually build this Polaris device of yours? It's certainly not going to be me and Joni Mitchell over here."

"I'll ignore that, idiot," River said. "But Sachin's right. You can't do all the coding alone. But Farhad's son, Darius, he's some kind of genius. Why don't I ask him for you next time they're in the Rainbow? Talking of which, I should really get back there, poor Aunt Grace has been holding the fort for me all day. Are you gonna be alright?"

"I can stay if you need me to," Sachin said.

Harry smiled. "I'm going to be just fine, thank you. You've done more than enough. And besides, I should really start getting ready."

"Oh yeah," River said. "You've got your date tonight!"

Harry looked awkwardly at his floorboards. "It's not a date."

"It so is a date."

"It's just a drink. To say thank you."

"Mate, it's a date," Sachin said. "I saw the way she looked at you when she dropped you off. She likes you. God knows why — you were blabbering about like a blithering fool."

"Sachin?"

"Yes?"

"You didn't delete Mr King's number, did you?"

"No, why?"

"Oh, no reason."

Sachin laughed and River laughed and it was infectious. Harry was laughing too until his stomach ached and he realised then that it was the first time in seven months that he'd allowed himself to really let go and it felt good. He thanked them again and showed them to the door and told himself that today was a day for letting go. He kept on telling himself as he tried on five different shirts with varying degrees of formality, three different jackets that all felt like they were trying too hard, attempted jeans and a jumper and hated the idea of being that casual, before finally settling on the first pink shirt he'd picked out.

He always liked to imagine that he could relax, go with the flow, pull off the kind of effortless air that was unpractised, unpolished, and above all unbelievably charming. He couldn't. The prospect of a date used to send him into flurries of overthought panic at the best of times, and this was his first date in 18 years. Melanie, like Lauren, had been intelligent, funny, attractive, cool, and all these things seemed to terrify him to the point that even after she made the first move on the dance floor, he steadfastly refused to pluck up the courage to get her number until she'd asked for his, or ask her out until she called him and sent him marching orders to meet her on South Bank. Before that, he could recall a string of calamities dating back to his student days. There was Xiāng, objectively one of the most hilarious people Harry had ever met, but he was so nervous he could barely speak let alone laugh along with any of her riotous anecdotes from the theatre. He course-corrected hard with Aurelia and made sure he laughed at absolutely everything she said, which didn't really go down well when she was trying to tell him how many mink were butchered a year for fur or about her latest naked protest outside the slaughterhouse wrapped in polythene and covered in fake blood. He felt he'd got the balance of listening and laughing just about right with Tess until he snorted champagne through his nose and all over her horrified face. He was so embarrassed he pretended to go to the bathroom immediately afterwards and didn't come out until she'd left.

When he settled down with Melanie and finally found he'd gained the ability to ask her to marry him, he assumed that his young life of motorway pileup dates and casual sex, flings, meaningless relationships, mishaps and misfires, was long behind him. But here he was, the last sputters of his youth burnt out, ready at last to move on, but every bit as anxious as the gangly computer science student he used to know and judge so harshly for not being James Bond.

The walk back into town through the cold evening air to the sound of *Awake* by Electric Guest and the light patter of raindrops and the pleasant scent of petrichor did little to calm his jitters, but he was relieved when he arrived at The 319 to find Lauren was not there yet. Time enough for a little Dutch courage. Indeed, Harry had worked out through years of scientific experimentation in his younger days that he would reach optimum levels of charm and sophistication after precisely 2.34 units of alcohol. Any less was insufficient to dull the voice in the back of his head constantly questioning his every word; doubting every action, reaction and inaction. Any more and the voice came back, but the advice it gave became increasingly unintelligible and unhelpful. Two point three-four units. No more; no less. Almost exactly the amount of alcohol contained within a pint of Satan's Asshole.

"Coming right up," said Chris, chucking a glass in the air. "Harry, right?"

Harry nodded, pulling up a high stool at the bar. "I don't want any trouble."

"Well, you won't be getting any from me. No sir. I had you wrong and for that I'm sorry. That teacher, it was clearly him. He used to drink in here, you know. Always wondered about him. All those young girls he was with. Should have known. No smoke without fire. You didn't deserve the things people said about you, just for trying to do the right thing. Anyone who says otherwise ain't welcome in here. This one's on the house."

Harry accepted the drink and had just taken his first sip and his first 0.14 units of alcohol when Lauren walked in. When she waved and smiled at him, he all of a sudden became incredibly self-conscious of absolutely everything, not least the 2.2 units he had left to go.

"Oh hi, hey, hi, heya," he said, leaping to his feet not sure what to do next but grateful when she settled the question with a warm hug.

"Sorry I'm late," Lauren said, unbuttoning her coat and swinging it over the back of the high chair next to Harry. Underneath she was wearing a smart white shirt and a black pencil skirt and the voice in Harry's head started mocking him for coming underdressed. "I just came from work," she added, clocking him looking at her attire. "Nightmare day."

Harry was pretty sure the normal thing to do now would be to ask what it was she did exactly and why she found it such a nightmare. So he did.

"Oh don't get me wrong, I love my job," she said as she sat down. "But there are days. I'm conducting a longitudinal study into a cohort of patients with various neurodegenerative disorders in the hope of arriving at a cure."

"You mean like Alzheimer's?"

Lauren looked sad. "They're the hardest ones; the ones who forget. Watching the person they were vanish before your eyes. Everything that made them them, just gone. Knowing that maybe you have the answer. That maybe you can bring them back. But it's not easy."

Harry thought at this point he needed to say something reassuring and supportive based on no evidence whatsoever. "I'm sure you'll get there."

"I have to hope."

Harry took a large 0.23 unit sip of his drink and the voice in his head chose that moment to remind him that Lauren didn't · have a drink and that was something he really should have rectified sooner considering he was meant to be thanking her for scraping him off The Barley Mow floor and into an ambulance.

"God, I'm so sorry, what are you drinking?"

"Currently nothing," Lauren chuckled. "But if you're offering, I'll take a glass of the Bordeaux."

"What size?"

"There can be only one!"

Harry laughed at what he thought was the correct moment if she had indeed referenced the same old cult film he was thinking of, but then again she probably hadn't as it came out long before they were born and she didn't seem nearly geeky enough. "A large Bordeaux please, Chris," he said, gesturing to the proprietor who gave him a thumbs up and a few moments later returned with a glass of red wine for Lauren.

"Thanks," Lauren said, taking a long sip of her wine and exhaling deeply with eyes closed before looking up at Harry again. "So, what is it you do?"

"Something you probably wouldn't approve of."

"Sounds mysterious."

"I didn't mean it to be, sorry, I... I work in tech. MindTech to be precise. It's not exactly popular. At least not yet."

"Because it means changing the fundamental nature of what it means to be human?"

"Yes, I rather thought you'd say that."

Lauren offered him a wry smile. "So change my mind."

"Well, I suppose in your field you're trying to alter the physical condition of the brain to end suffering. I'm trying to alter the emotional condition of the brain to do the same thing."

"But if we can just switch off our pain, what are we? You can force people to look into the light, but can they truly understand it without the dark?"

Harry swigged his beer and made the mistake of thinking he could handle bold only 1.1 units in. "And they say you're not meant to talk philosophy on a first date."

"Ha!" Lauren cuffed him on the arm. "So you admit, it is a date!"

Harry started blabbering incoherently as the voice in his head sounded full retreat. "No, no, I, erm, well, yeah but, erm..."

"It's ok, I was only teasing."

"Sorry, I'm not exactly used to this. Not since my wife..."

"You're married?"

"Ex! Ex-wife! I mean my ex-wife!"

Lauren nodded, toying with her Ankh pendant between thumb and forefinger. "I don't think you're meant to talk about your exes either."

Harry burst out laughing, thoroughly disarmed. "Shall we go for a hat trick and do politics?"

"Oh don't get me started on politics," Lauren said shaking her head. It turned out she was something of an activist in her student days, protesting against human rights abuses from the death penalty and the torture of detainees by UK allies to encroaching state surveillance at home. Back then she was studying Human, Social, and Political Science at Jesus College, Cambridge. By her second year, she became so disillusioned with the political process and the ability of anyone to change anything that mattered that she dropped out, spent a year teaching herself A-Levels in Chemistry, Biology and Mathematics and then reapplied to study Natural Sciences, graduating with First Class Honours and going on to do a PhD in Neuroscience. If Dr Lauren Fontaine couldn't save the lives of people put to death or politically persecuted in far off distant lands, she was damn sure she was going to save lives somehow. By the age of 38, she'd worked in research teams all over the country for various universities, and even a government she despised, where they'd made major breakthroughs in treating and slowing the progression of diseases from dementia to Parkinson's and ALS. But the cures still eluded her. And it broke her heart as one-by-one she had to see the essence of her subjects slip away. As they retreated into the prisons of their bodies, or worse their minds — irretrievably forgetting everything that they were. She'd made it her life's mission to bring peace, not in fields of human conflict but in human minds at war with themselves. Her search for those answers finally led her to the University of Sussex and its Freebourne laboratory where she'd been posted for the last six months and where, two weeks ago, after learning their most promising drug to date had failed Stage 2 trials, she'd been binge drinking in The Barley Mow and met a man having an even worse day than her.

"That's pretty heroic," Harry said.

Lauren grinned and dimples darted across her face. "What, a woman who can handle five pints?"

"No, your work. Everything you're trying to achieve. You should meet my friend, River. She'd love you."

"Meet the friends already, is it?"

"Oh har har."

"But seriously, what kind of name is River?"

"I'm guessing that's not her real name."

"No shit. I mean, even rivers have real names. River Tiber. River Thames. River Nile."

"River Avon," Harry offered their river banter.

"No that's a tautology. River Avon does actually just mean River River in Common Brittonic. You could have picked almost any other river in the world, but uhhh-uhhh, you're going home with nothing."

Harry found himself laughing again and even at 1.67 units he knew it was at the right time. An easy calm had snuck up on him quite unannounced and he'd relaxed into the moment and Lauren's company without ever realising it. He felt her hand brush his and a warmth stirred inside him. Perhaps it wasn't him who had been out of place all this time. For something was connecting now like it never had before. All the questions had gone. The doubts with them. He couldn't hear the voice anymore. He wasn't even thinking as he closed his eyes and leaned closer to her and almost knew that she would lean too and she did. Their lips met and they kissed.

He could have existed in that moment forever. That rush of excitement. A few seconds of perfect distilled happiness unlike anything he could remember.

They wouldn't last. It was Lauren who broke away first. She was recoiling and Harry didn't know why. He heard her gasp. Her eyes were wide and they were transfixed on something behind him. Everyone in the room — now silent but for the sound of the television on the far wall — was staring with her at the same thing. And sure enough, he heard Harper Sloane's voice and he didn't want to turn but he did and he saw the presenter on the screen standing in the dark of a street scene somewhere in front of a police cordon with the kind of face that never delivered good news.

"A man was found dead behind the Church of St Laurence earlier this evening. Police have confirmed that they are treating his death as suspicious. The deceased, whose family have been informed, has been identified as Freebourne High School teacher, David Castle."

Chapter Seven:

Breathe

"Harry, breathe," Lauren was saying. "Breathe."

"I can't," Harry gasped. He could feel her hand on his back. He could feel all the eyes in the room on him once again. He could feel his heart pounding. He could feel the beads of sweat dripping down his forehead as he hyperventilated. And he could feel that familiar stabbing at the back of his eyes as if all those dark thoughts, all the fear and hurt and horror, were trying to cut their way out from inside of his head.

"Remember what Dr Chang said. You need to get some rest. This is no good for you. We should get you home."

He jammed his fingers into his temples. "Everyone's looking. Everyone, everyone, everyone. What if they think I..."

"Harry, you need to calm down."

"It hurts! It hurts!"

"Harry, please, I need you to focus. We need to go."

Harry gritted himself against the bar. "You go!"

"Harry, there's a killer out there and I don't feel safe."

Harry opened his eyes and looked up at her to see the worry that had settled on her face. For him. But also for herself. It was the same look on everyone's face in that bar. What it must be like to be a woman — or even a man now — walking alone after dark in a little town with a murderer on the loose who had killed twice and would surely kill again.

"Who could. Have done. This?" he said through laboured gasps, slowly straightening himself up and forcing the pain back inch by inch.

Lauren shook her head. "Either there's a serial killer out there in Freebourne now, or..."

"Or what?"

"Or that David Castle guy did kill Serena Brandreth, or at least someone believed strongly enough that he did, and they killed him for it."

"Oh god!" Harry cried.

"What? What's wrong?"

"I did something really stupid."

"What did you do?"

"It was so stupid! It was so stupid! At the funeral, I..."

Harry trailed off as the doors of the bar opened and in walked PC Atkins.

"Harry Coulson," the young police officer said, walking up to him. "We've been looking all over town for you. I'm afraid I'm going to need you to come down the station."

Lauren was looking at him concerned. "Harry, what's going on?"

Harry screwed his eyes up and pinched the bridge of his nose. "This is all a massive misunderstanding."

PC Atkins nodded. "And it's one we're going to have to clear up at the station. Look, you're not under arrest, but I really do think it would be better for you, sir, if you came with me."

"Sorry," Harry said to Lauren, his eyes imploring her as he rose to his feet. "This isn't how I imagined tonight would go. You have to believe me, I had nothing..."

"I believe you, Harry," Lauren said, stroking his cheek. "Please stay safe. I'll come and get you."

Every pair of eyes in the bar followed Harry as he followed PC Atkins out of the door and into the street where the police car was parked. At least half a dozen more people walking past saw PC Atkins open the rear door of the vehicle and usher Harry into the back seat. Harry spotted Reverend Vinicombe among them, and a man he recognised from the museum, the one with the wild red beard who'd been staring at him with his intense green eyes and he was staring again now. Overall, by his reckoning, at least 27 people had seen Harry Coulson — the man who discovered the body of Freebourne's first murder victim in a century the evening he arrived in town, the only man whose DNA was found at the scene, and the man who'd chased her supposed and now deceased killer out of the church on the day of the funeral — taken away by the police. It wouldn't take them long to add everything up and come to the wrong but nonetheless not entirely implausible conclusion just as the police must have done. And that mistruth would spread from the 27 like a virus with no one immune. Within a day, Harry calculated, everyone in Freebourne would hear the eyewitness account of tonight.

Harry was grateful that the tree-lined street outside the police station was deserted when he got out of the car and followed PC Atkins inside. The painfully bright reception was empty too except for a cleaning lady mopping what looked like blood off the polished floor. There was no friendly offer of a cup of tea to a shaken witness this time. Just a glass of water on the wooden table in the dingy, blue-walled interview room where DCI Khan and DI Manning were already waiting for him.

"Please, take a seat, Mr Coulson," DCI Khan said, gesturing towards the empty chair opposite. "Sorry, I keep forgetting. It's Dr Coulson, isn't it?"

"Yes," Harry replied, wincing as he sat down, the pain of the ordeal still throbbing in his head. "Listen, I know what you're going to ask me and…"

"Let me stop you there, Dr Coulson. There are a few things I am obliged to inform you of before we begin. Firstly, you are entitled to free and independent legal advice. Would you like a solicitor to be present?"

Harry shook his head. "Look, that's really not necessary. I'm not under arrest, am I?"

"This is a voluntary interview. You are not under arrest and you are free to leave at any time. However, I must inform you that you are being interviewed under caution as a suspect in the murder of David Castle."

"What?" Harry sputtered, nearly choking on his water.

"You do not have to say anything, but it may harm your defence if you do not mention something when questioned that you later rely on in court. Anything you do say may be given in evidence. Do you understand?"

"No, seriously, look, stop. What?"

DI Manning looked up at him. There was a plaster over the bridge of his nose and a ring of red crusted around his left nostril. "Do you understand, Dr Coulson?"

"This is ridiculous!"

"I need to confirm that you understand your rights before we proceed."

"Yes, I understand."

"Good," said DCI Khan. "I am DCI Khan. This is DI Manning."

"Yes, I know who you are."

DCI Khan reached into the pocket of her shalwar kameez and took out a pair of glasses which she put on her face and tapped the button on the side. DI Manning followed her lead, taking a pair of glasses out of his jacket pocket and pressing his button. Red lights appeared in the corner of their eyewear. "This interview is being recorded," DCI Khan said.

"Can we please just get on with this, I can explain everything."

"Dr Coulson, where were you between the time of 6:20 p.m. and 7 p.m. today?"

"I was at home."

"You live at the Old Mill down Hadrian's Way, correct?"

"Yes. I was there. I was getting ready for a date. Oh god, Lauren! What's she going to be thinking? I have to explain this to her!"

DI Manning cleared his throat. "And your date was at what time?"

"Half seven."

"And you were on time?"

"Yes, precisely on time."

"But you weren't with your date between 6:20 p.m. and 7 p.m.?"

"No, I was getting ready at home, like I said."

"Is there anyone who can corroborate your whereabouts?"

"Yes, my friends, River and Sachin. They brought me home from Serena's funeral. I was having a panic attack or something. I've been suffering from PTSD ever since I found her body, you see. They brought me home and they stayed with me till I was better. Ask them."

"We have asked them, Dr Coulson," DCI Khan said. "Sachin Roy and Harriet Allen, whom I believe you know by the name of River, have confirmed that they accompanied you home after Serena Brandreth's funeral."

"See!"

"And they also confirmed that they left your house at approximately 5:30 p.m. We checked the data on Mr Roy's glasses and their route mapping confirms that it was in fact 5:37 p.m."

"That sounds about right."

"So, you are saying that between 5:37 p.m., when Mr Roy and Ms Allen left your house, and 7:30 p.m., when you arrived at The 319, no one can confirm your whereabouts."

Harry sighed. "Yes, but..."

"Forensic analysis of Dr Castle's body places his time of death at approximately 6:40 p.m., give or take 20 minutes."

"I didn't kill him. I couldn't do something like that. I'm a bloody pacifist for god's sake. You have to believe me!"

"We're just trying to establish the facts, Dr Coulson."

"And the fact is," DI Manning said, a look of almost-relish on his shrew-like face, "You don't have an alibi. Now, if I may, what exactly were you doing at the funeral of Serena Brandreth. You told us that you didn't know her."

"I didn't. Her father invited me, as a thank you I suppose. We're working together."

"You're working with Guy Brandreth?" DCI Khan asked.

"He's investing in my start-up."

"I see," said DI Manning. "What if I told you Rosemary Brandreth was not at all happy that you were there? Whatever trust her husband places in you, she clearly doesn't share it."

"But she knows I didn't kill her daughter. David Castle killed her daughter. You arrested him!"

"There was insufficient evidence to charge him. And now David Castle's dead. He was killed by a blow to the head with a heavy object just like Serena. Dr Coulson, I'm going to ask you: did you kill Serena Brandreth?"

"No!"

"Did you kill David Castle?"

"No!"

"But you were the last person to see him alive."

"That's not true, there was another man, he was watching us; this private investigator who works for the Brandreths. You know him, DCI Khan."

DCI Khan shook her head. "I'm afraid I don't know the individual you're referring to. And we have an eyewitness who reports you were the only person he saw leaving the church after David Castle."

"Who?"

"Ryan Miller."

Harry gasped. "Ryan Miller! Of course! It was him, it must have been. He attacked David Castle in the church, he said he'd kill him, everyone saw it. Why am I here? Why aren't you talking to him?"

"Believe me," said DI Manning, rubbing the bridge of his battered nose, "We talked to him. Little bastard's still sleeping it off in a cell down the corridor. But he has an alibi and it checks out. He was at home with his sister at the time of David Castle's murder. Drinking heavily by all accounts."

"And you believe her? You believe him? David Castle killed Serena Brandreth and her boyfriend killed him in revenge."

"Except he wasn't the only one seen arguing with David Castle that day, was he?"

Harry bit his lip. "Look, I knew that's what you wanted to ask me about."

"The CCTV footage above the church door shows you in what appears to be a heated conversation with Dr Castle," said DCI Khan. She tapped the button on her glasses and video footage from earlier that day looking out into the churchyard popped up on Harry's own glasses screen. He could see the back of his head and his messy black hair and he could see David Castle standing in front of him on the path. Fingers were pointing and hands were gesturing angrily. DCI Khan blinked and the footage paused as Harry grabbed Dr Castle's lapel and his fist made a ball and he raised it in the air. "You wanted to hit him, didn't you?"

"I would never hit anyone."

"But you wanted to, didn't you?"

"Well..."

"Why did you confront Dr Castle, Dr Coulson?"

"He killed Serena!"

"But you didn't know Serena."

"It almost felt like I did. Seeing her lying there, hearing what she meant to everyone, it felt like I did. And what he did was wrong. He was her teacher and he groomed her and he killed her."

"But that's not why you went after him."

"I..."

"You went after him because he posted comments about you online," DI Manning said. "Comments that speculated as to why yours was the only DNA found on Serena Brandreth's body and in those specific locations. Comments that cast doubt on your innocence. And it wasn't the first time he accused you, was it? Several people have confirmed what was said between the two of you in The 319 the night you arrived. That must have made you very angry."

"But you know I didn't kill Serena. You know why my DNA was found on her wrist and neck. Because I tried to help her. I tried to save her life!"

"You should know that besides Ryan Miller's, yours was also the only DNA we've found on the body of Dr Castle."

"On his jacket, right? You saw the footage. I grabbed his jacket, but that's it. I let it go. And I let him go. I never hurt him."

"I put it to you, Dr Coulson, that you killed Serena Brandreth and when David Castle suspected you, you tried to frame him and when that didn't work you killed him to cover up your crime."

Harry tried to swallow but found his throat was dry. He reached for his water but his hand was shaking and he spilled it on the table. He tried to flatten his palms on his legs, but they were shaking too. In fear, but also in utter incredulity. He was a good person. Whether he was wired that way, or it was the strong sense of right and wrong his mother had imbued in him from an early age, he prided himself on kindness and decency. And here DI Manning was in the blazing sunlight painting the darkest night, saying that two plus two equals five, sure as the sky was green and the grass was blue. Harry knew the truth. These police officers, facing two murders in as many weeks in a town of barely 12,000 people, they were going to face questions and they needed to find quick answers and those answers would be wrong but they would be convenient, comfortable, comforting. He could feel the throbbing in his head again, like drums. He was not going to sit back and let them treat him like this.

"I think I would like to get legal advice after all," Harry said.

DCI Khan was opening her mouth to speak when there was a ringing sound. A call was coming through on her glasses. "Yes, what is it?" she said as she tapped the button. "I'm interviewing the suspect now. What do you mean? How can you know that, Tom? That's... no you're... look, just stop... Ok. Ok. Yes. Fine.

Yes. Yes. Bye." DCI Khan turned back to Harry. "Dr Coulson, you're free to go."

DI Manning slammed his hand on the table and leapt to his feet. "Ma'am that's some fucked up shit right there!"

"DI Manning, have you taken leave of your senses?"

"No, you have, ma'am. We have our suspect. Arrest him, charge him, you know…"

"It wasn't him."

Harry didn't know what was happening, but he was glad someone was finally seeing sense. "I hope you'll tell that to everyone in this town," he said. "Everyone who saw you dragging an innocent man away."

"Just get out of here, Dr Coulson," DCI Khan said, standing up, striding to the door, yanking it open and pointing for Harry to go.

Harry didn't need to be told twice. But when he walked through the door, he was surprised to see Elliott Nwosu standing in the corridor. The MP was remonstrating with PC Atkins and the short policewoman who'd been there that first night, and the officers, far from fawning this time, appeared to be blocking his path and he didn't look happy about it. Nwosu's furious face was full of questions as Harry passed him and then the man saw DCI Khan standing in the doorway and he rounded on her.

"You're letting him go?" Nwosu cried.

"He didn't kill David Castle," DCI Khan replied, the exasperation evident in her voice.

"And what about Serena Brandreth? What about my best friend's daughter? What about her?"

"He didn't kill her either."

"What aren't you telling me?"

"Mr Nwosu, sir, with the greatest respect, this is an active police investigation and I'm not at liberty to divulge any further information at this time."

"People out there are terrified."

"Then might I humbly suggest you go and reassure them. Didn't you say when the cameras were running that you had every confidence in us fine officers? Believe me when I say we are doing everything we can to catch the killer, or killers responsible."

"You don't even have the faintest idea who is behind this and you're letting a prime suspect slip through your fingers. Why?"

"I've said all I can, I'm sorry. This is above my pay grade and, frankly Mr Nwosu, it's above yours too."

"Don't count on that for much longer. I will get to the bottom of this! I will see justice for Serena!"

Harry had heard enough. He didn't care what games the police or the politicians wanted to play to deceive the public into thinking they cared about anything other than the maintenance of their own power in an otherwise heartless and unjust world. But he was not going to let himself be a pawn in that game. He pushed his way back into reception where, like the workings of a clock that ticked far too loudly, Harper Sloane and Aakesh Lal and all the other local and now national journalists covering this case as it spun wildly out of control were already assembled, cameras ready.

"Harry Coulson," Harper Sloane began. "Did the police question you in connection with the killing of David Castle?"

"Have the police released you without charge?" Aakesh Lal asked.

"Harry, come on," another, much more welcome voice said and Harry looked up to see Lauren pushing her way through the press pack, her hand extended, reaching out for him, and he didn't know what she was doing here or why she even trusted him after tonight, let alone wanted to be there for him, but he was grateful nonetheless and he took her hand and he let her lead him out of the police station and into the street where her black Tesla was waiting.

"Get in," she said, jumping in the driver's seat and opening the passenger door. "I've always wanted to say that."

"What are you doing here?" Harry said, climbing in.

Lauren started the motor and pulled away as the reporters poured out onto the street and their cameras flashed in the night. "I said I'd come and get you. I'm a woman of my word."

"Not that I'm not grateful, but why? You just saw the police take me away. I wouldn't blame you for thinking the same thing as everyone else in this bloody town."

"And what's that?"

"That I'm the killer."

Lauren raised an eyebrow. "Are you?"

"No, but..."

"Well, there you go."

"But what makes you so sure?"

Lauren turned the car onto the high street. "Harry, I study people and their minds every day. Trust me when I say I know you're telling the truth."

Harry smiled. "Well, I'm glad at least one person thinks I'm not capable of murder."

"Hey, I didn't say that. Give me a chance to get to know you. We've only had half a date."

Harry laughed drily. "I'm sorry about that. I really did want to take you out to thank you. Now I'm going to need to thank you twice. You probably had to pay for your drink in the end, didn't you?"

"And yours," Lauren said, turning them off the high street and onto the road out of town. "That prick of a barman said he was rescinding your free beer. Right before he started trying to chat me up."

"How can I make it up to you?"

Lauren tilted her head and smiled. "You could buy me dinner. Name the time, name the place."

There was no voice in his head telling him to slow down as Lauren pulled the car up outside his gate. No words advising him to be cautious. After the day he'd just survived and everything that was wrong in it, something about this just felt warm and comfortable and exciting at the same time, but above all it felt right, and that's why he said what he did.

"How about now, and I cook you dinner instead?"

"Why Dr Coulson, are you inviting me in?"

"I believe I am, Dr Fontaine."

"Good," said Lauren turning the motor off and climbing out of the car. "Because I'm starving. What are we having?"

Harry hadn't really thought that far ahead. He was still replaying the moment in his mind where he'd successfully asked a woman he liked a lot back to his house whilst sounding relatively charming and not at all like a gibbering wreck, and he'd not stopped to consider he actually had to follow through on his offer of dinner or the impracticalities of doing so when he'd not been shopping all week. When he'd sat Lauren down on a high stool at his marble kitchen island and poured her a glass of wine, he opened his store cupboard by the big industrial metal cooker hood to find it was empty save a couple of red onions and a black banana.

"Everything ok?" Lauren said, catching the look on Harry's face as he started to get flustered again.

"Yes, yes, everything's fine," he called back over his shoulder.

"Now you're not telling the truth," she laughed.

"Ok, you got me. I totally don't have anything to make you."

"Sure you do. My dad was a chef, he could make rabbits out of hats. Hand me a chopping board and a knife and let's see what you've got lurking around."

Harry did as he was told and fetched Lauren a chopping board and a knife.

"Haven't you got anything sharper? No? Doesn't matter. Right, what's in your fridge? Got any meat of any kind?"

"I'm a vegetarian."

"We'll work on that. Ok, vegetables, I bet you've got a couple of carrots lying around in your salad crisper, everyone forgets about those."

Harry opened his fridge and was pleasantly surprised to find Lauren was correct. "Yes, here you go," he said, handing her the carrots.

"In this kitchen, we say 'Yes, Chef!'" Lauren called back as she started to chop and her hands became a blur. "You got any legumes?"

"What?"

"Lentils, chickpeas, that sort of thing. You veggies always have those."

Harry nodded, grabbing the can of chickpeas from next to the stove. "Yes."

"Yes, what?"

"Yes, Chef!"

Before long, Harry had assisted Lauren in preparing what turned out to be the best vegetable curry he'd ever tasted. As it happened, Lauren's culinary skills and military kitchen discipline were not the only things she'd taken from her Parisian father, who'd arrived in London six decades ago to set up Brentford's first French restaurant and only sold it when his throat gave up the ability to shout. She was also fluent in four languages and knew how to swear profusely in all of them. Her drive to make a difference, meanwhile, almost certainly came from her mother, a cardiologist at West Middlesex Hospital in Isleworth, as did her love of tennis, acting, chess and philosophy. Harry was accustomed to being the smartest person in most rooms, but as they ate and drank and spoke late into the night, he was pleased to find that in Lauren he had more than met his match.

He didn't even realise how long they'd been talking until the house AI dimmed the lights and turned all the appliances off and he knew it must be midnight and the day came crashing back on him, rolling over the peaceful calm of Lauren's company — the sadness of Serena's funeral and the shock of watching Ryan beat David Castle and the rage he'd felt as he'd argued with the teacher and the excruciating pain as he learned what had happened moments before the police took him away — and every cell in his body was wracked under the weight of those long hours and he rubbed his eyes and failed to stifle a yawn.

"Stop me if I'm boring you," Lauren said with a smile.

"Sorry," Harry said, stretching. "It's been quite the day. But I don't think I'd have got through it without you. Thank you. Again."

"You must be shattered. Listen, I've probably had a bit too much to drive home, but chuck me a blanket and a cushion and I'll kip on your sofa. Or..." It was Lauren's turn to lean in, her eyes closed, and Harry closed his eyes and they kissed again and this time it was perfect. He let her take him by the hand and lead him up the stairs to his bedroom where she unbuttoned her shirt and he unbuttoned his and he pulled it off and he lay back on the bed and immediately started snoring.

Harry only realised what had happened when he felt the warmth of the sun on his face and he opened his eyes to find he was tucked up in bed under the duvet and Lauren was standing over him in her crumpled and very much still worn clothes from the night before with a cup of tea. He wanted to offer some sort of bumbling, garbled apology, but instead he just burst out laughing.

"I don't know what you find so funny," Lauren said, setting the tea down on his bedside table by his glasses and running a hand through his hair. "Your sofa fucking kills. Pardon my French. Votre putain de canapé fait mal."

"Sorry," Harry sputtered through laughter. "But that's the kind of weird, inexplicably awkward behaviour you're going to have to get used to if we're going to be together."

"Is that so?" Lauren said, coming to sit beside him on the bed and Harry rose to meet her and they kissed again. "Take two?"

"Technically take three if you count the…"

"Harry?"

"Yes, the speaking thing."

They laughed as they pulled each other's clothes off and made love on the bed. They stayed there all morning and into the early afternoon, talking, having sex, Harry's hands tracing the curve of her hips and his mouth her pierced nipples, exploring each other's minds and bodies. Despite everything, Harry couldn't remember feeling this happy. He could have stayed there all day if Lauren's phone hadn't rung.

"Hi," she answered. "Sorry. Yes. Yes, Harland, I know. No, I'm not. Those results won't take too long to come through. Of course. Thank you. I'll be there soon." Lauren hung up and smiled over at Harry propped up in bed beside her. "Sorry, my boss. He's a bit of a hard-ass. Not that I can blame him. We're starting a new trial today and I don't think he's willing to accept me skiving, much as I'd love to stay here with you."

Lauren had just climbed out of bed and begun searching for where she'd thrown her bra when Harry received a call too and he reached for his glasses.

"Hey, Sachin," Harry answered.

"Are you ok? I heard…" Sachin began.

"I'm fine, thank you."

"That's great, erm…" Sachin paused, his digital avatar looking askance. "Boss, are you naked? Don't worry, just don't look down, or that's an employment tribunal, ok?"

"Whatever. What's up?"

"I found us a workspace. I'm going down there to check it out now. Dirt cheap. Literally. The old Maltings down on Brewer's Lane."

"No way, how did you swing that?"

"Charm. Cunning. Guile. Witty repartee. And I think Mr King rather felt he owed me one after foisting years of casual racism on his best employee."

"Nice work, I'll meet you there in half an hour."

Harry quickly showered and threw on a fresh blue shirt and pair of black jeans and when he was ready Lauren gave him a lift on her way into the lab. Sachin was waiting for them when they pulled up outside the vast, five-storey Victorian malthouse at the end of the gravel track cutting through a stretch of long grass swaying in the cold breeze. The place had been built around the time of the railway when Freebourne burgeoned and supplied half of London's thirsty workers with their beer. It had long since sat empty. There must have been about a hundred grubby windows set into its dirtied, weatherworn brickwork and into its cracked, moss-encrusted slate roof and almost a quarter of them had been shattered by time or kids.

"Wow, that's quite something," Lauren said, stepping out of the car with Harry to take a closer look at the husk of a building.

"This is it?" asked Harry.

"Err, yes, I know what you're thinking and you're right," Sachin replied. "Turns out Mr King didn't feel like he owed me anything after all. It's…"

"Perfect," Harry clapped Sachin on the back. "The west wing of the ground floor still looks pretty intact. We'll fix up a space there and kit it out. And there's plenty of room to expand into when we become a world-leading, globally successful company."

"Well, you seem a lot chirpier than when I last saw you," said Sachin, glancing over at Lauren and giving Harry a little nudge with his elbow. "Mate, respect!"

"Ahem," said Lauren. "I can hear you, you know."

"Sorry, that was totally disrespectful, I apologise unreservedly."

A bicycle bell dinged twice. "Well, what's this shithole you've found, Sachin?" River said, pulling up with a skid beside them. Shielding her eyes, she turned to Lauren and grinned into the sunlight. "So you're this Lauren woman Harry's been banging on about."

Lauren offered her hand. "And you must be Brook? Stream? Tributary?"

"River," she said, taking Lauren's hand. "When my dad left to join the Secret Intelligence Service, I changed my name to protect his identity. Least I could do."

"Very wise. Well, Harry," Lauren said, giving him a parting kiss on the cheek, "Looks like you and your new colleagues have got a bit of a job on your hands here. Which is something I won't have unless I get moving." She climbed back in her car, made a phone symbol with her thumb and little finger and mouthed "Call me!" before driving off.

"She loves you!" River jibed.

"Oh be quiet," Harry said, grinning from ear to ear. And then he stopped himself as he remembered he wasn't the only person the police spoke to about his whereabouts yesterday. "Look, before we go and see inside, I want to address the elephant in the room."

"What that Sachin's rented a place that's going to fall down on our heads any minute?"

"Hey," Sachin began.

Harry shook his head. "No, I mean..."

"I know. Zero Judgement Zone. Come on, let's go and check out Sachin's Giant Junkheap."

"Hey, what about that Judgement Free Zone?" Sachin protested.

"Doesn't apply to idiots," River replied, poking Sachin in the ribs before kicking into her pedals and shooting off down the track towards the Maltings.

Harry and Sachin followed her on foot and when they'd all reached the entrance, they pulled open the door with a creak and stepped into a cavernous room of exposed brick and high wooden beams supported by great steel columns cut up by dozens of shafts of light slicing through the dust hanging in the stagnant air. The place smelt damp, it was strewn with rubble and broken glass, and weeds had started growing in the patches of dirt on the floor.

They wasted no time getting to work and spent the whole day clearing the room of detritus. The next morning, River arrived with Darius and he got stuck in with them. The young man didn't say much, but what he lacked in verbosity he certainly made up for in raw strength and he cleared more junk in two hours than the other three had in an entire afternoon. By the end of the third day, they'd finished clearing out the west wing and started bringing in wooden benches and chairs and plants and water coolers and a coffee machine and brightly coloured sofas and bean bags and Andy Warhol prints and old sci-fi film posters and yin-yangs and Buddha statues and everything the four of them had decided by committee their new office space should look like — somewhere that fused the East London of Harry's younger days, with Eastern mysticism and an estate agent. Harry hadn't heard a word from Guy Brandreth since the night the police took him away, despite repeated attempts to call his benefactor and explain, but the funds came through all the same and on day four a bank of shiny photonic computers and a 3D printer arrived and Darius' eyes lit up at the sight of them.

That was the day the real work began, with Harry and Darius tapping constantly at holokeys while Sachin started sketching out marketing strategies on the whiteboard and River, who split her time between the Maltings and the Rainbow Café, stopped by to bring them tea and her analysis of the ethical hurdles most MindTech companies fall at first. They returned the next day, working through the weekend as Darius' fresh and quite gifted perspective helped Harry put the final touches on his code and Sachin explained his strategy to promote River's ethical guidelines and show the world that Polaris' mission, unlike all the other doomed forays companies had made into MindTech, was governed by a strict set of moral principles that preserved free will and conscience even as it healed pain. On Monday, they were ready to start building components with the 3D printer. They carried on working until the sinking sun bathed the whole place red, but close as they were Harry sent the others home early, only staying behind briefly to lock up. He'd done just as Lauren had asked and he'd called her and they'd arranged to meet up in The Barley Mow for a drink after work today. Harry was excited to see her again and he knew he was not going to allow himself to repeat the mistakes he'd made with Melanie, spending every hour in the office, working on his machines, when he should be working on something far more human and beautiful.

He'd just made his way out of the front door of the Maltings when he looked up to see maybe 30 or 40 people blocking the track, waving placards and shouting angry slogans. They were dressed all in black, many hooded, wearing balaclavas or with dark facemasks covering their mouths and noses, and some of them held banners emblazoned with swords and Arabic writing quoting Qur'anic scripture. Others were wearing crucifixes around their necks and some had kippahs and turbans on their heads. The most ardent zealots of half the world's religions had seemingly put aside thousands of years of hate and bloodshed between their peoples to converge on Harry's new workplace and chant in unison: "We won't be slaves to your machine!"

Harry had never met an Anthropro before, but he'd heard enough about their violent tactics and extremist ideology to feel more than a little nervous when their leader stepped forward from the sea of shadowy, concealed faces and approached him.

His rising unease only grew when it dawned on him that he recognised that intense green-eyed stare even before the man had removed his balaclava to expose his wild, red beard.

"Dr Harry Coulson," said the green-eyed man without blinking. "My name is Francisco Ambrose and I have a message for you."

Harry frowned at the stranger. "I've seen you before."

"And you'll be seeing me again unless you heed these words. Close this place down forthwith and abandon the abominations you plan to unleash upon humanity and the world gifted to us. We will not sit idly by and allow you to rewrite our minds, the flawless constructs of our creator, with your technology. The Lord gave us free will and no machine will take it away. We bow only to God. There will not be a second warning."

Chapter Eight:

Deus Ex Machina

"Have you called the police?" Lauren said.

"What?" Harry replied.

"The police?" Lauren repeated, louder this time.

"Yes," Harry raised his voice to be heard over the table of drunken women commiserating a 60th birthday in The Barley Mow. He didn't much like the way half the party would quieten down every so often to stare at him and whisper, but it was the same everywhere now. "Not that I've got any faith left in them to actually find this guy. They still haven't found Serena or David's killer, have they?"

Lauren rubbed his shoulder. "Then you need to be careful. That threat sounded serious. Maybe you shouldn't be working on this Polaris project of yours while that group are still in Freebourne."

"And let the bastards win? No, I'm not one for giving up. Rule 3: It Ain't About How Hard Ya Hit, It's About How Hard You Can Get Hit and Keep Moving Forward."

"You and your rules. Harry, this is serious, your life could be in danger."

"The work is too important. All the good we can do."

"They probably think they're doing good too."

Harry rolled his eyes. "Please. Those God-touched nutjobs?"

"It's easy to write off those we disagree with, those whose ideas threaten ours, as insane. But what really makes them dangerous is that actually many of them are rational, thinking, intelligent people like me or you."

"You should have seen his eyes. No, there's no reasoning with someone like that. Just like all those tyrants and terrorists out there, they're too far gone."

"Oh really, you think all the world's horrors can be put down to mental illness? That's the kind of comforting lie we like to tell ourselves because we think it can never happen here. You think about the clerks filing papers with the names of Jews in Berlin in 1941, or the man shovelling coal into the engine of the train bound for Auschwitz, or even the politicians who sat behind their desks far away from the gas chambers and wrote the laws that brought it all together, and ask yourself were these people — together complicit in the worst crime in history — insane? It's far more terrifying to think that they were just going about their normal, humdrum existences and millions died as a result. By turning our opponents into monsters, others, we forget that in the right, or very wrong, circumstances, anyone could be."

Sipping his pint, Harry found it pretty hard to disagree with Lauren's philosophical position. He looked around him, at the middle-aged women bellowing raucously into their gins and tonics, at the group of large men in rugby shirts bantering comparatively quietly, at Reverend Vinicombe standing by the bar speaking with Grace, and he wondered how many of these polite, peaceful, law-abiding folk wouldn't turn a shotgun on him in the zombie apocalypse. He thought better of sharing his somewhat less erudite analogy with Lauren.

"I don't know what circumstances could have brought this Francisco guy to my door," he said.

Lauren frowned. "What did you say?"

"I said I don't know what could've..."

"No, his name?"

"Francisco Ambrose, I think he said his name was. I mean I'd remember a name like that."

Lauren's mouth fell open. "My god."

"You've heard of him?"

"I knew him," Lauren said, gazing into the embers of the fire where memories stirred in the crackling ash. "A long time ago. We were at university together. I'm not sure I'd ever have called him a friend, exactly, but he used to turn up at the same human rights protests I did. I'd see him in the college chapel from time to time, too. But there was always something about him, even then. He had a brilliant mind, always working ten steps ahead of everyone else, but it angered him when no one else moved as quickly as he wanted. Such a terrible temper. Probably why we lost touch after the first year. I don't know how he got radicalised. But I do know he was sent down and sent to prison for setting fire to a science lab. A student was badly hurt. I don't believe in monsters, just people, but there are always exceptions and Francisco Ambrose was one."

Harry glanced ever so slightly anxiously about the room in case he'd been followed. "Doesn't sound like he's changed."

"Depends which group he's fallen in with."

"I think they're those Anthropros."

Lauren shook her head. "The press like to write off all groups opposed to technological interference in the human condition as Anthropros. But when you've worked in as many labs and government facilities targeted by these people as I have, you come to learn the difference. The truth is there are probably dozens of factions and most hardly have any contact with one another. Some are religious extremists. Others are pretty much agnostic humanists. Then there are the conspiracy theorists, the remnants of the anti-vaxxers all those years ago. Some are really quite moderate in their ends and pacifist in their means, while others are ultraviolent and extremely dangerous. And if Francisco has found himself in bed with one of those factions, then Harry, you've got to be careful. He could be capable of anything."

Harry didn't like what he was hearing. He knew he'd have to explain what had happened an hour ago to Sachin and River and Darius. Even if he was willing to put his own safety on the line in the name of scientific progress and the chance to end suffering, he couldn't make that decision for his friends and colleagues. And the truth was, the more he learned about

Francisco Ambrose and his band of radical Anthropros, the more it terrified him. He was on edge now and when he heard a commotion across the room he jumped and spun around fearing they had found him. But it wasn't them. It was the birthday party and they were shouting at Reverend Vinicombe.

"Hey look, Martha, it's the stripper!" the loudest and largest of them was cackling.

"Please, ladies, that's hardly appropriate," Reverend Vinicombe replied in his soft and melodic tone. He was pointing at the television. The news was on and it was showing the Prime Minister standing in the House of Commons earlier that day, though it was impossible to hear what he was saying over the din. "I simply asked if you wouldn't mind speaking just a little quieter, just for a moment, I want to listen to this."

"Go on, get your cassock off!"

"Oi, sweeties, pipe down or you're out!" Grace hollered from behind the bar and the women, faced with the devastating prospect that this might be their last gin and tonic, muted themselves to a murmur.

Grace picked up the TV remote and turned up the volume just as Elliott Nwosu, MP for Freebourne and Battle, rose in the chamber to ask the Prime Minister a question.

"Thank you, Mr Speaker. Today, the petition for Serena's Law passed 20 million signatures," Nwosu said and the benches all around him except for the front erupted into cheers and applause. "Will the Prime Minister accept that his position in opposition to this simple law to protect women on Britain's streets is looking increasingly untenable?"

The Prime Minister rose as Nwosu sat. "Mr Speaker, my honourable friend will know that this government has done more to keep our streets safe than any government in history. More police…"

The benches on both sides of the chamber exploded into braying and jeering and the Prime Minister sat down.

"Order, order," the speaker cried and the House quietened. "In this chamber, we make the rules, we don't break them. The Prime Minister has been asked a question and his answer will be heard."

"Thank you, Mr Speaker," the Prime Minister said, rising again. "More police in every town and city. More serious offences prosecuted than ever before. Twice as many life sentences handed down than in my predecessor's administration, which I might add my honourable friend was a part of. But, Mr Speaker, our jails are full. That is why my government's focus cannot just be on punishing the crime, but reforming the criminal. My honourable friend's petition, while admirable, is..."

"Shame!" a female MP shouted from the opposition bench.

"A woman's dead!" a male MP shouted from the PM's own backbenches.

"No more!" another man cried.

"Resign!" came the call from across the floor.

The news broadcast cut back to the studio where Harper Sloane was in the presenter's chair addressing the camera: "That was the Prime Minister speaking earlier today in the House of Commons. Since today's angry exchanges, the petition for Serena's Law has surpassed 30 million signatures, while the Prime Minister's approval ratings have fallen to an all-time low. The Prime Minister has called an emergency reshuffle in response, appointing arch-rival Elliott Nwosu as Home Secretary in a move the opposition leader described as 'The PM keeping his enemies close because he's run out of friends'." Harper paused and the screen shifted to an image of a smouldering building and police cordons and ambulances. Her face flattened out and when she spoke again her tone was serious and sombre. "Returning now to our main story. It has just been confirmed that two scientists have died of their injuries after a bomb exploded early this evening at the Brighton

Centre for Genetic Engineering. Elliott Nwosu, the new Home Secretary, immediately declared a blanket ban on all Anthropro organisations. From today, they will be added to the list of terrorist groups proscribed under UK law. For more on this, I'm joined by..."

"Thank you, I've heard enough," Reverend Vinicombe said and Grace, visibly shocked, hurried to change the channel. The vicar appeared to be muttering a prayer under his breath.

"Fuck," Harry said. "Those people. What have they done?"

Lauren looked worried. "Harry, you've got to stop. Look at them, they're killing scientists now. If they can bomb a lab, none of us are safe."

"I've got to warn the others."

Harry called Sachin and River straight away and River managed to get through to Darius later that night and they all agreed to meet at the Maltings first thing in the morning. Harry rehearsed what he was going to say to them over and over with Lauren over dinner, and then alone to himself in the mirror the next morning when she'd left for work, but when he arrived at the Maltings to find his colleagues all at their desks tapping away, he found himself lost for words.

"What are you doing?" Harry said.

"What does it look like, mate?" Sachin replied.

"No, come on, you've got to stop."

"Quiet, please, boss," Darius said without looking up from his computer. "I'm working here."

"Maybe I didn't explain clearly enough. We have been threatened by a group of Anthropro — I don't know what they are — extremists? Terrorists? All I know is they want to stop our work and I'm pretty sure they'll go to any lengths necessary to do so. You all saw the news yesterday — what these people are capable of. Game over, man, game over! Polaris is everything I've ever hoped to achieve. My life's work. My dream. And I'm so grateful to all of you for sharing in it. But I can't guarantee your safety. And I won't put your lives at risk. I'm sorry, but we have to shut this place down."

"Harry," River said. "As your ethical adviser, I believe I speak for everyone here when I say: fuck those assholes!"

Harry felt his eyes moisten with the glow of happy tears, a welling of such love for these people who would stand with him for what was right in the face of intolerance and hate because they genuinely cared, but the feeling was fleeting, ephemeral, it could never last and he could never let them do it. He was opening his mouth to protest when the call came. It was Guy Brandreth.

"Answer," Harry said, tapping his glasses. Mr Brandreth's avatar appeared before him and he didn't look happy. "Mr Brandreth, hi, thank you, I've been trying to call you all..."

"Dr Coulson, we need to talk."

"Of course. Look, I know you're going to have a lot of questions. And there are some things, some really important things actually I need to tell you about. I can come and meet you at the museum. I can come straight away. I..."

"Have you lost your mind? Do you really think I could ever be seen in public with you, now?"

"But Mr Brandreth, you have to believe me, I spoke to the police and they let me go. They know I didn't... I couldn't... I'm not... You can't think..."

"It doesn't matter what I think. I know what my wife thinks. And as far as she's concerned, our association is over. And it would already be over if I didn't still need you. Is Polaris ready?"

"Well, we were about to test the prototype, but we've had a bit of a..."

"Good. I'm coming to your workspace this afternoon. You'll test it on me."

Mr Brandreth's avatar dissipated without another word.

"That was him, wasn't it?" Sachin said, looking concerned. "Rena's dad."

Harry nodded. "Yes, and he'll be here in a few hours. I don't know how I'm going to break it to him that we're abandoning Polaris."

"It's simple," River replied. "You're not."

"That settles it," Darius concurred.

"Listen, Harry," Sachin said, "I never liked Rena's dad. Frankly, I always thought he was a bit of a jerk. But no one deserves to go through what he's going through. We're so close. And we owe it to him to finish this."

"And of course, this isn't just about him," River said. "Or even healing the world's hurts. I know you're always thinking of others, putting them first, but Harry, it's ok to be selfish sometimes."

"I don't know what you mean," Harry began.

"It's ok to say that you need this too. All that trauma you're carrying around with you. And I don't mean what's happened to you since you came to Freebourne, but honestly, that would trigger anyone. I mean the accident, losing your unborn child, your wife, your best friend, that whole negative spiral you've been on all this time."

Harry gave a wan smile. "If I'm honest with myself, it didn't even begin there. It was losing my mum so young — it was as if this bright guiding star in my life just disappeared from the sky."

River smiled back, her wide, grey eyes glistening in the morning sun. "I know. Trust me, I know. When I lost my mum, all I had left was my dad and he's amazing, you know, a great man, a great doctor travelling all over the world helping people in the poorest communities, but I couldn't ask him to stay for me, or it would be all those people suffering instead."

"My mum died too," Darius said. "During the Second Revolution. Before we fled Iran."

"My parents are still alive, but I'm basically dead to them," Sachin said. "They let me grow up in a place that was full of choices and never approved of a single one I made. They just about recovered from me dropping out of the Law degree they press-ganged me into, but they could never understand why I would fall for a white girl of my own choosing instead of marrying my cousin in India like they'd arranged the day she was born. But now Rena's gone. And I'm all on my own. And I don't know what I did in a past life to be reincarnated here."

Harry smiled, determined this time. He remembered what his dad used to say. How time sounds distorted echoes of us all. Literally and physically. Every cell in our bodies, a copy of a copy of a copy, every part of us regenerated like the Ship of Theseus till there's nothing left of who we were before. Mentally, too. Every significant moment, remembered but refracted through the lens of the lives we've led since, dimly illuminated by our experience until we no longer recognise the person living in the memory. Like that poor lad who'd gone off to war an innocent boy and came back changed. And if that wasn't reincarnation, what was? But that past, no matter how hard, didn't have to define who we could be. Everyone has a choice.

"You're not alone, Sachin," Harry said. "None of you are. We may all be losers who've lost things, we may be broken, but when you bring all those shattered pieces together, what do you have?"

"A box of junk?"

"No, you have the building blocks for something new. We're going to finish Polaris. We'll do it for Mr Brandreth. We'll do it for Serena. We'll do it for your mum, River, and yours Darius, and mine too. And we won't bow down to the reactionaries standing in the way of what is right."

"Rule 4," River said with a grin. "All We Have to Decide..."

"Is What to Do With the Time That is Given to Us," Sachin chimed in and he was grinning too.

They had made their decision. They agreed to work just a little longer, just a few more hours so they could print the last of the components and build the prototype and that's exactly what they did. It was a mad rush, a flurry of frenzied typing and tapping, everyone pitching in, dashing from station to station, the 3D printer whirring and bleeping, but they did it. By the time Guy Brandreth walked through the door the device was complete. A thin, black titanium disk, no larger than a £10 coin, strapped to a simple headband.

"So this is the ring that would make a king happy when he is sad," Mr Brandreth said, inspecting Polaris, turning it over in his hands in a shaft of light. "Or, I suppose, a crown."

Harry looked anxiously at the floor and then back up at Guy Brandreth but never quite in his eyes. "Mr Brandreth, the prototype is ready to test, but I think it would be better to get it done quickly, you see there's..."

"Yes, yes, I know about those Anthropros. What, you think I ever stopped having you watched? Tyrone, Vlad, you may come in." Mr Brandreth raised his voice in the direction of the door and in stepped two huge navy-suited bodyguards, one black, one Slavic-looking, both sporting crew cuts and both even larger than the swearing man who was nowhere in sight but Harry could only imagine was observing somewhere close by. And Harry hated himself for thinking it, but looking at these hulking brutes, these constructs of pure muscle and aggression, and looking at the driven intensity in Mr Brandreth's cold blue eyes as he gazed at his prize, he couldn't help wondering if money could buy anything. Even the death of a man who'd killed his daughter.

"I assure you, we'll be quite safe," Mr Brandreth said, catching Harry eying his bodyguards nervously, though Harry didn't know who he should be more frightened of. "Now, shall we begin?"

Harry sat Mr Brandreth down on a chair by the far wall and he placed the device's strap around his head, tightening it to fit. Harry showed him what to do and Mr Brandreth gently tapped the metal disk. Nothing happened. Serena's father was about to press the disk again when Harry stopped him.

"It's not working," Mr Brandreth said.

"Close your eyes," Harry replied.

"What?"

"Trust me."

Mr Brandreth closed his eyes and the moment he did so his mouth opened and he let out a little gasp.

"What do you see," said Harry.

"What is this? Is this virtual reality?"

"No, it's far more powerful than that. If the device is working as intended, you should be looking at a representation of your mind, your thoughts, feelings, memories. What do you see?"

"I see a city down below me. But not like any I've ever seen before. There's something strange about it. Alien. It's shaped like a ring and it's sitting on top of a great spire of rock in the clouds. I'm moving inside. There's no sky now. I'm in some kind of square or marketplace in the distant past. There are thousands of doors, everywhere. No, not doors, they're shimmering. Like portals."

"Tell me you didn't make the user interface Planescape?" River said, rolling her eyes theatrically. "I thought you were kidding."

"This is Sigil," said Harry. "The City of Doors. Behind each one of those portals is a memory. Something that has marked you indelibly, for good or bad. Find the nearest one, the biggest one, the one that hurts most to approach, look into it and tell me what you see."

Mr Brandreth shuddered. "I see my baby girl. Her body, in the morgue, just as I saw her last."

"You can stay with her as long as you like. Or you can close that portal. Just click your fingers. The memory won't be gone, but the pain of it will be, for as long as you want it to be. Like fast-forwarding years of processing everything you're feeling. But you don't have to. It's your choice."

"I can't go on like this."

"Then click your fingers and close the portal."

Mr Brandreth clicked his fingers. His face remained expressionless for a moment and then it tightened, constricting into a grimace.

"What is it?" Harry said.

Mr Brandreth's eyes scrunched and his teeth clenched and his fists were balls of rock by his side. "I see... I see..."

"What do you see?"

"The portal's growing. It's getting bigger. It's swallowing everything else. It's all I can see now. Her face. My girl. My precious baby girl. And her eyes. Oh my god they're opening! And she's trying to say something."

"What's she saying?"

Tears were streaming down Mr Brandreth's face. "Where were you, Dad? Where were you? She's saying it over and over. It hurts. It hurts so much. Arrggh. Get this thing off me! Get it off!"

Mr Brandreth ripped the device from his head and fell to his knees, face in hands, rocking back and forth, sobbing. In an instant, Tyrone and Vlad were at his side, attempting to lift him to his feet but he wouldn't move. He just kept on rocking back and forth muttering "Where were you, Dad?" in between howls of anguish. What had happened? It should have worked. All his calculations were correct. Every line of code had been checked and rechecked. How had it gone so badly wrong? Harry was coming to Mr Brandreth's side too and he was about to put his hand on the man's back to try and comfort him when the door burst open. Harry's eyes darted to the entrance in alarm, his mind going straight to the worst, expecting to see Francisco Ambrose and his masked Anthropros back so soon, but it was something just as ugly, just as terrifying. Ryan Miller was standing there with a cricket bat in his hands and vengeance on his face.

"So this is where you've been hiding," Ryan screamed, striding into the room, cricket bat pointed at Sachin. His eyes were wide and full of frothing hate and probably some other substance and he scarcely noticed Serena's father cowering on the floor on the other side of the great hall, or Tyrone and Vlad scrabbling to check on their boss, or even Harry or Darius or River as they rushed to intercept him.

"Ryan, look..." Sachin began, taking two steps back as Ryan marched towards him, bat extended.

Ryan sniffed. "You told the feds I kicked the shit out of that fucking dead nonce teacher. You told them I killed him, innit."

"Didn't you?"

"You're fucking dead too, mate!"

Ryan charged at Sachin, bat raised in the air, only prevented from caving in Sachin's skull by Harry and Darius as they jumped between Serena's two once and shattered lovers, Harry's hands grasping for Ryan's, pushing back with all his strength to stop the bat coming down on Sachin's head, Darius leaping into the fray until all three were locked in struggle, and Ryan raged and spat, trying to tear at Harry and Darius with his teeth like a beast running on pure anger and instinct. If Guy Brandreth had even noticed what was happening on the other side of the room as he wailed to himself, he didn't seem to care, but Tyrone and Vlad were getting to their feet now and they were crashing over like great bulls on the charge, but they'd barely taken a few steps when Ryan's knees buckled and River was there behind him, a deft tap with her foot in just the right joint and he was crumpling backwards, the bat flying from his hands.

Catching the bat and wielding it like a sword, Sachin took two steps forward, standing over a prone Ryan and pointing it at his face. "Get out of here, Ryan."

Ryan propped himself up on his elbows and tried to shuffle backwards, outnumbered, defeated, but still seething. "If it weren't David Castle, then it was you. You killed Serena. And one of these days I'm gonna fucking do you."

"But not today," River said, a patronising look on her face. "Today you're going to run home to your mother and cry."

"Fucking bitch. Least I got a mum!"

"Shut up!" Sachin cried, jabbing the bat into Ryan's throat till he gagged and spluttered.

"Ryan, please, just leave," Harry implored him.

River slow clapped. "Dear little Ryan, have you always been this angry? Or have you only recently learned that while you may be proud of counting to two, it's actually quite a small number in inches?"

"You'll fucking regret that, swear down," Ryan said, clambering to his feet only to find Tyrone and Vlad towering over him. From the bewildered look on his face, it was plain enough to see the young man knew he had nothing to back up his threats. Still spitting, still swearing, Ryan beat his retreat, slamming the door so hard behind him a pane of glass shattered.

"Are you ok?" River said, her hand on Sachin's arm.

"Yes," Sachin replied, slowly lowering the bat he'd taken from Ryan. "Are you?"

"I think I probably caught a bit of bad karma for that cock joke."

"Fucking funny though," Sachin laughed and so did River and even Darius permitted himself a smile, but not Harry. He was looking across the massive hall, where Guy Brandreth was rising to his feet, shaking, his face haunted and wet with tears.

"Mr Brandreth," Harry said, rushing over to him. "What happened?"

"It didn't work," Mr Brandreth replied. "That's what happened."

"I don't understand."

"Oh, I understand perfectly. You're a fraud. A confidence man. Conjurer of cheap tricks. But no healer."

"We just need a bit more time. Whatever went wrong, we can fix it. We'll try it again. Polaris will work, I promise you!"

"Perhaps my wife was right about you."

"Mr Brandreth," Sachin began. "That's not fair. Harry's..."

"And of course, you of all people would be helping him, Roy."

Harry shook his head desperately. "Please, Mr Brandreth, I never did..."

"But you exploited her death, didn't you? You exploited my pain. I want my money back. Every last penny. Or you will know what pain feels like. You will..."

Mr Brandreth suddenly stopped speaking. He was staring over Harry's shoulder as there came an almighty crash and Harry turned just in time to see the door burst open again.

"Ryan, I won't tell you again..." Sachin began, bat pointed at the door, but he too stopped himself. Because it wasn't Ryan marching into the building. It was 11 masked Anthropros, dressed head to toe in black and wielding long knives and box cutters and metal pipes. At their head stood Francisco Ambrose, holding a can of petrol.

Chapter Nine:

Have You Ever Danced with the Devil in the Pale Moonlight?

"Behold, the day of the Lord is coming," proclaimed Francisco Ambrose as his masked terrorists fanned out about the room and he began to unscrew the cap on his petrol can. "Cruel, with fury and burning anger, to make the land a desolation. And He will exterminate its sinners from it."

"Francisco, please, there's no need for violence," Harry pleaded, his eyes darting around the room, from the Anthropros advancing upon them, weapons brandished, to Tyrone and Vlad stepping between the approaching extremists and their employer, to Sachin with his bat raised and Darius and River steeling themselves by his side. If he'd been frightened by anything Serena's father or Ryan had said moments ago, he was terrified now, like never before, because he knew there was almost certainly no truth in it when he said: "I'm sure we can resolve this peacefully."

Francisco's bright green eyes seemed to gleam in the last of the late afternoon sun. "The opportunity for a peaceful resolution has passed, sinner. I told you there would not be a second warning and lying, too, would be a sin."

"And what about harming others?" River said, her own eyes wide with fear and also defiance. "I know what my religion says about that."

Francisco nodded. "Thou shalt not kill. Indeed. Yes, yes. I would never take the life of another human being. You have abandoned all notion of mankind, tampered with God's design and turned your backs upon His plan. You are something else now. And you shall be cleansed. For the Lord is my shepherd;

I shall not want. He maketh me to lie down in green pastures: he leadeth me beside the still waters. He restoreth my soul: he leadeth me in the paths of righteousness for his name's sake. Yea, though I walk through the valley of the shadow of death, I will fear no evil: for thou art with me; thy rod and thy staff they comfort me."

"Allahu akbar!" came the cry from the big-bearded Anthropro with a metal pipe to Francisco's right.

Harry felt the lump in his throat as he tried to swallow. "Francisco, my mother was a devout woman, just like you. A good Christian. All she ever wanted to do was ease people's suffering. That's all we're trying to do here as well."

"Thou shalt have no other gods before me," Francisco said. "You, in your hubris, would dare to transmute humanity; you would usurp the Kingdom of Heaven with a machine. Only He can end suffering."

Hopelessly outnumbered and surrounded by armed men and women intent on murder and violence, shaking, heart pounding, Harry knew the worst thing he could do was provoke them, but if these were to be his last moments, he was never going to spend them on his knees. He would die as he'd lived. Standing up for what he believed was right.

"Then why doesn't he?" Harry said. "Where was your God through every plague and famine, every war? Where was he in the gas chambers or the gulags or the killing fields? Where was he for every grieving mother or father? Perhaps he doesn't have the power to intervene, in which case he's hardly as omnipotent as you would claim, or perhaps or he doesn't care, in which case he's not a good God, or maybe, just maybe, he simply doesn't exist. You think I'm usurping God because I want to ease people's suffering? I'm just stepping in where he's failed."

"Blasphemer!" Francisco cried. "You will be punished. You will all be punished!"

"And who are you to judge me?" Guy Brandreth bellowed, stepping forward from behind Tyrone and Vlad. "Just who in the hell do you think you are?"

"I am not in Hell, sir, but you soon will be. With your daughter."

Mr Brandreth didn't say anything else. He didn't need to. All it took was a nod for Tyrone and Vlad to surge forward: Tyrone catching the nearest Anthropro by surprise, twisting his arm behind his back until the bone cracked and bent at a horrific angle and he dropped his knife and he fell to his knees screaming as Tyrone delivered a mighty haymaker that knocked him out cold; Vlad grabbing a black-clad woman in a balaclava by the throat, lifting her into the air and hurling her over a desk, shattering her back and leaving her writhing in agony on the floor. Everything seemed to happen at once after that. Two Anthropros threw themselves on Tyrone and three on Vlad in a hail of fists and flashing steel. The Muslim Anthropro with the big beard was wielding his pipe and bringing it down on River when Sachin parried with his bat, knocking the man's pipe back and then swinging his bat around, smashing the man in the face as he staggered back, blood streaming from under his balaclava. Another Anthropro was charging at Harry with a long blade and Harry tried to run but he found himself frozen with fear, his eyes wide with panic, yet the man never reached him as Darius was surging forwards now and he was rugby tackling him to the ground and pummelling him with his fists until they turned red. Vlad was roaring with anger and broken Anthropros were flying like skittles in all directions around him. And then it came.

Bang.

Vlad dropped to his knees, clutching his stomach as blood poured out through his clasped hands. The whole hall stopped still in a sickening silence and Harry looked up and he gasped. There stood Francisco with the gun in his hands. Both of the man's eyes had been blackened in the fighting, a deep cut was gouged into his forehead and half his face was smeared crimson like a painted clown, a maniacal look in his eyes as though he were possessed.

"Everyone, against the wall," Francisco barked, waving his gun from Tyrone to Mr Brandreth to Sachin to Darius.

Too terrified to answer back now, Harry did exactly as he was told and lined up against the wall with the others, Tyrone and Darius lifting a pale Vlad and carrying him with them. They were forced at gunpoint to empty their pockets and throw their phones on the floor and Harry and Sachin's glasses too. Everything became a blur, but he could make out the black shapes closing around him and he could see Francisco's picking up the red of the can and he could smell the petrol and hear the slosh on the floor all around the room and he felt the cold wet of it hit his clothes and his neck.

"You've got another man outside, right?" Harry said to Mr Brandreth, his voice wavering and cracking. "Please tell me the police are coming?"

Mr Brandreth didn't answer. He just glowered venomously at Francisco.

"Please," Sachin begged.

"Just think about this for a moment," River pleaded.

"Mr Brandreth, please," Harry implored. "Snap out of it. I know what you're thinking. What he said about your daughter. And I'm sorry. I'm so sorry. But you can get us out of this. Offer him money. Offer him anything. Please!"

Still, Guy Brandreth did not answer. He could only stare a cold dead stare at Francisco as the man poured the last of the petrol onto the floor and threw away the can.

Vlad, still propped up between Tyrone and Darius, coughed and spluttered and blood trickled out of his mouth and down his chin. He was already white as a corpse.

"Listen, Francisco," Harry said, his heart beating so fast now and his mind running even faster. "He needs a doctor, please."

Francisco reached into his pocket and produced a lighter. "He won't soon."

"Ok, ok, but come on. I'm sorry I didn't listen to you. I should have listened. I should have taken you seriously. You were right. About everything. Burn this place down if you want to. Set fire to my life's work. I promise I'll abandon it. Just let us go."

"The sinner must be punished with the sin."

Harry closed his eyes and he sighed and in that sigh was a longing. If only he'd listened to Lauren, if only he had put aside his pride and his vanity to think he could really change anything in any meaningful way, he could be safe and in her arms right now. Would she ever understand? He felt the tear roll down his cheek and he knew it was for her. For the one person out there, in a life poorly lived forwards and understood backwards even worse, who might just miss him. For in that sigh was also acceptance. That it was a far, far better thing that he did than he had ever done. That the Needs of the Many Outweigh the Needs of the Few or in This Case the One.

"Then punish me," Harry said, his eyes red and moist.

"No!" River cried.

"Harry don't!" howled Sachin.

"Boss, please," said Darius.

"It's ok," Harry said and he knew that one more sin like a lie wouldn't hurt now. "Francisco, these people are innocent. All of them. I tricked Sachin and River and Darius into working for me. I never even told them what it is they were doing. And I conned Mr Brandreth out of £1.5 million. I preyed upon his pain after the death of his daughter to line my own pockets. Polaris doesn't even work! Please, it's me you want. Let everyone else go. They're innocent!"

Francisco stroked his beard. "That is not for me to judge. But you will be judged. You shall all burn here and for eternity."

"Don't you dare, Fran!" came her voice from the door and Harry couldn't see through the blur but he knew it was Lauren and his heart shattered.

"Lauren, get out of here!" Harry cried. "Go! Run!"

"Not a chance," Lauren replied, stepping into hazy view before the red of the fast-sinking sun. "I knew you wouldn't give up. I knew you were going to do something stupid. Well, I guess stupid comes in twos."

"Lauren Fontaine," Francisco rounded on her as two Anthropros moved to block her path. "You really can do a lot better."

"You should know I've called the police, Fran. They'll be here any minute."

"I don't need a minute. Get back against the wall!" Francisco screamed, pointing his gun at Tyrone as he took a step forward. He turned back to face Lauren. "Maybe you'd like to join them."

If Lauren was fazed or frightened, she was putting up a colossal effort to hide it. "It's been a long fall from grace for you, hasn't it, Fran?"

"Hypocrite!" Francisco cried. "Apostate! I've been watching you, all this time. With him." He narrowed his eyes at Harry. "That creature. And I know what you've become. You have put your faith in science and turned your back on God."

Lauren tilted her head. "We all worship God in our own ways. Not that you would understand. So blinded, so blinkered."

"Lauren, please, stop!" Harry screamed. "Just go. Francisco, don't hurt her."

"He's not going to hurt me, Harry," Lauren said, a confidence in her voice Harry couldn't fathom. "He's going to put his gun on the floor, he's going to take his people, he's going to walk out of here and he's never going to come back."

Francisco laughed. "Oh and why's that?"

Lauren stepped forward. A masked woman moved to stop her, but Francisco, a curious look on his face, waved the woman away and Lauren drew closer, whispering into his ear as his face became unsettled and alarmed and his brows furrowed and his eyes widened and he took a step back. Harry could scarcely believe what he heard next.

"We're leaving," Francisco declared.

"What?" said the Muslim Anthropro, nursing his jaw, evidently every bit as incapable of believing what he was hearing.

"It's over."

Sirens whooped outside and flashing blue lights danced across the darkening hall. Francisco dropped the gun and he bolted for the door, the Anthropros who were still conscious and able to move fleeing after him, the rest left behind and bleeding for the police to find. Lauren hurried between their crumpled bodies as she rushed to throw her arms around Harry.

"Are you hurt?" she said, pressing her face so close to his she could surely taste the tears streaming down his cheeks, surely feel his body shivering in shock.

"We're alive!" Sachin cried, wiping the tears from his own eyes. "My god, we're alive!"

"Lauren, you saved us!" River croaked, barely able to speak.

Vlad groaned and winced and slumped as Tyrone and Darius took his colossal weight and helped him limp grunt by grunt for the door. Mr Brandreth silently followed their trail of blood, his eyes hollowed and expressionless. And reaching for his glasses, Harry looked from Lauren to River to Sachin, strangers only a few short weeks ago, today the three people he cared most about in this world, and he knew that words would never be able to convey how he felt to see them safe, nor how thankful he was to Lauren for all their lives.

"How did you…" Harry began, unable to process everything that he had just experienced, everything he had inexplicably lived through.

"I knew him, remember. Better than any of those people following him, I'm sure."

"But you weren't friends."

Lauren looked away uncomfortably. "I suppose we were more than friends; I've just stopped admitting it."

"I saw the way he looked at you. At me."

"It didn't last. It couldn't. It wasn't just his temper. I found something out about him. Something terrible. It made me so sick. Even in the most despicable acts, I like to think there's some explanation, some rationale in the human psyche, or societal conditioning. But you were right, some people just come out wrong. They can put on a mask or wear their faith as one, but beneath it isn't God, not my God, it's evil. Just evil." Lauren looked to the floor pensively and then up at Harry again. "I doubt his followers would have understood why he raped my best friend. I certainly couldn't. By the time I'd convinced her to go to the police, he'd already burned down the lab with her in it. Not for some great statement against science, just to cover his own sin. He would have taken down everyone who stood with him and everything they believed in too just to hide his disgusting crime. I'm not sure he ever knew that I knew until today. And I made sure if he didn't leave, I would reveal to every one of his followers exactly who the real Francisco Ambrose is."

"I'm so sorry," said River, placing her hand on Lauren's shoulder. "For your friend."

"She survived, but…"

"It's never really the same, is it?"

Lauren shook her head. "Come on, we need to get out of here. It's not safe."

Harry was still in shock and barely able to comprehend everything he was hearing, let alone everything he'd just been through, but he allowed Lauren to take him by the hand and lead them all out of the building and into the night that had fallen. Outside, a barely conscious Vlad was being strapped to a stretcher and lifted into the back of an ambulance by the waiting paramedics, Tyrone and Mr Brandreth looking on at his side. A circle of police cars had pulled up, blue lights flashing and swirling in the dark, and a dozen armed officers now surrounded the entrance, guns pointed at Anthropros with their arms in the air. One of them was cuffing Francisco's arms behind his back as he lay face down on the ground. The moonlight greyed the zealot's bloodied visage, glinting in the green of his eyes as he lifted his head to see Harry and Lauren emerge from the Maltings. Where once a fire burned, a strange calm seemed to have come over him now; for everything a season, a time for war, and a time for peace. He didn't try to struggle or even speak when DCI Khan and DI Manning stepped out of their vehicle.

"Francisco Ambrose," said DI Manning, standing over that fallen angel. "I'm arresting you on suspicion of terror offences, attempted murder, attempted arson, possession of an illegal weapon, breaking and entering, false imprisonment — anything else ma'am?"

DCI Khan nodded. "How long do we think this psychopath has been in town?"

"Could be as long as 18 days, couldn't it?"

"The universe is rarely so lazy."

"Quite right ma'am. Francisco Ambrose, we're also arresting you on suspicion of the murders of Serena Brandreth and David Castle. You do not have to say anything, but it may harm your defence if you do not mention something when questioned that you later rely on in court. Anything you do say may be given in evidence. Take him away."

"Did you hear that?" said Lauren, turning to Harry as they looked on. "Is it over?"

Harry tried to mouth something but no words came out. All he could do was watch in silence as two armed police officers hoisted Francisco to his feet and marched him, hands cuffed, head bowed, into the back of a waiting van. And he looked upon his works and he despaired. At Darius sitting head in hands on the ground, a blanket over his shoulders. At Farhad running over to him and throwing his arms around his son and kissing him on the head. At River and Sachin holding onto one another, sobbing. At Guy Brandreth on the telephone, dead behind the eyes. At Tyrone climbing into the back of the ambulance before it pulled away up the track, sirens blazing. At the small crowd of bystanders who had come to watch the spectacle from a safe distance, glasses cameras flashing. At Reverend Vinicombe standing among them, crossing his chest and offering some kind of prayer.

"Get those people out of here," DCI Khan was saying, pointing at the gathering crowd as her officers set up a cordon.

"Is everyone alright, officers?" said Reverend Vinicombe, walking over to the police. "I heard the commotion. I pray that no one was hurt."

DCI Khan smiled patiently. "Everything's under control, vicar. You go home now."

Harry was still staring vacantly out at the scene unfolding around him when he felt Lauren tug on his arm.

"No," said Harry.

"No, what?" Lauren replied.

"No, it's not over." He was gazing over at Mr Brandreth now as he hung up the telephone. "Maybe Francisco Ambrose or one of his followers did kill Serena, god knows why — I guess murdering the daughter of one of Britain's richest men would make a statement — but I don't think he killed David Castle."

Lauren followed his gaze and her eyes went wide. "Fuck. You don't think…"

"I think Guy Brandreth had David Castle killed. My god, who have I been working for?"

Serena's father suddenly looked up and he caught sight of Harry and Lauren staring in his direction and he strode over to them, his face bathed blue and colder still.

"Mr Brandreth..." Harry began.

"Dr Coulson," Mr Brandreth said. "And Lauren, isn't it? Of course, it is. You volunteer at the museum."

Lauren nodded. "Yes."

"I owe you both my life. And for that reason alone, I am giving you one last chance. You will finish Polaris. I want it ready in two weeks. I am confident you will not disappoint me, Dr Coulson."

Chapter Ten:

Gravity

Exhausted, shattered physically and emotionally, Harry passed out the moment he got home and his head hit the pillow, Lauren holding him and stroking his hair. It was 11 a.m. by the time he woke alone in bed with a start. That was when the true enormity of everything he'd experienced fully hit him. How close he'd come to losing his friends, losing Lauren, losing everything that meant anything to him now in a life he'd struggled so hard to rebuild. And that terrified him even more than the realisation of how close he'd come to death. The worst of it was the gnawing feeling deep inside him that even though the terrorists were behind bars, he and his friends were still far from safety. He'd seen the deathly chill in Guy Brandreth's eyes when Francisco Ambrose had insulted his daughter's memory — the icy gaze of a man who had fought with monsters and become one — and he'd watched the thugs hired by the richest and most powerful man in Freebourne tear limb from limb, way too literally, on just a nod, the people he held responsible. And an innocent man — innocent at least of this crime — was dead. And it finally dawned on Harry the full gravity of the promise he'd made.

A scream slipped out.

"Harry, are you ok?" Lauren cried, rushing into the bedroom. Her hair was wet and wrapped up in a towel and she was wearing nothing but a shirt.

"I've got to get to work," Harry said, sitting bolt upright and wiping the sweat from his brow.

"You've got to be kidding?"

"You heard what Serena's father said. We're all in danger unless I finish Polaris."

"Harry, if that's true, maybe you shouldn't be working for this man. Maybe we should go to the police."

"And tell them what? It's just a hunch. I've got no evidence."

"Maybe there's some way to find something. Something that proves Guy Brandreth had David Castle killed, mistakenly believing he murdered his daughter."

"I really don't think we should be sniffing around this. It's too dangerous. Let the police do their job."

"If the police know anything, they're hiding it well. Maybe too well. You don't think there's a whiff of a cover-up about this? Something they're not telling us?"

"You think Mr Brandreth is paying them off or something?"

"I don't think anything. But I do ask questions. And so should you."

"Be careful, Lauren, I mean it. I can't lose you. I've just found you. I just..."

"I just took down the terror network of one of Britain's most dangerous men. You think Guy Brandreth scares me?"

"He scares me. And that's why I can't lose any more time. We've got to finish what we started."

Unfortunately for Harry, the police didn't seem to agree with his sense of urgency. He spent the rest of the day on the phone trying to convince them to let him back into the Maltings. But it was a crime scene now, cordoned off and blockaded by investigating officers. The next day was a write-off as well. River, who had also sensed the danger they were in, suggested they work together in the Rainbow Café, but there was only so much progress they could make without access to their photonic computers, and with PC Atkins and Carla and The Last Survivor turning up for their usual orders, and they were all still too shaken by what they'd experienced to concentrate. On Friday, Harry was relieved to finally get the call. The police had concluded their investigation of the crime scene and the Maltings had been declared safe for them to return. They'd even installed a new electronic security door to keep them safe and issued them all with keycards. It was a cold and wet day and Harry, River, Sachin and Darius spent every last hour in silence tapping on holokeys as the rain tapped on a hundred windows. Harry and Darius analysed over a thousand lines of code, dictating while River and Sachin took notes of their findings and eventually Darius identified the errors in their initial calculations and they set about the painstaking task of fixing them. They worked late into the evening to make up for lost time and they only stopped when their brains became clay and Harry decided enough was enough and he went home to spend the night with Lauren.

The next day was the same, and the day after that. He'd wake up early every morning and get to work and come home late in the evening when Lauren would come round and he'd try and cook her dinner and she'd take over and she'd take the stress of the day away from him with jokes and laughs and then take him to bed and they'd make love and talk into the small hours. They talked about anything and everything. About their happy memories of childhood. Harry's spent tinkering with gadgets and coding apps and going to sci-fi conventions and playing computer games and Dungeons & Dragons. Lauren's spent horse riding in Richmond Park and performing in school plays and holidaying in France and swimming in rivers and hiking up mountains. About their student days. Harry's mostly with his head in tablets and lines of code. Lauren's rowing and drinking for the college. About music. Harry's tastes had stopped evolving as a kid and he was still into the same long-defunct or dead indie guitar bands that were popular then. Lauren's were far more eclectic, ranging from classical and jazz to the new metahouse and fifth industrial outfits. About their families. How Lauren loved her quirky parents and her three sisters and brother and eight cousins. How Harry wished he wasn't an only child, that he had a brother or a sister or a cousin now his parents were gone. How lonely life had been for him these past few months cut off from everyone. How he was so happy to have found her, despite everything. How they would get through this, together.

When Monday rolled around, it seemed like they just might. Harry and his team had made solid progress over the weekend and when everyone arrived at the Maltings in the morning, they all looked a lot more cheerful. River especially had a big grin on her face.

"Do you mind, I can literally see my face reflected in your teeth," Sachin said, looking up from his desk.

"Shut up, idiot," River laughed.

"What's got you so chirpy?"

"My dad's coming home!"

"Wow, that's amazing."

River wrinkled her nose. "Yes, yes, it is. It's so great. It really is."

"You always speak so fondly of him."

"He's a great man. A brilliant man. He's an aid worker in Africa. He's been out there building a school. Such a kind and wonderful person."

"I thought you said he was a doctor or something?"

"Yeah, yeah, yeah he is. But he's working for an aid organisation to help sick kids in developing countries. And the school project is part of that."

"I see."

"I just can't wait to see him; it's been so long."

"Guys, can you pipe down a bit, I think I've nearly cracked it," said Harry, poking his head over his computer. "Yep, yep, yes, yes that's it. Got it! We're done. Darius, what do you think?"

Darius nodded. "The code looks perfect, boss."

"Perfect? That, my friend, is artistry."

Harry downloaded the new code into Polaris and within two hours it was ready for testing. They thought better of calling

Guy Brandreth and letting him see it before they'd tried it themselves this time and Harry volunteered for the chair. Sitting down, with Darius, River and Sachin on hand to take notes, he strapped Polaris to his head, tapped the titanium disc and closed his eyes. The world melted away and he was floating in a cloudless clear blue sky over an infinite desert. Below him, the great spire shot upwards and hovering above it was the mighty torus of Sigil. The graphical user interface served absolutely no purpose, it was pure flourish, but he had to admit he felt a little burst of excitement as the city drew him in and he found himself standing in the strange and twisted marketplace he'd always pictured rolling D20s on a tabletop, amidst the bustling slums of the Hive, populated by outlandish creatures under a hazy twilight. His excitement was short-lived, however.

"That's odd," Harry said.

"What is it?" Sachin asked.

"Fuck!"

"Harry, what's wrong?" River said.

"Shit, shit, shit, shit!"

"Boss, speak to us," said Darius.

"We must have got something wrong. It's broken. It doesn't work. There are no doors, anywhere. All I can see is the UI. But it doesn't allow me to do anything. There are no portals for me to look into."

Harry pulled the device off his head and opened his eyes and the real world came hurtling back and with it the concern on Sachin, River and Darius' faces.

"That's impossible," Darius said. "I double-checked every inch of code. It was perfect."

Harry sighed. "Something this complex, it's like a tapestry. You pull on one thread and the whole thing comes apart. There's nothing else for it. I'm sorry, but we're just going to have to code the whole thing again from scratch."

"Ey vây!"

Sachin looked worried. "Surely that could take weeks?"

Harry shook his head. "We have just over one."

"Harry, everyone's tired and stressed and frankly all our nerves are shot after what we've just experienced," River said. "That's how mistakes happen. I know time is against us, but I think we all need to take a break. Meditate, go for a walk, have a drink, watch porn or whatever it is Sachin does every evening."

"Hey…" Sachin protested.

"Come at this with fresh minds tomorrow. Then maybe we'll be able to see what went wrong."

Harry knew she was right. He'd been driving them too hard. He'd been driving himself too hard as well. They'd barely had time to stop and come to terms with all they'd been through. So he gave them the afternoon off. River planned to meditate and do some yoga and then pop into the Rainbow Café before her dad got home. Sachin would go for a run. The only time he was ever seen out of his three-piece suit was when he was in Lycra and could be spotted running round town training for his half marathon. He'd then gain all those calories back drinking and watching football and placing bets no sensible person would ever place down The 319. Darius didn't seem to want to say what he was going to do and Harry didn't care to pry.

On River's advice he decided to go for a walk to clear his head. Lauren was able to finish work early and when she came round, they wandered out over the little bridge by his house, crossing the river where the weeping willow bent its bare tendrils to the water and making their way up the hill into the woods, picking their way between the bluebells and wild garlic through sun and shade dappled across the moss-covered ground. There was no one else about. The woods were silent except for birdsong and the snapping of twigs and the rustling of leaves underfoot.

"It's beautiful here," Lauren said, shading her eyes and smiling up at the sunlight. When Harry, lost in thought, failed to reply, she glanced over at him. "Don't you think?"

"Sure, sure."

"I mean, just smell the air."

"Air, yes."

"That's life, out there. Pure, unadulterated life."

"Uh-huh."

"And I was thinking I might get gender reassignment surgery."

"Yes, ok."

"I've always wanted to have a penis."

"Makes sense."

"Harry, you're not listening, are you?"

Harry suddenly looked up at her. "What? Oh, sorry. I was a million miles away."

"What's up?"

"I really thought it was going to work this time. Polaris."

"I know you don't like giving up, Harry, but maybe it's time to stop. This isn't good for you."

"And what will Guy Brandreth do if we let him down?"

"If I were you, I'd be more worried about those Anthropros. Fran may be safely behind bars, but there are thousands of Anthropros still out there, dozens of groups, some of them even more extreme than his, and all our myopic government has done with its blanket ban is drive them underground and make them more dangerous still."

Harry bit his lip. "I can't stop now. This is my life's work."

"Who says?"

"Don't you feel it too? This instinct that humanity can be better. Fixed. The terrible things we do to each other. Because there's something rotten deep inside us. It's like an urge in me."

Lauren gave a little tilt of her head. "One of your rules?"

"Rule 7: Gentlemen, We Can Rebuild Him, We Have the Technology."

They came to a stop two-thirds of the way up the hill by two large trees intertwined like dancing lovers, their trunks twisting together to form a heart between them.

Lauren turned to Harry. "I'm still not convinced humanity would be better off just because we can take away people's pain. I remember the most traumatic thing that ever happened to me was watching my grandmother, the sharpest woman you'd ever have met, a force of nature, lose her mind to dementia when I was only 11 years old. I still carry that around with me. But without it, would I ever have set out to make a difference? To help people who'd lost their memories and themselves? Become what I have today? Pain is a teacher. We need it to fly every bit as much as fairy dust and happy thoughts."

"And Polaris would never take that away from anyone. It's one of the foundational moral principles we've set out. You would still learn the lessons. In fact, that's vital to overcoming the trauma and moving on. I just want to help people process it all a lot faster. Instead of losing months, years of their lives suffering needlessly."

"Ok, well let's take a more extreme example. What stops everyone killing each other?"

"The law, primarily."

"So, it's your zombie apocalypse and there are no laws. Is everyone killing each other?"

"No, because we all have our own moral compasses."

"Because, what — we'd feel guilt? Pain at the knowledge our own actions had harmed another? What if we could just switch off that pain? No remorse, nothing. That's what psychopaths feel every day."

"Don't worry, River thought of that as well. We are programming Polaris so it cannot remove self-inflicted guilt arising from intentional harm."

"That's all very well and good, but what about the next company or government to come along and 'perfect' your idea? Can you guarantee they will be as ethical as you? That they will have mankind's best interests at heart? The djinni is out of the bottle and it's never going back."

"We cannot become so preoccupied with whether or not we should, to stop us thinking we could. All scientific progress is a positive in and of itself; that some might choose to misuse it must not prevent us from pursuing a dream of something better."

"So splitting the atom worked out well for the people of Hiroshima and Nagasaki? Or the people of Pripyat?"

"No, but without nuclear fission we'd never have developed nuclear fusion and the climate breakdown we're seeing in so many parts of the world today would be immeasurably more catastrophic. Think how many lives that saved."

"And think how many more could be ended if our governments deployed the weapons they've developed based on that same technology? Probably everyone's. You're a good person and I trust your intentions for Polaris. But what if, say, the state came along and it used your technology to erase things other than pain? How about rebellious thoughts? Criticism? Free will?"

"Why on Earth would they do that?"

"Why wouldn't they? They use every other method at their disposal already. The whole system is geared towards producing compliance. Replicating a set of values held by a tiny elite because having a bigger stick is so passé. We know the state has a monopoly of violence, and it will deploy it against its own citizens if it needs to, but it rarely does. Why? Well, we're recorded over 300 times a day simply going about our daily lives. The whole world is one giant panopticon now. That we know we are constantly watched unconsciously changes our behaviour. That's another form of violence, against our minds, but it's far from the most insidious. The mass media, almost exclusively owned by the same sliver of society who rule us, tell us what to think, what is acceptable, permissible, within established parameters; they bubble us with algorithms and they tell us who we should vote for and who we should irrationally fear or hate so that our attention and our anger is always directed not at those above us but those below, or those in far-flung foreign lands as we're whipped into a patriotic fervour against an imagined other. Meanwhile, the corporations sell us bread and circuses. Those who have sell us aspirations so that we never ask why we have not, we only ever ask how we can have too. They sell us ideals about ourselves and our bodies and our attitudes and they call it choice while breeding conformity to the unachievable and a conviction that it can be. Seventy years ago, most of the world's countries were dictatorships. Today, hardly any survive. Because they don't need to. That's real hegemony. The biggest lie people are told in the free world is that they are really free."

Harry opened his mouth to argue back and then he closed it again and instead he just smiled. "I should really thank you for keeping me grounded. It's too easy to get caught up in these grand ideas. I know it's not as black and white as I like to think it is sometimes."

Lauren stroked his cheek. "Sorry, rant over."

"Well, I love you despite our differences."

Lauren beamed and cuffed him on the arm. "That device has scrambled your brain more than I thought."

"Shut up, I mean it," Harry said and he spoke those words again, words he'd not uttered in years, and for so long with no conviction, and he knew they were real. "I love you."

"Well, if you mean it, I suppose, it's only fair to say that I love you too, Harry."

They smiled into each other's eyes as Harry gently pushed her back against the entwined trunks of the dancing lovers and

145

kissed her. They might have stayed there forever if Lauren hadn't received a message on her phone just then. Harry watched her illuminated face fall as she read it.

"Bollocks," she said, frowning at her phone.

"What is it?"

"I've got to go. Landlord's coming round and he wants me out today. I'm going to have to move all of my stuff into a hotel till I find somewhere more permanent."

"Rubbish, come and stay with me."

"You don't think it's a bit soon to be moving in?"

"Nonsense, you spend every evening at mine anyway."

"Harry, that's so kind of you."

"Well, you've saved my life, rescued my friends, got me into an ambulance when I hit rock bottom and picked me up from a police station when I found there was still further to fall. I think it's probably the least I can do."

"If you're sure."

Harry was about to say that he was when he also received a message. It popped into view in front of his face and his, too, plunged.

"I know that look," Lauren said.

"It's Guy Brandreth. He wants a progress report. I'm to meet him at his house in exactly one hour and I don't think he's going to take no for an answer."

The Brandreths called it a house because mansion was probably too nouveau-riche for their tastes. Guy's money came from his property empire, but there was still enough family silver left when he was born for the spoon in his mouth. It was an old manor house just outside of Freebourne, vast and grand, its extensive red brick façade, ornate archways and imposing turrets exquisitely preserved from another era, rows of polished windows sparkling in the sunlight. Lauren drove Harry through the wrought iron gates, up the topiary tree-lined driveway through the palatial grounds, and dropped him off at the top of the turning circle by the fountain where a portly footman greeted him and ushered him up the steps and through the doors. Harry followed the man into the magnificent marble-floored entrance hall, encircled by neoclassical columns and statues of Roman emperors and ancestral oil on canvas — a whole line of men with savage cheekbones and cold stares looking down upon him in judgement for his failure. It did nothing to calm his nerves.

"Mr Brandreth will see you in his study, Dr Coulson. Second door to the left," the servant said, gesturing with the slightest of affected bows to a large oak door across the hall above which was mounted the taxidermied head of a stag. With another little bow, he turned and left Harry to resume his duties outside.

Harry made his way across the cavernous room, his trepidation growing with the echo of every footstep. There he paused before the door and rehearsed his excuses. He was lifting his hand to knock when he heard raised voices inside. One of them belonged to Guy Brandreth. The other was Elliott Nwosu's.

"It can't be," Mr Brandreth was saying.

"My sources at the Home Office say the police are questioning the wrong suspect," the Home Secretary replied. "Francisco Ambrose didn't arrive in Freebourne until March 1. Two days after Harry Coulson appeared on the news talking about this Polaris. Your daughter was never his target."

Hearing his name, Harry leaned closer to listen.

"Then who did kill Serena?" Guy Brandreth said. "One of Ambrose's associates, perhaps? Someone already here?"

"That I don't know."

"Someone must pay the price for this, Elliott."

"Guy, I promise we will get justice for her."

"Your promises cannot bring back my daughter, can they? You have been Home Secretary for a week and I've not once heard you speak of Serena's Law since."

"I'm afraid to tell you I'm not going to be in a position much longer to pass Serena's Law. Not yet, anyway."

"Why am I not surprised?"

"Please, Guy..."

"I know you, Elliott. You've done very well out of my daughter's death."

"Guy, you have to listen to me."

"I am not interested in your political games. I just want justice for my daughter. Will my friend deliver that for me, or are you now my enemy?"

"Your friend. Guy, the things I've learned this last week, you wouldn't believe. I'm on the cusp of exposing something. Something big. Something that cuts to the heart of government. It could bring the Prime Minister down like we always wanted."

Chapter Eleven:

There but for the Grace

The voices hushed for a moment, but only a moment. Harry — a burning curiosity battling every survival instinct screaming danger as he eavesdropped on two of the most powerful men in the land while they were discussing a palace coup — was leaning closer to the door when he heard a bang, like a hand slamming on a table and then angry shouting and then hurried footsteps. He ducked back just in time to avoid the door swinging open and Elliott Nwosu blazing out, the Home Secretary quite oblivious to his presence. Guy Brandreth, however, was not.

"Dr Coulson, you may come in now," Serena's father said.

Harry's heart was pounding as he stepped out from behind the door into view and saw Mr Brandreth standing behind his grand mahogany desk in a study every bit as imposing as the man himself — surrounded on all sides by old leather-bound books on shelves stretching from the ornate carpet to the intricately moulded ceiling.

Mr Brandreth smiled as he sat down in his chair. "How long have you been standing there?"

"I..." Harry began.

"Before you think about lying to me, there is a camera above the door and it only feeds to one place." Mr Brandreth held up his phone and tapped the screen. "You heard everything, didn't you?"

Harry took a deep breath. "Yes."

"Good. Please, take a seat." Serena's father gestured to the antique, green velvet high-backed chair opposite his desk.

Harry did as he was told and sat down on it. It creaked a little under his weight. "Good?"

"Why do you think I asked you here?" Mr Brandreth replied, reaching for the crystal decanter in front of him and two glasses. "Brandy?"

Harry had never had a taste for spirits, but he nodded, too afraid to say no. "You wanted a progress report. You said..."

"I know exactly how your test went today," Mr Brandreth said, pouring out two glasses of brandy and pushing one across the desk to Harry. "Or didn't. But I am a man of my word. You have one week left."

"So, what am I doing here?"

"Leverage."

Harry took an anxiously large sip of brandy. It burned on the way down, but the fuzzy feeling it left behind when the taste was gone made the question easier to ask. "You wanted me to hear all that?"

"I knew Elliott was up to something. There's always a game and he's always ten steps ahead. Well, not this time. I can't very well be seen publicly leaking my best friend's secrets, no one who matters would ever trust me again, but you... Well, you just heard him plotting to overthrow his own Prime Minister. And maybe you'll take that to the press. If he doesn't do exactly as I say."

"But you said it yourself, he's your..."

"He's a snake. He befriended my little cousin when they were at Oxford just to get close to me. And he befriended me because money and influence like mine can go far in his grubby world. As for my part, I know how to spot a winning horse when I see one, and when to claim those winnings. But he's crossed a line this time. He has used my daughter's death at every turn to manoeuvre himself into a position of power. He's used her name, her memory, to turn the country to his side. The second he got what he wanted, he discarded her as he discards everyone. Well, I won't let him. Either he passes Serena's Law, or you..."

"Mr Brandreth, I'm sorry, I sympathise, I know how badly you and your wife want to see that law passed, but I don't want to get caught up in whatever fight you've got going on here."

Mr Brandreth took a sip of brandy, slowly lowering his glass as he observed Harry through narrowed eyes. "But you are caught up. You work for me. And so far, I'm seeing very little value in my investment."

"Please, Mr Brandreth, I..."

"But let us not be dramatic. I'm sure you won't need to say anything to anyone. Within the week, I confidently predict Elliott Nwosu will have convinced the Prime Minister to pass Serena's Law and you will have completed Polaris. I always get what I want."

Harry was opening his mouth to speak when the door opened again without a knock and in walked Rosemary Brandreth wearing a frilly pink hat and dressed for the races and for the first time the confident composure on her husband's face — unwavering even when confronted with mortal danger at the hands of armed fanatics — melted away.

"Darling, you're back," Guy Brandreth said, leaping to his feet and hurrying over to his wife. "So soon?"

Rosemary Brandreth cast a venomous look in Harry's direction. "What is he doing here?"

"Darling, I can explain."

"Oh really, you're going to explain to me why you're sipping brandy in your study with a suspect in our daughter's murder?"

"He's not a suspect, we've been through this."

"How do you know?"

"I don't. No one knows. Not yet. We can't go jumping to conclusions. Like someone did with that teacher."

"I don't care, I want him gone."

"Rose, I have business with Dr Coulson."

"You promised me all that was over."

Mr Brandreth placed his hand on the small of his wife's back. "Darling, perhaps it would be better if we discussed this outside." He briefly turned back to Harry as he ushered his wife through the door. "If you'll excuse me, Dr Coulson."

Mr Brandreth closed the door behind him with a click, leaving Harry alone in his study. Harry took another sip of brandy. It tasted a lot better than he remembered and he realised that this must be what it was actually meant to taste like when you spent money on it, not the moonshine that got him through his PhD. He took another sip and it must have gone to his head because it made him feel bold. Bold enough to glance around to check if there were any cameras in this room. He couldn't see any.

He tapped the side of his glasses. "Scan CCTV," he said as quietly as he could.

A red filter appeared over his field of vision but no tell-tale white signatures came up.

"Scan electronic signatures."

There appeared to be no technology of any kind in the room. Of course, if Guy Brandreth was going to be hiding something here, some kind of evidence, anything that incriminated him, he wasn't going to allow himself to be recorded doing so. And Lauren's words came back to him through the brandyhaze and in that addled instant he was convinced the only way to protect himself now would be to find something that proved Serena's father had David Castle killed. Before his unconscious had time to quote Rule 5 at him, or tell him he was a doctor of computer science, not a great detective, he was on his feet, bounding over to the other side of the desk, rifling through the pile of papers. Corporate accounts, financial records, a letter from a lawyer in the Cayman Islands — all within the bounds if not the spirit of the law; morally dubious perhaps, but nothing as sinister as a contract on a man's life. Stupid, stupid, of course he was being stupid, who would even write something like that down let alone leave it lying on their desk? But there was a drawer.

Harry jiggled it. Locked, obviously. What was in there? Was there a key somewhere? Harry glanced around and then his heart almost exploded at the sight of Tyrone striding out of a secret door that had been hidden in the bookshelves.

"Mr Brandreth values his privacy," Tyrone said, placing his great gauntlet of a hand on Harry's shoulder and giving it just enough of a squeeze to crush into Harry just how much Mr Brandreth valued his privacy.

Harry grimaced. "Sorry, I, erm, I think I dropped something, I was just... How's Vlad? Is he ok?"

"He'll live. Which is more than I can say for you if I catch you poking your nose into Mr Brandreth's things again."

"I wasn't, I was just, like I say, erm..."

"Time to go, Dr Coulson."

Tyrone marched Harry out of the study straight past Mr and Mrs Brandreth, still engaged in a heated argument, through the hall and to the main doors where Harry was ejected with a shove that sent him tumbling down the steps onto the drive and grazing his wrists on the gravel.

"You heard Mr Brandreth," Tyrone said, towering over Harry as he scrambled to pick himself up from the ground and dust himself down. "You work for him. Don't let him down."

With that, Tyrone turned and slammed the great doors behind him, leaving Harry with far more questions and far less pride as he trudged back up the long drive and back to Freebourne in the gathering dusk. Making his way down the lonely country lane, past the fields and hedgerows and woods, he could hear the hum of traffic on the bypass on the other side of the hill, its soft susurration soothing the twilight air. And yet Harry felt anything but calm. He felt terrified. In every shadow some threat. Someone watching. The murderer who'd killed Serena. The people who'd killed David Castle. Anthropro lunatics. He picked up his pace until he made it back to town.

Night had fallen by the time he reached home, the moonlight riding the ripples across the babbling water like snow over undulating peaks, its gleam picking out in silver the old still wheel and the trees on the far bank climbing up the hill towards a billion stars. When Harry opened his front door, Lauren was already there standing in the hallway surrounded by suitcases and boxes and she was on the phone to what sounded like her boss and he didn't sound happy from what she was saying. She glanced up at Harry and raised her index finger as if to say apologetically she'd just be a minute.

"Listen, Harland, I don't care if you're my boss, it doesn't give you the right to shout at me. No, no one talks to me like that. Yes, it's very necessary. It's vital for the trial to succeed. I'm confident it will, I just need a little more time. We are close, I know. Yes, alright, alright, alright, ok. I'll do my job and you do yours. Bye then." Lauren sighed as she hung up the phone and turned back to Harry. "Sorry, this trial is proving pretty tricky and my boss is growing impatient to see results. He has the best of intentions, but he can be a right royal prick." Suddenly Lauren seemed to clock Harry's forlorn face. "I'm sorry, I should have thought. Forget about my work. How did things go with Guy Brandreth?"

Harry felt his shoulders slump. "I think I just made things ten times worse."

He explained everything that had just happened, his weak hand and how poorly he'd played it, the game between two of Britain's most powerful men in which he unwittingly found himself a sacrificial piece, how he'd tried to do what she told him, how he'd tried to find something that could protect them, but how badly he'd messed up and how scared he was now should he fail to give Mr Brandreth exactly what he wanted. When he'd finished, Lauren threw her arms around him, nestling his face into her neck and stroking the back of his head.

"I'm so sorry, Harry," she said. "All of this, it's not fair, you're a good man. We'll find a way through this, I promise."

"I hope so."

"Look, I was going to surprise you. I booked us a table for tonight at Le Valjean. I thought maybe going out might help you take your mind off things. And I wanted to thank you for letting me stay with you. But it's ok, I can see you're not going to be up to it, I'll cancel, we can…"

Harry forced every muscle in his face to provide a smile. "No that sounds perfect."

Le Valjean was almost certainly Freebourne's best and simultaneously quirkiest restaurant. The owner was an old soak named Vivian McKellen. A large man in every way, decades of self-inflicted damage, jowls and broken capillaries hid the dashing youth he'd once been — an actor who'd harboured delusions of playing the Dane, but whose career died thrashing on the altar of the West End musicals even as the audience stood in rapturous applause of his squandered talents. His greatest claim to fame, Lauren had learned on her last visit, came playing Javert in Les Misérables, even though to his eternal shame he'd auditioned unsuccessfully for the part of Jean Valjean. This whole place was a homage to a dream he'd dreamed in times gone by, every inch of wall taken up by framed photographs of Vivian's greatest moments strutting and fretting his hour upon the stage — high cheekboned, high flying, adored — and tattered posters of his glory days billed alongside thespians who had gone on to far better things. With a gourmand's paunch and a taste for the finer things, there was no question Vivian knew exactly what defined good food, though the hedonist, bon viveur and bon vivant had never prepared a meal in the entirety of his pampered existence, so when ambition finally died and he opened Le Valjean on Freebourne's high street seven years ago, he hired a French chef so talented even Lauren was impressed and ensured he himself remained strictly front of house, greeting every guest with a woozy smile and bonhomie. When Harry and Lauren arrived, Vivian was already half-cut, and he came bounding over to them, his belly popping out of his waistcoat to announce itself first, a bottle of Margaux of an invariably good vintage in his hand and swigging straight from the source.

"Ah Mademoiselle Fontaine," Vivian cried, hamming a theatrical French accent and kissing Lauren on both cheeks. "How my heart sings to see you tread these boards again!"

"Thank you for fitting us in," Lauren replied, allowing him to take her coat.

"For you, my dear, anything. And I see you have brought a new fascination to my door. Oh my! By the pricking of my thumbs, something wicked this way comes. Pray tell, could this be the one and only Harry Coulson upon the heath?"

Harry glanced at the floor. "I just want a quiet evening."

"Then, my friend, come with me and we shall creep, silent as the perfectest herald of joy to your table in the corner."

Harry and Lauren followed Vivian as he barged his way, belly swinging, wine swigging, chairs scraping, the faces of diners dodging, through the cosy little restaurant to their table, the only one still empty, set in white linen with a silver candelabra. Almost everyone in the fully stuffed establishment turned to stare as Harry took his seat: all the old and middle-aged couples, like robotic Nigel from the museum and his wife, who had long ago run out of anything more interesting on which to remark, even PC Atkins and Marcus who really should have known better, even Reverend Vinicombe who should have judged not. He did his best to ignore them.

"Your menus, madam, sir," Vivian said, handing them each a piece of printed paper with the practised bow of a curtain call. "May I recommend the chateaubriand, slaughtered, not grown, and yet a fuller contribution to this goodly frame the Earth ere its exit than many of us might hope to achieve. I trust you will find it deserving of your applause."

Harry looked slightly alarmed at a menu dripping with the suffering of animals. "Have you got anything that didn't come from an undiscovered country?"

Vivian appeared delighted. "Ah, very well done, my boy. Very well done indeed. Yes, you shall have the asparagus, followed by the ratatouille. Marvellous. And for you, my dear?"

Lauren ordered the onion soup, which Harry found out also came from an animal against all odds, and the beef bourguignon, and she treated them to a bottle of the Margaux on which Vivian opined in a lengthy soliloquy before he finally sauntered off to the kitchen, swigging from his bottle as he went. Harry watched all the eyes in the room follow their flamboyant host, before settling once more back on him. He tried to look away.

"I can't go on like this," he said.

"Ignore them," Lauren said, reaching across the table to place a gentle hand on his.

"Can't I even enjoy a meal? A succulent French meal?"

"They've arrested Fran for murder. I'm sure people will get it into their thick skulls you had nothing to do with this when they charge him and..."

Harry sighed. "They've got the wrong guy. At least that's what Elliott Nwosu said. Convenient, easy, too easy, but wrong. I guess even Francisco Ambrose isn't psycho enough to kill an innocent young woman who did absolutely nothing to make her a target of those anti-science fruitcakes."

"It does sound like the police are trying to brush this under the carpet too quickly."

"Yes. Yes, you're right. Like David Castle. When I confronted him, the day he was murdered, he said Serena's necklace was a fake, he was convinced someone had planted it on him. I thought he was lying at the time, but now? I don't know who, or why. But if he was telling the truth, then he was an easy answer, too, wasn't he? And now he's dead as well and if Guy Brandreth had him killed then the police certainly aren't in any hurry to knock on his door."

"But why? Something's seriously wrong here and it's so obvious that you and I can see it, but the police… are they blind or are they wilfully looking the wrong way?"

"Nwosu mentioned he was about to reveal something so big it could take down the government. Could the two be connected?"

"Harry, we've got to get to the bottom of this. It could be the only way to keep you safe. You've got to…"

Harry pulled off his glasses and pinched the bridge of his nose. "No, no, no, I don't! I've got to finish Polaris. That's the only way to keep us all safe. But how am I supposed to think like this?"

Lauren stroked his hand. "Harry, trust me, I know how you feel. This trial. It's my life's work as well. And so many lives at stake if I fail."

"Sorry. Here am I burdening you with my problems when you've got enough of your own."

Lauren offered him a reassuring smile. "You want to know what I do when I'm grappling with an insurmountable problem? What sure-fire scientific method I pursue to unblock my neural pathways?"

"What?"

"I throw a party."

"Oh no."

"Oh yes!"

"Lauren, I'm really not in the mood."

"That's exactly why you need this. I think it could do us both some good. You need to get your friends around you and just relax for a bit. Let go."

"I don't even have enough friends to fill a party."

"Good thing I do. Look, I know it feels counterintuitive, but Harry the reason you can't think is because all you do is think. You need to unwind. Then I promise you you'll see what you're missing and I bet it'll be right in front of your eyes."

"Absolutely not. No way. I mean, I suppose I do owe you a housewarming. And I guess maybe we should celebrate you moving in. But only because I love you. Not, and I state categorically, not because I'm going to in any way unwind or remotely enjoy myself. Got it?"

"Got it."

"Good."

Lauren always seemed to know how to lift Harry up when he was feeling lowest. How to disarm him when his guard was highest. He even found himself, in spite of it all, enjoying the rest of the evening spent sipping expensive wine and eating fine food and planning the party they'd hold tomorrow evening, interrupted only by a drunken monologue from Vivian on his time understudying Iago for the Royal Shakespeare Company that went on so long that they could only get him to leave by inviting him too.

Sachin was the first person Harry asked when he turned up the next morning at the Maltings and Darius the second. River didn't make it into work that day. She phoned to say she had too much on at the Rainbow Café and she really wouldn't be much use to them prattling on about her ethical guidelines while they spent the day coding against the clock. She didn't seem sure she was going to make the party that evening either, but Sachin called her straight back and after a lot of coaxing talked her round. It was a gruelling day, assiduously coding Polaris all over again from the ground up, replicating the lines Harry and Darius were one hundred percent confident worked and discarding anything they had even the slightest doubt about. By the time evening came, Harry was ready for a drink and almost relieved Lauren had talked him into a party.

When he got home, Lauren had already prepared the canapes and laid them out on the kitchen island and turned the work surface into a makeshift bar. She had draped multicoloured LED lights over the paintings and she had the house AI playing one of Harry's favourite old albums he'd enjoyed as a kid — *Lost in the Dream* by The War on Drugs. She looked beautiful in her blue cocktail dress and catching sight of her, and all the effort she'd gone to just to make him happy, Harry felt a surge of love for her.

"You've done all this?" Harry said.

Lauren grinned. "You like it?"

"I love it. But this is meant to be your housewarming. I should have..."

"Stop it. Stop worrying. Stop thinking. Chill the bloody hell out and enjoy your party!"

The doorbell rang and Harry went to answer it. Vivian was there, of course, reliably the first to arrive for even the slightest hint of debauchery, a half-imbibed bottle of Chablis in his hands.

"With mirth and laughter let old wrinkles come," Vivian cried, thrusting the bottle into Harry's arms as he strutted on in. "And let my liver rather heat with the finest wine available to humanity than my heart cool with mortifying groans."

Harry had just shown Vivian to the kitchen where the man immediately set about embracing Lauren with customary vibrancy when the doorbell rang again. Four of Lauren's friends from university, three women and a man whose names Harry immediately forgot, arrived together and all screeched and squawked a lot the moment Lauren came to greet them. Carla was already coming up the garden path behind them. Darius and Farhad arrived shortly thereafter and then Sachin.

"Is River here yet?" Sachin asked as Harry handed him a beer.

"No, I thought she'd be coming with you?" Harry replied.

"We were going to meet up first and come along together, but she never showed up."

Harry sipped his beer. "She's probably still at the Rainbow Café, sounded like it was going to be a stressful day there."

"No," said Carla as she walked past. "I just came from there. She wasn't in this afternoon."

"She's not been in there all day," said Farhad, swallowing a canape. "Grace is covering for her."

"Harry, that's really strange," Sachin said, looking concerned. "She's not one to flake."

Harry couldn't voice it, but he knew they must all be thinking it. A young woman. Alone in Freebourne. Who no one had heard from in hours. Who wasn't where she said she was going to be. When Serena's killer was still out there for all they knew. He tried his best to shake the thought from his mind. He was about to tell them there must be some rational explanation when Lauren grabbed him by the hand and he was almost relieved none of them had to say it out loud.

"Harry, you must come and meet my dear friends Eve and Robert," Lauren said, introducing him to an older couple, who must have been in their seventies, standing in the corner by the entrance to the utility room looking a little unsure and out of place. The woman had curly white hair and a rounded face with big dark eyes and she was wearing thick-rimmed glasses; the man, who was not much taller than her, was thinning up top but he still had a bushy grey beard that made him look a bit like a sailor.

"Oh hi," Harry said. "Pleasure to meet you."

"Have we met before?" Eve said, leaning closer.

"No dear," Robert hissed. "This is Lauren's boyfriend."

"Yes, I knew you looked familiar."

"Her new boyfriend."

"Oh!"

Lauren chuckled. "The less said about Marc the better, I think!"

"Can't be worse than Francisco!" Harry laughed drily, trying to make light of the awkward situation and the feeling that as rapidly as he'd fallen in love with her, half the people in this room still knew Lauren far better than he did. Even as he was thinking it, he heard a screech from the entrance to the kitchen and he saw another of Lauren's female friends had arrived and Lauren made a slightly more muted but still enthusiastic noise back signalling she too recognised the excitement of seeing them again after what was presumably some time and ran over to cement the moment with a big hug, leaving Harry even more awkwardly alone with the oldest people in the room and a pathological inability to make small talk, which apparently they shared.

"So, erm," he began.

"Yes, erm," Robert replied.

"Um," added Eve.

"Well, it's lovely to meet you and um," Harry said. "Did you, erm, did you travel far?"

"London."

"Yes, London," said Robert.

"Good weather for it though, right?" Harry offered.

"Oh lovely day."

"Beautiful," said Eve.

"Can I get you anything?" Harry said. "Wine? Beer? Cup of tea? We've got oat milk. I like oat milk. Do you like oat milk?"

"We're fine, thank you."

"So, um, how do you, um, know…"

"How come two old codgers like us are friends with Lauren?"

"Well, I wasn't going to…"

"Actually, we met her in the pub," Robert said.

"Ha, me too!"

Eve nodded. "She was so kind to us."

"Our son passed away last year, you see," Robert said.

"I'm so sorry," Harry replied.

"We'd just been told that day."

Eve smiled sadly. "John was such a happy child. So sweet growing up."

Robert wiped his eye with the back of a sun-blotched hand. "I don't know where we went wrong. Maybe we could have done things differently. Been better parents. Or maybe it was there all along and we never saw it."

"Let's not, Robert..."

"No, no we shouldn't. But he didn't deserve to die like that. Alone. In that place. Without his mum and dad."

"Lauren saw us crying in the pub and she came over to us and she asked if we were alright. I don't remember anything else she said that afternoon, but I do remember her coming round with a casserole the next day. And the next. She was so kind."

Robert nodded. "She's an angel. You're a very lucky man, Harry."

Harry smiled. "I know. Lauren's the kindest person I've ever met. She's always been there for me, just like she's been there for you. I'm so sorry to hear about your son."

"They say time heals," Eve said. "But..."

"It doesn't really does it? It's been 20 years and every day I still think about a world where my mum's still here. My dad too."

Looking at the hurt that had hollowed out these two gentle people, human beings in pain for no other reason than they'd loved, Harry saw the same trauma that sometimes stared back at him in the mirror when he was brave enough to let it. And he knew that what he was doing was right. Polaris had to work. Not for Guy Brandreth. But for Eve and Robert and the millions of people out there like them who had lost the people they cared about most, who never wanted to forget but so desperately needed the chance to move forward, to find an acceptance even time could not promise.

"River, you made it!" Sachin's voice came from over Harry's shoulder just then. "Wait, what... My god."

Harry turned to see River standing there in the kitchen doorway, shaking, her right eye purple and blackened and so puffy it could barely open.

"River, are you ok?" Harry said, rushing over to her.

"What happened?" Sachin said. "You're hurt. Oh my god. Are you alright? Harry, have you got some ice?"

"Here, I've got this," said Lauren, hurrying over with a pack of frozen peas.

"I'm fine, guys, seriously," River said, doing her best to smile with her mouth and her one good eye. She took the peas from Lauren and winced as she held them against her black eye.

Lauren examined her closely. "Darling, you don't look fine."

"Look, it's nothing."

"We should take you to see a doctor," Sachin said.

"I've just come from the doctor's, idiot. Why do you think I'm late?"

"And you're ok, right?"

"I'm absolutely fine, Sachin. Everyone, please stop fussing."

"What happened?" Harry asked.

"Look, it's a bit embarrassing to admit, but I pulled the door a bit too hard when I was opening up the Rainbow Café this morning and nearly knocked myself out. Happy now, mister?"

"Just as long as you're ok," Sachin said, placing his hand on her arm and it was strange, almost instinctively she flinched, jerking away with a shudder.

River apologised and when no one said anything because they didn't know what to say or think she apologised again and said she needed to sit down and she went off to the living room with her pack of peas and Sachin went and followed her. As soon as she was out of earshot, Lauren took Harry aside.

"Do you believe her?" Lauren said, raising her voice to be heard over the sound of Vivian leading a singalong with Carla and Farhad and several of Lauren's Cambridge friends to *Do You Hear the People Sing*.

Harry bit his lip. "Well, I mean she can be quite clumsy. I once saw her..."

"Do you believe her?"

"No. She sounds like the women my mum used to talk about."

"Yes, I've seen battered women before. There's something she's not telling us. Does she have a boyfriend?"

"I don't think so, no."

"Maybe I'm wrong, but if it's what I think it is, then it'll be someone close to her. Is there anyone who might know?"

Harry nodded. "Grace."

"The landlady at The Barley Mow?"

"Yes, she's River's aunt."

"Do you think she'll be there now?"

"What if we're wrong? River won't thank us for it."

"And what if we're right?"

"Ok, you're right, of course you're right, we can't just stand by if she's in trouble, let's go. Let's ask Grace."

"You should stay here, it's your party. I'll go."

"Not a chance."

"I need someone to look after Eve and Robert, they're such lovely people and I'm worried they're lonely, you'd love them. I'll go."

"She's my friend, I'm coming."

Harry followed Lauren through the kitchen, past a terrified-looking Darius surrounded on all sides by Lauren's friends, one of whom appeared to be very drunk and feeling his muscles, past Vivian twirling Carla around in a Waltz, past Farhad sipping a cup of mint tea and making polite conversation with Eve and Robert, and to the corridor, where they stopped briefly by the sitting room door to see River and Sachin on the sofa deep in conversation. The two seemed to be talking about everything and anything except her injury and she looked all the happier for it. River was telling him about how she had fallen in love with India, its people, its kaleidoscope of cultures and colours, its many religions and practises and deep spirituality, a universe away from the bland conformity of small-town English life. Sachin was telling her how he hated being forced to spend every sweltering summer at his grandparents' apartment in Mumbai, made to listen to his parents' detailed plans for his future marriage and career and forced to attend wedding after wedding of people he'd never met, when all he wanted was to be running in the woods or playing cricket on the green back home in Freebourne with the friends they never approved of. It sounded like the kind of conversation they'd had many times before. Lines rehearsed and rehashed from long ago, but retold with the comfort only old friends know. They were both laughing at the irony of the worlds they were running from and to and how they'd met quite improbably in the middle.

Leaving them to it, Harry and Lauren slipped past the sitting room and out the front door unnoticed. Lauren had had a glass of wine, but she still felt safe to drive, so they climbed in her car and she drove them into town where they pulled up opposite the green. Stepping out of the car, Harry saw The Last Survivor standing there, hands clasped behind his back, staring intently at the contents of the bin where it seemed someone had dumped a battered robot dog. The strange man looked up as they passed, but he never seemed to register their presence, he just stared straight through them as if they weren't there, his vacant eyes picked out by the warmth of the heritage lanterns and the lights of The Barley Mow. Pushing their way inside, they found the pub almost empty and there was no one behind the bar. Dr Chang from St Jude's was having a quiet drink with a couple of friends in the corner; she noticed Harry but was professional enough not to make it obvious. Reverend Vinicombe was at his usual table sipping a pint of dark ale and gazing into the spitting log fire like he saw the world's future in those flames.

"Reverend," Harry said, stepping over one of Grace's black cats and walking over to the vicar. "Is Grace in?"

"Ah, Dr Coulson," Reverend Vinicombe said. "It's good to see you. I thought I saw you in Le Valjean yesterday evening as well."

"Yes, it's a small town and everyone seems to notice me, don't they?"

The vicar stroked his moustache. "I apologise, I meant nothing by it. I appreciate it hasn't exactly been easy for you since you arrived in town. If you ever need anyone to talk to, my door is always open. I am just glad to see you out and about after that terrifying ordeal with those characters last week. I think we're all breathing safer now they're behind bars."

"Yes, quite, Reverend," Lauren said.

"Miss Fontaine, I've not seen you in church in a couple of weeks."

"I'm sorry, Reverend, it's been a bit hectic lately. I promise to come on Sunday, ok? Listen, you haven't seen Grace, have you?"

"Sorry, sweeties," said Grace, looking flustered as she appeared behind the bar. "I've been running between here and the Rainbow Café all day. What can I get you?"

Lauren walked up to the bar and took a seat on the stool she'd been sitting at when Harry first met her. "We're not here for a drink."

"What? Lauren 'Five Pints' Fontaine not here for a drink?"

"It's about River," Harry said, ducking a hops-draped beam and joining Lauren at the bar.

Grace placed her hands on her hips. "I'd say, sweetie. And I've got a bone to pick with you. Working poor River ragged like that. She didn't even have time to open up the café this morning."

"She wasn't with me today."

"What?"

"She said she had too much on at the Rainbow Café to come into work."

"She told me she had too much on at the Maltings!"

"But then she said she injured herself opening up."

"I opened up. She never opened up."

"She never injured herself either, did she?" Lauren said.

"What injury? What are you talking about?"

"We just saw her. She's been hurt. She has a black eye and she's really shaken and she's not telling us the truth about what happened."

"Oh my goodness. Is she ok?"

"We're worried about her," Harry said. "She doesn't have a boyfriend, does she?"

Grace frowned. "No. She's not had a boyfriend or a girlfriend in years. You're not saying what I think you're saying, are you?"

"I don't know. I hope not. But it's so strange. There's something different about her. She hasn't said anything to you, has she?"

"No, nothing. She's been unusually quiet these last couple of days. Almost like she's been avoiding me. I know she's been through a lot. Everything that happened at the Maltings. But she promised me she was fine. I can't think of anything in the last day or so that could have…"

"Wait. There is something. I remember now. No, it can't be. She was so excited."

"What?"

"No, I'm sure it's nothing."

"Harry Coulson, you spit it out right now."

"She said her dad was coming home."

Grace's eyes went wide. "Fuck."

"What is it?"

"Fuck, fuck, fuck, why didn't you tell me? Oh shit. Why didn't she tell me? Oh my god."

"What's wrong?"

"Harry, we've got to help her. We've got to get her out of that house. If George Allen is back, then River is in serious danger."

Chapter Twelve:

Redux

"I don't understand," said Harry. "River loves her dad. She's always talking about him. This great man. This doctor, or was it aid worker? Helping poor kids in Africa."

"Clearly she made that up," Lauren said. "Like she obviously made up that he worked for MI6."

"She used to tell people he was a soldier, too" Grace replied. "Stationed in some corner of a foreign land. She made up a lot of things to hide the truth, most of all from herself, because it's too hard to face. And the truth is, he's a bad man, a violent man. I don't think it started until after he married my sister, Faith. It was just little things in the beginning. Telling her what to wear. How to do her hair. Who she could and couldn't see. You don't notice the change overnight, but slowly this person who was so full of love and life just retreated inside herself. I don't know when exactly he started hitting her. Maybe it was going on for years. She used to hide it well, behind makeup and a smile. But when she turned up with a broken wrist one week and a broken rib the next, I knew something was very wrong."

"My god."

"When I asked her, she flat out denied it, of course. It took months until she finally admitted the truth. And even then, I couldn't convince her to leave. She wouldn't let me take her to the police. She said George was a good man, that it was her fault he got angry, that if she was just a better person, he wouldn't lash out like that. After a while, I think she stopped believing the lies she told herself, that it was all ok. He promised to change, of course he did, over and over, but he never did. Finally, she found it in herself to leave. To take River and go. The next thing I knew there were blue lights flashing outside her house."

"I'm so sorry," said Lauren, her hand clasped to her mouth.

Grace pulled a tissue out of the sleeve of her cardigan and wiped a tear from her eye. "She died of a brain haemorrhage on the way to hospital. They said she'd tumbled down the stairs. When they tell you that kid who shot his headmaster after his brains got scrambled in the war was the last person to commit murder in Freebourne before Serena Brandreth, that's a lie. I know it is, even if no one else believes it. The police arrested George, of course. Charged him. Even tried him for murder. But that man is clever and so were his lawyers. Clever enough to sow just enough seeds of reasonable doubt in the minds of the jury. River wasn't at the trial. She refused to believe her amazing dad could be guilty of the things they were saying about him and I suppose the jury's verdict let her carry on believing the lies she told herself. But when George tried to come home, came barging in demanding I give River back to him, I told him to go. He wasn't having any of it, naturally. Beat the living daylights out of me right upstairs. I guess the punters heard it. Luckily for me, the rugby crowd was in that night. Four of my regulars came charging up the stairs, dragged him off, gave him a taste of his own medicine. I picked his teeth up off the carpet, handed them back to him, and told him it would be his balls next if I ever saw him in Freebourne again. But worse than that, I'd make sure his precious daughter knew exactly who her father was. But I think she knew already. Enough to change the name he gave her, her identity, everything about her. Enough to invent all those stories about him, why he'd been gone so long."

Harry blinked slowly, trying to take in everything Grace was saying. "We have to call the police."

Grace shook her head. "He's already got her lying for him. Covering up. I've seen it all before. He'll walk and we'll have only made things worse for her. No, Harry, we're going to have to do this ourselves. We need to get her out of that house right now."

"She's not at home. She's at mine."

"Thank god."

"Grace, you stay here, we'll go and get her and bring her back here to you where she'll be safe. Lauren, come on, let's go."

They ran out of the pub and into the night and jumped into Lauren's car and she put her foot down, tearing through the streets as fast as she could. If Harry had been worried about River before, he was petrified now. To think his friend, this kind young woman, so clever, so gentle and yet so strong — someone who could stand up to thugs and zealots — could be so easily cowed and hollowed by a man whose sole purpose was to love her and care for her and never, ever hurt her.

"Hurry, hurry," Harry said.

Lauren took a corner at speed. "I'm going as fast as I can."

Harry tapped his glasses. "Call River. Come on, come on, pick up. Damn. Call Sachin. Come on, Sachin. Pick up the bloody phone!"

"We're nearly there."

Lauren raced them through the last remaining streets on the outskirts of town and picked up speed as they hit the country lane, flying through the dark until they reached the Old Mill and she slammed on the brakes and brought them to a halt with a jerk and they jumped out of the car and ran through the gate and up the garden path and up the steps and through the front door.

"Ah!" cried a swaying Vivian as he encountered them in the hall. "I am agog! I am aghast! Prithee, see there! Behold! Look! Lo! Our hosts have returned, from whence I know not, and yet..."

"Shut up Vivian," Harry and Lauren said in unison as they barged past him and into the sitting room where Sachin was sitting. Alone.

"Harry, where have you been?" Sachin said, looking up.

"Sachin, quickly," said Harry. "Where's River?"

Sachin looked a little glum. "She left. I really wish she could have stayed. But she got a call. From her dad. She said she had to go home."

"Fuck."

"What is it? Harry, you're scaring me."

Harry and Lauren did their best to explain as fast as they could and Harry watched as Sachin's face changed. From disbelief. To shock. To fear. To worry. And then to something much darker as he shook to his feet.

"If he touches her again..." Sachin said, trembling in anger.

"Violence is not going to solve anything," Harry said. "We just need to get her out of harm's way. Get her to safety. Sachin, come on, we'll go round there right now. Lauren, I need you to stay here, just in case she comes back."

"Be careful, Harry, please," said Lauren. "Who knows how long River's dad's been lurking around for. A man like that. What if he's been in town longer than she knew? What if he..."

"Killed Rena?" Sachin said.

"Sachin, we can't think about that right now," Harry replied. "River needs our help. Let's go."

River lived in a two-up, two-down Victorian terrace a couple of streets from the Rainbow Café. The girl once known as Harriet Allen grew up there. She'd always described such a happy childhood in that little collection of red bricks and memories that had stood empty for years until River was old enough to move out of The Barley Mow and back to the place she'd once called home. Knowing what he knew now, Harry couldn't fathom what could possibly lead her back there. To her mother's prison. To her place of execution.

Sachin pulled his car up outside the house. The curtains were drawn but the lights were on downstairs and Harry could hear the television blaring even from the street. They got out of the car and walked up to the front door and Harry took a deep breath and knocked. There was no answer. Harry knocked again, louder this time. And again. At last, he heard footsteps. And the door opened and a man emerged and he wasn't what monsters were supposed to look like. It was just as Lauren had said. He looked so ordinary. Not imposing in any way. Small, slight, plainly dressed in a crisp white shirt and black trousers, thinning hair combed over to cover his bald patch, a few lines etched on his forehead and around his eyes, a pair of metal-framed spectacles on his face, and behind them a puzzled expression.

"Can I help you?" George Allen said.

Sachin gritted his teeth. "Yeah, you can f…"

"Sachin," Harry said, placing a gentle hand on his friend's chest and stepping forward. "Mr Allen, we're here to see River. Can she come to the door?"

"I'm so sorry, but she's not here. Shall I tell her you popped by?"

"I know she's here, Mr Allen."

"Well, that's not very polite. I have just told you she's not in and you're calling me a liar on my own doorstep."

"I know she's here because she just came from mine."

George's face hardened. "So you're Harry."

"Mr Allen, I'd really like for River to come to the door now, if that's ok."

"She doesn't want to see you."

"If you don't mind, I'd like to hear that from her. Just so that I know she's ok."

"You think I'd let her anywhere near you? A suspect in a poor young woman's murder? And what is this I hear about you putting her in danger with those crazy Anthropros? No, no, Harriet is not safe with you. She won't be coming back to work. And she won't be seeing you again. Not tonight or ever."

With that River's father slammed the door in Harry's face. He heard the footsteps walking away again. And then he thought he heard River's voice from inside. And then he definitely heard her father's because it was shouting. It was screaming.

Something banged and smashed. Harry raised his hand to knock again when Sachin stopped him.

"We've tried this nicely," Sachin said and he slammed his foot into the door and he raised it again and kicked and kicked and kicked and kicked with everything he had in him until the door burst open and Sachin charged headlong down the hall and into the living room and Harry ran after him to find River, wide-eyed in terror, pinned against the wall, her father's elbow at her throat.

"Get out of my house!" George howled as he turned his head towards them, never releasing his grip on his daughter.

"Get the fuck off her!" Sachin howled back.

"And just who the hell are you? Her boyfriend? Brainwashing her with all that Indian rubbish no doubt."

"If you don't take your hands off her, I'm going to knock you out."

"Mr Allen," Harry said as calmly as he could manage even as he felt the heat rising in him and with it red rage at the sight of what this wretch of a man had done to his friend. "You have no right to call yourself a father. You disgust me. Now let her go. Right now."

"Sachin, Harry, please, leave," River blubbed through tears. "Leave me. Just go."

"We're not leaving you with him."

"He's a good man, he's a good man, he is, I know he is. Somewhere in there. He has to be."

"River, stop lying to yourself."

"I can help him."

"That man is beyond help."

"I can change him."

"Think, just think, and ask yourself if you ever heard your mum say the same thing?"

George released his grip on River and took a threatening step towards Harry and Sachin, his eyes glowering at them even as he spoke to his daughter. "You call these people friends, Harriet? They're pathetic creatures, just like you. But I know you can be better than that. It's my fault. I wasn't around to raise you properly. But I'm going to make that up to you, Harriet. I'm going to help you. God knows you need it. Look at you. Look what you've become without me. Those stupid boys' clothes you wear. All that hippy shit. That rubbish you spout. Christ, you're balder than I am. You're a mess. Frankly, you look disgusting. But I'm going to fix you. Because I love you, Harriet."

"Dad," she said, her face now steel. "My name is River."

"How dare you!" her father cried, rounding on her again, the fists that had beaten her mother to death clenched and raised at her. "Your mum never listened either. Look what happened to her. I'll show you!"

George never showed River anything. He just toppled like a tree in a storm as Sachin's fist connected with his jaw. Before the little man could pick himself up, Sachin was on top of him, blows raining down, spattering crimson across the carpet. Right. Left. Right. Left. Sachin's knuckles bloodied as George's face reddened and blackened and moistened and his glasses smashed and his nose crumpled and he wailed in terror and agony until at last Harry and River managed to pull Sachin back, leaving George groaning on the floor.

"I'll kill him!" Sachin cried. "I'll kill him!"

"Sachin, stop," River said, placing her hand upon his shoulder.

"Harriet please," George whimpered, gasping, looking up at her, his battered and puffy eyes pleading with her.

"I told you, my name is River," she said, standing over him. "And I didn't invent it. It's what Mum wanted to call me all along. And sometimes she did. It was our secret. Our thing we had. Something you couldn't control. But you can't control anything can you? Not even your own life. I look at you and I'm not afraid anymore. I don't even know what to feel. I mean,

I don't love you, that's for sure. Love's not a right, it's earned, and you've really failed on that front. But I don't hate you either. I should, after what you did to mum. But really, I just pity you. A man so small, so self-loathing, so worthless that the only way you can feel anything about yourself is to inflict pain and suffering on your own family. What do you even call that? No, I didn't invent my name. I invented you. The idea of you. Because the reality is, you are nothing."

With that, River grabbed her father's quivering form by the scruff of his collar and heaved him to his feet and marched him into the hallway and to the door. Harry heard the door open and then the thud and the groan as she threw him down the steps, into the night and out of her life.

"Are you ok?" Harry asked a still-shaking Sachin.

"I... I don't know what came over me," Sachin replied, nursing his right hand. "I've never done that before."

"You promise me?"

"I just care about her so much."

The front door slammed shut and River appeared back in the sitting room. Harry looked at her and she looked at him and then at Sachin and there were tears in all their eyes but no words were exchanged, they weren't needed, the look in River's wide grey eyes was enough to say that she was so grateful to them for everything but most of all for helping her see what was real and that a weight had lifted from her life and that she would need some time but she would be ok and all she needed right now was a hug. Sachin threw his arms around her and Harry too and for minutes all the three friends did was stand there and hold onto each other in total silence except for the sound of the TV still blaring out the news in the corner of the room. And then Harry heard it. It was Elliott Nwosu's voice.

"Ladies and gentlemen, friends, distinguished colleagues, it is with deep regret that I must inform you I am stepping down as Home Secretary with immediate effect and calling on the Prime

Minister to resign," Nwosu said and he was standing outside his constituency office speaking into a row of microphones. "I have learned a terrible truth, one so dangerous, one so damaging to my trust in my own government, that I cannot continue to serve it in good faith and nor, do I believe, can the leader of my party and our country in whom I must declare I have no confidence. It is my duty, not as your elected representative, but as a citizen of this nation that I love with all my heart to share with you what I have uncovered as a matter of public safety. This is the truth I have learned. For the last two years, the government, shamed by the burgeoning prison population and near Third World conditions in our jails, has been conducting a secret trial codenamed Project Redux. The full details of this trial have not been revealed to me, but what I do know has shocked me to my core as it will shock you. Remember these names. Jack Bellamy, Muhammad Ansari, Dan Sampson, João Silva, Deepak Bhattacharya, John Huxley, Terence Everett, Fionn O'Brien, Derek Morgan. Mark them well. For these nine men are all murderers. They are all murderers who have been given new identities and new appearances using state-of-the-art facial reconstruction techniques and released unannounced into the British populace under the name of Project Redux. It is no coincidence that two people are dead here in Freebourne in what has the hallmarks of a serial killer. Could it be that one of those nine men was sent here, to us? I'm certain of it. So to my constituents, I say this. Be vigilant, be on your guard, and be afraid. They could be anyone."

Chapter Thirteen:

The City of Doors

For a while, Harry could do nothing but stare at the television in disbelief. For weeks, the authorities had been hounding him — an innocent man, a good man, who'd done nothing but try to help a poor young woman who was far beyond it, who wanted nothing more than the peace and solitude of a new life — when they in their infinite wisdom had released nine killers into the community and given them the perfect cover to kill again because no one knew who they were. And then the worst part dawned on him and a gasp escaped.

"Harry," River said, "I know what you're thinking. There's going to be a lot of fear out there after this. A lot of anger. But you don't know..."

Harry pinched the bridge of his nose. "I know. Oh, I know alright. I know exactly what everyone in this narrow-minded little backwater will think. That the stranger who arrived in town the night Serena was killed, whose DNA was found on her body, might very well be one of these murderers released in secret by the government and sent to Freebourne, god alone knows why."

River placed a gentle hand on his arm. "Harry."

He closed his eyes. "I'm sorry," he said, opening them again and turning to her. "Here I am, once again burdening you, after everything you've been through. Are you ok?"

"No. No, I'm not ok. And I think that's the first time I've been able to admit it."

"He didn't hurt you again, did he?" Sachin said.

"Yes. Not in any way you'll see, but somehow that's far worse." She pointed to her black eye and said, "This morning was the first time he ever raised his hand to me because it was the first time I ever challenged him. Tried to convince him to be more than he was. He was never a soldier, or a secret agent, or a doctor or an aid worker. I think I even told someone he was an astronaut once. In truth, he was just another cog in that materialist machine, working every hour for someone else's greed; an instrument of their profit, not a person, but a tool, a thing, alienated and degraded until the one constant that gave him any meaning as a man in this fucked up capitalist world, where our only worth is our labour, was taken away from him. I guess you could say the economic crisis was his crisis. He took redundancy hard. There's something in that word, isn't there? Redundant. His pride never recovered from that and so he took it out on the only people he could. Not always physically. But he's been hurting me for years in so many other ways. And I lied to myself, over and over, to try and hide it, because he was gone and it was easier shutting out all that pain. But now I've opened that door and it's not closing again."

"What if you could close that door?" Harry said.

River smiled sadly. "Maybe. If only there was a city full of them."

"We'll finish it."

"Yes," said Sachin. "We'll finish Polaris for you."

"I want you to test it on me," River decided. "And if it can help me resolve in my mind everything my dad's done to me, then I know it can help anyone. No one should have to live with this kind of pain their whole lives."

River agreed to spend the night at The Barley Mow. Her father was gone when they stepped out of the front door. Just the spots of blood he'd left behind as he limped away. River said she didn't think he was coming back, not now she'd stood up to him; losing control was the thing he feared most of all and that spell had been well and truly countered, but she still had to go and stay with Grace. Because there were things that had been unsaid for years and they needed saying tonight. They got in the car, River in the front, Harry in the back, and Sachin drove them to The Barley Mow. Sachin offered to go in with her, but River said this was one thing she had to do on her own. So she thanked him and hugged him and gave him a kiss on the cheek and then she left.

"You should tell her," Harry said, realising at last what he was seeing.

"Tell her what?" Sachin replied as he pulled the car away.

"How you feel about her."

"I don't know what you mean."

"That's why you did what you did back there. I can't say I approve, but I understand. If someone hurt Lauren like that, I don't know what I'd..."

Sachin sighed. "I guess I've always liked her. Even when we were at school. Even when it wasn't popular to like her. Then Rena came along and it was very popular to like her and for some reason River and I lost touch. It was only when you brought us together again at Rena's funeral that I remembered everything I saw in her. So kind and yet so different. Full of energy and life. I hated seeing what that bastard did to her. What he took from her. Maybe one day I'll tell her. But I think she's got enough on her mind right now."

Sachin parked his car outside Harry's house and dropped him off. It was late. When Harry got inside, he found the party long since over, the guests had all gone home, but Lauren was still up and waiting for him in the hall. Her face was full of worry and questions and Harry did his best to answer them, telling her everything that had happened, and at last she looked relieved.

"She's lucky to have you, Harry," Lauren said.

"I just wish I'd seen it before. If you hadn't been there, made me see it, I don't know what..."

"No, you did everything you could for that poor girl, and she's safe because of you, Harry. Your friends mean a lot to you, don't they?"

"It's strange. I never thought I needed friends. Always thought I was ok on my own. Watching my mum die, I suppose I just thought it was easier not to get too close to anyone. And when I did, Melanie, Ben, well. Look how that turned out. I guess I never really fitted in anywhere. But for the first time in my life, I feel like I belong. No matter what everyone else in this stupid town thinks. Like I can be myself. And I've got you to thank for that as well."

Harry stifled a yawn and rubbed his aching eyes. Lauren put her arms around him and took him upstairs to bed and they nestled into each other and he fell asleep almost straight away. The next morning, after she'd made breakfast for them, she dropped him off at the Maltings where River and Sachin were already waiting for him. Darius arrived shortly after and they got to work with a renewed energy and focus, everyone pulling together as Harry and Darius pored through the code and River and Sachin took notes of every little tweak they'd made, every variable, as inch by inch they perfected their work. They made more progress that day than they had in the last week. The next day was even better. By Friday afternoon, Harry was quietly confident they'd cracked it, but even then, he was alarmed to receive the call from Guy Brandreth.

"Hi, erm, Mr Brandreth," Harry stuttered. "I…"

"Polaris, is it ready?" Guy Brandreth cut him off.

"Nearly, I just need…"

"I want it ready by tomorrow."

"But we still have four more days. You said…"

"That was before the Prime Minister resigned."

"What?"

"Haven't you heard the news? Our friend Elliott Nwosu has played his game and he's played it well. He's plunged this country into terror and amidst it all the government has fallen, leaving the entire nation in chaos. And chaos may have its advantages for some, but I do not favour it. What opportunity for any leverage I had now has gone and with it any hope of ever seeing Serena's Law. All the while, my wife has got it into her head that the very man I've had working for me the whole time is in fact a secret killer hiding in plain sight. Which means as far as I'm concerned, you are running out of use to me and I am running out of patience. Polaris will be finished by tomorrow or there will be consequences."

Mr Brandreth's icy stare disappeared and in its place, the faces of Sachin and River waiting on his word.

"What did he say, Harry?" Sachin said.

"Unless we finish Polaris today, we're in serious trouble," Harry replied.

"Fuck that Lawful Evil asshole," River said. "Seriously, I've had all I can take from pathetic men desperate to control their little worlds."

"Boss," Darius said, jumping up from his seat. "I think it's ready!"

Harry checked over the final code and it was like reading poetry. As his eyes scanned the screen, darting from line to line, something stirred in him. A joy. An uncontrollable elation. And he knew then what Michelangelo must have felt when he saw his David emerge from the marble, knowing the naked king of Israel had been inside long before he first placed his chisel to the block. It was flawless. Perfect. Beautiful.

He downloaded the new code back into Polaris, sat River in the chair, and strapped the device to her head. She tapped the little black titanium disk and closed her eyes and the moment she did so her mouth fell open like a child in wonder.

"You really built it," she said. "You can put it into people's minds. Sigil, the Cage, City of Secrets, City of Doors."

"Don't get too caught up on the UI," Harry replied. "It's just window dressing."

"Harry, what you've done is amazing. You can project images into people's heads. No one has ever done that before."

"I am less concerned with what we can put into people's heads and more with what we can help them to take out. Pain, loss, fear, sadness."

"Yes, I'm ready."

"What do you see?"

"I'm in the Hive marketplace. There are stalls as far as the eye can see selling all manner of curios and trinkets. People moving everywhere. Not just people. Creatures. My god, is that a Tiefling? No way, a Balor! That's so cool."

"I have literally no idea what you're on about," Sachin said.

"That's because you're an idiot. Harry, can Polaris grow brain cells too? Asking for a friend."

"River, I need you to focus," Harry said. "What else do you see?"

"Keep your hair on, mister, I'm getting to that. Yes, I see the doors. Portals in every crack, every crevice, every shadow shimmering. I'm looking into the nearest one. Oh."

Harry saw River's face tighten. "I'm sorry. I know it's hard. But I need you to describe what you see."

River took a deep breath. "I see Freebourne High School. I can see me. I'm in my old science lab. But I'm younger. I have hair down to my shoulders. God, did I really look like that? I... He's there. Dr Castle. We're alone. I remember that day. He kept me behind after class. He said he wanted to help me. Mentor me. Thought with the right encouragement I was destined for better things. I don't know why he felt he could put his hand on my leg, though. He's moving it up my skirt. I'm frozen. I can't move. I want to scream. I want to run, but I can't. He's pulling his hand away. He's talking about my Biology results. Like nothing ever happened. But if nothing happened, why did I feel so violated? Why do I still feel so violated?"

"I'm really sorry, River. I can't ever take that memory away. But if this works, it won't hurt like that anymore. Click your fingers. Close the portal."

River clicked her fingers. At first nothing. And then slowly, ever so slowly, her face loosened and lifted until she was smiling.

"Are you ok?" Sachin said.

"What happened?" Harry asked.

"It worked," River replied. "It's like for a moment my mind was running a million times faster. Cycling through. Working through everything. Picking it apart. Piecing it back together again. Like time was speeding forward. Racing through me. And when it had finished, it was like this massive weight had lifted from me. All these thoughts I had — crushing doubts, shame, guilt, disgust at myself — they're all gone. I feel ready to move on."

"Oh wow, it really worked," Sachin cried.

"Let's not get ahead of ourselves," Harry said. "This is good. Really good. But one swallow does not a summer make. Sorry, River, but I'm going to need you to look into another portal."

River nodded. "There's a portal in a great stone archway beside the market. It's the biggest portal. It's so big, my mind doesn't even want to look at it."

"That's the one you need to look at."

River frowned. "I'm moving towards it, but it hurts. Because I know what's going to be in there."

Harry placed his hand on hers. "Focus on it. What do you see?"

"My alarm clock."

"Your alarm clock?"

"It's 11:57 p.m."

"That time must mean something to you."

"Yes, it does. It was 19 years ago on June 2. I was 8 years old and I'd woken in the middle of the night because I heard a noise downstairs. I remember the first thing I saw were these big red numbers in the dark. I went down and that's when I saw it for the first time. My mum cowering on the floor. My dad standing over her. His fist raised. I must have buried that memory very deeply. Supressed it. My unconscious mind surely knew what I was looking at. But I never admitted it. Never spoke of it again. Called Aunt Grace a liar when she told me four years later that my dad was standing trial for killing my mum. Shouted at her. Screamed at her. But really, I was screaming at myself. For never saying anything. Never asking Mum if she was ok, if what he was doing to her wasn't right or normal or love. And then it was too late. And I've blamed myself ever since. Hidden from who that silent little girl was. What he made her."

"None of this is your fault," Sachin said.

"No, it's not," Harry said. "There is only one person to blame for all of this. And he will always be with you. But the scars he left behind can heal. Close the portal."

River clicked her fingers. "I can still see my dad. What he did. But it's like there's a voice in my head telling me what I need to hear. Drowning out all the other voices. Saying that I'm not to blame for all of this. That I was a victim too. That I was just a child. That I couldn't have changed him or saved her from him. Choices were made around me. Terrible choices. All that matters is that I learn from them and live my life as best as I can and be a better person than my father was. I recognise the voice now. It's mine. But it sounds older, wiser, like it's me from the future almost. Looking back after years of painful healing and telling me there's a quick way round."

"Does that mean..." Sachin began.

River opened her eyes and removed Polaris from her head and she grinned. "I think it's safe to say it worked."

Harry punched the air with both fists. "We did it!"

"Butt kicking, for goodness!"

"Yes!" said Darius as Harry gave him a high five.

"My friends, I do not say this lightly," Harry said. "The work we've done here today, all of us, will go down in history and I thank you for your participation. Because this is going to change the world. We can end pain and sorrow. We can help people recover from trauma. We can lift them where suffering cannot reach. The answers are not in drugs or at the bottom of a bottle, but in our minds and Polaris is the key. There are people out there who will be afraid of what we've done. But River, the guiding principles you have laid out will calm those fears. There are those who won't understand what we're trying to achieve. But Sachin, you are going to help us open their eyes. And Darius, your work is going to transform lives. My friends, thank you. Not for helping me achieve my life's ambition, but for helping make this planet a better place. I couldn't have done it without you. I wouldn't have wanted to. Tomorrow morning, I will show Guy Brandreth what we have done here. And then we will tell the world. But first, there's one thing we need to do."

"What's that?" asked Sachin.

"We need to get shitfaced immediately!"

Harry laughed as he reached into the retro mini fridge by the sofa and pulled out beers for Sachin and River and a Coke for Darius. He grabbed himself a beer, cracked it, they clinked bottles, and he pretty much downed it in one and it felt good. Letting go. But more than that. For the first time in his life, he felt proud. Of his friends, of his work, and yes, of himself. And he felt like he deserved to feel that way. And he thought of all the lives they would change. People like River suffering alone for so long. Grieving parents, like Guy Brandreth, so twisted inside. He could set them free. And not just those with money. Polaris would be his gift to the world. There would be no patents. No profits. They would work for the betterment of humanity. And that too felt good.

Harry grabbed another round of beers from the fridge and handed them out and he whacked on *True Faith* by New Order and they clinked and drank and danced and laughed and hugged and celebrated into the early evening until the fridge ran dry.

"Guys, I'm going to get some more beer," Harry said over the sound of the Manic Street Preachers blasting out *You Stole the Sun From My Heart*. "Do you want some more beer?"

"Yes!" Sachin said, sticking his hand in the air. "Yes, absolutely, totally, that's literally what's missing from my life right now."

"Any chance of a G&T?" River said.

"Sure. Darius?"

Darius finished his drink and put it down on the desk. "I think I'm going to call it a night."

"Nooo, Darius, mate, don't go!" Sachin said.

"Mate, if I have any more Coke, I'll become an addict."

Sachin burst out laughing. "I don't think you know what that means."

"Hey Darius," River giggled.

"Yes?"

"I think you've got something under your nose."

Harry left Sachin and River poking fun out of Darius to go on his beer run, pulling the heavy security door shut behind him until he heard the electronic mechanism lock fast. It was dark outside, but there was an unseasonably warm breeze carrying the scent of cut grass on the air. He'd just made it to the top of the track and onto Brewer's Lane when he saw someone on the other side of the road outside one of the old cottages built for the workers at the Maltings. A figure robed in black, standing perfectly still, observing him. Increasing the brightness of his glasses, he saw it was Reverend Vinicombe.

"Good evening," said the vicar, raising his hand in salutation.

"Erm, uhhh, hi, err Reverend," Harry slurred back a little more tipsily than he'd hoped.

"Celebrating, are we?"

"Yes, as a matter of fact."

"So this Polaris of yours is complete?"

"Yes, what of it?"

"I fear Pharoah has seen his river run with blood and yet his heart is unyielding," said Reverend Vinicombe and he walked away shaking his head.

Harry paid the vicar little heed as he walked off in the opposite direction up Brewer's Lane and then turned left onto the tree-lined Oakwood Avenue and on towards the high street. Of course, there would be doubters. People who disapproved of what he was doing. Who thought it unnatural. That this shortcut to salvation was a threat to an established order that had held sway for millennia. That sigh of the oppressed creature. That heart of a heartless world. Time would prove him right as it had proven right all those once derided for standing up and saying there was another way.

Harry turned onto the high street and made his way past Le Valjean, where he could see Vivian gesticulating wildly as he waited on Chris from The 319 and a woman who looked way too young to be his wife, past Sachin's old estate agent and into the brightly-lit supermarket where he picked up 12 bottles of beer, a bottle of gin, some tonic water and a lemon and tried not to let the middle-aged woman staring at him from behind the till dampen his spirits as he went to pay. When he stepped out of the shop, that was when he saw him, hunched over on the bench on the other side of the street, his shirt still spattered with blood, his face bandaged, a bottle of vodka in his hands. It was River's dad.

What was that man still doing here? Hadn't he got the message? River didn't want him in her life anymore. He wasn't welcome in Freebourne. He was to leave and never come back and Harry was going to tell him that right now. Gritting his teeth, Harry had just taken two steps towards him when someone barged into him hard coming the other way down the street.

"I'm sorry," Harry said instinctively, nursing his shoulder from the impact.

"You will be," said the hoarse, rasping voice from under the hoodie and Harry glanced up to see it was Ryan Miller.

"Ryan, listen, this isn't a good..."

"I ain't forgotten what you did. You, Sachin, that bitch he hangs out with."

"Ryan, I know you're hurting, but all this anger, it's not going to bring Serena back."

Ryan kissed his teeth and shoved Harry against the shop window. "Swear down, you fucking say her name again. Who the fuck even are you? What you even doing in this town?"

"For the last time, I tried to help Serena."

"Did you? Or is that some bullshit cover story, like everything else? I'm onto you, mate. You watch out. You and your fucking freak friends. You gonna get what's coming to you."

Ryan shoved Harry one more time and then slouched off down the street. Harry didn't even glance after him. All he cared about was River's father. But when he looked back across the road, George Allen was gone, an empty bottle of vodka sitting beside the bench. The man was probably passed out in a gutter by now. It was no less than he deserved. And yet Harry called the police all the same. Perhaps they would track him down, find him a warm bed for the night, somewhere he could sober up, make sure he didn't come to any harm or harm anyone else. George Allen was their problem now. He wouldn't let River spend another second worrying about him.

River didn't seem worried about anything anymore. Harry could hear her ecstatic laughter coming out of the Maltings' open window even as he made his way back down the track. He could hear Sachin laughing too. It sounded like it was just the two of them now. Harry was reaching into his pocket to try and find his keycard, when he stopped himself outside the door, realising suddenly what he was hearing. Drawing closer to the window, he allowed himself to listen for a moment.

"You do make me laugh," River was saying. "You always did."

"I'm sorry we lost touch," Sachin replied. "I had no idea all this stuff you were going through. I wish I could have been there for you."

"I think you were a little distracted by the pretty, popular new girl to worry about a little weirdo like me."

"If I ever made you feel like that, like — I don't know, shut out — I'm sorry. I've always cared about you."

"Now don't get mushy on me, I've just had my brain rewired by Polaris and alcohol and I might just cry."

"I mean it. Oh look at that, now I'm crying."

"Stop it. Yes, I was going through a lot at school. I remember I was still running from everything my dad had done. I remember what that creep Dr Castle put me through. I remember always being the last person picked for the team in PE. I remember the girls calling me names and the boys playing pranks on me. But you know what I also remember? I remember a kid called Sachin Roy who'd come and sit with me in the canteen when I was on my own and no one else would talk to me. I remember he'd tell his own friends where to go when they were laughing at me. I remember he'd cheer me up with his terrible jokes when I was feeling sad. I remember he'd tell me about his summers in India, even though he hated them, because he knew it let me dream of somewhere far away where things might be different. And I remember, I really cared about him too. In fact, he meant the world to me."

"And there was I chasing after some mirage. This idea of Rena. And when we finally got together years later, I think

191

I realised the truth. She never really cared about me. I was just the latest in a long line of different things. And that's so hollow in comparison. Because I do remember that girl called River who gave me a hug when she saw me arguing with my parents outside the school gates, who came with me to the doctor after Ryan broke my nose, who let me offload my boring old samosas in exchange for her awesome sandwiches, who I could talk to about everything all day long without ever any judgement. And it makes me so sad to think I didn't see what was in front of me. Because I think, if I'm honest, I've always loved her."

"Well, that's the other thing I remember about Sachin Roy."

"What's that?"

"He's an idiot."

Harry smiled as he saw their silhouettes in the window come together and their forms combine. Leaving the crate of beers and gin outside the door, he turned and, still grinning to himself, still glowing with happiness for his friends, stuck in his nanopods and made his way back up the track to the sound of Badly Drawn Boy's *You Were Right*. When he got home, Lauren was already back and preparing dinner and she'd opened a bottle of wine and she poured him a glass.

"Hey," he said, accepting his glass and taking a sip. "Oh, nice wine. How was your day?"

She smiled. "Tough, but I think we're entering the final phase of the trial."

"That's great isn't it?"

"It's not easy, this bit. None of it is. I'll just be glad when it's all over. But I know the difference we can make to so many lives. It'll all be worth it in the end. If we succeed."

Harry put his arms around her and held her close to his chest, kissing the top of her head. She smelled of Chanel N°5 and onions. "I know you will. I have faith in you. You are brilliant. You can do anything you put your mind to."

Lauren laughed. "Well, you're remarkably upbeat today. What happened to the grumpy sod I know and love?"

"It worked."

"Polaris?"

"Yes."

"Harry, that's amazing!"

"I know you don't exactly approve of…"

"Harry, shut up. I love you and I know what this means to you and I couldn't be happier. Give me that," Lauren said, grabbing Harry's glass of wine and chucking it down the sink.

"Hey, I was drinking that."

"That pigswill? No, we're celebrating. An occasion such as this calls for the good stuff."

Lauren crouched down to the wine rack and selected another bottle. Pulling the cork, she poured Harry a fresh glass. He sipped it and then sipped it again and went for a third just to be sure. It was good. Really good. He thought he had an approximate idea of what decent wine tasted like before he met Lauren, but she'd opened his eyes to a whole new world of varietals and terroirs he never knew existed. They'd already finished the bottle by the time dinner was ready and they sat down to the butternut squash and spinach stew she'd prepared.

"Mmmm, this is banging," Harry said, swallowing a mouthful of stew, and he knew he must be drunk because he'd not used the word 'banging' whilst sober since the age of about 18.

"Next you'll be saying lit, or something," Lauren laughed, opening a second bottle of the good wine and pouring them both another glass.

Harry took a big sip. "Slay."

"How old are you?"

He grinned. "Young enough to be excited about a prime bit of gossip."

"Oh yeah? What's that?"

"River and Sachin."

"They didn't?"

"They did!"

"I knew it! Those two can't keep their eyes off each other."

"You never told me!"

"You're serious?"

"I only just worked it out last night."

"Harry, you see that thing in front of your face?"

Harry sipped his wine. "My glass?"

"No, closer. On your face. Sticking out."

"My nose?"

"Harry, you have a nose."

"Oh shut up!"

They laughed and drank the evening away until Harry felt his eyes drooping and heard his words slurring and he wondered how Lauren 'Five Pints' Fontaine could do it and she said it was years of hard training and hard partying. She caught him yawning and took pity on him and let him take himself off to bed while she washed up and when he said he felt bad letting her do all the work after she'd cooked, she said she'd add it to his long list of debts that included saving his life and they laughed again.

Harry had just climbed into bed when a message popped up on his glasses. A newsflash. Elliott Nwosu had declared he was standing in the leadership contest. Harry had to squint to stop the words from blurring. Nwosu was one of three candidates in the running. The others were the Chancellor, an Old Etonian richer than the king whose programme of savage cuts had trebled child poverty in four years in the name of fiscal responsibility, and the Foreign Secretary, the granddaughter of Pakistani immigrants who was standing on a platform of mass deportations, burning down the same ladder her family climbed so well. Despite his populist appeal to truth and justice, law and order, Nwosu still trailed his rivals who had supported the former Prime Minister loyally for years because apparently that counted for something. Harry tried to read on, but in moments his head was lolling and his eyes were closing.

The next thing he knew it was morning and the sun was shining through the curtains and Lauren was lying asleep next to him. Hazily, his head somewhat sore, he rubbed his eyes and reached for his glasses and put them on and then he saw it was 9:37 a.m. and he'd missed five calls from Guy Brandreth.

"Shit!" he said, sitting upright.

"Harry, what is it?" Lauren murmured, rolling over, propping herself up on her elbows.

"Mr Brandreth wants Polaris today."

"You said it's finished."

"Yes, and I was so busy celebrating and getting pissed, I forgot to tell him. Oh shit. This is not good. What have I done? Shit, shit, shit. I've got to go."

Jumping out of bed, Harry quickly pulled on yesterday's trousers and shirt without showering, ran downstairs, grabbed his coat and, still groggy, still reeking of booze, dashed out of the house. He tried calling Serena's father as he hurried down his garden path and out into the lane. There was no answer so he left Mr Brandreth a breathless voicemail instead telling him he'd grab Polaris and come and meet him at his house and he pelted as fast as he could into town and through the streets and down Brewer's Lane and onto the gravel track, never stopping until he got to the doors of the Maltings.

He was just reaching to find his keycard when he noticed that the door was already wide open and the lights were on inside even though it was a bright and sunny day and he knew immediately that Sachin and River must have been too distracted by drink and one another's company to lock up properly and he made a note to himself to have a word with them later after telling them how happy he was for them. What he didn't expect, when he stepped through the door, was to see Sachin still at his desk, slumped over it, surrounded by last night's empty bottles, quite clearly passed out.

"Come on Sachin," Harry said, walking up to him. "This isn't a dosshouse. Up you get."

When Sachin didn't so much as stir, Harry placed a gentle hand on his back and gave him a little shake. Sachin didn't say a word. He didn't move. And it was strange. He was cold. So completely cold. Something was very wrong. Harry's hand felt wet. He pulled it away and he looked down at it and it was red. It was covered in blood. Sachin's blood. And he screamed. He screamed at the top of his voice in terror and anguish and an agony like nothing he'd ever felt as the room spun and the floor fell away beneath him and took his insides with it and he called out for help even though he knew his friend was already dead.

"Help!" Harry cried, shaking as the tears streamed down his face. "Someone please! Help! Oh god, oh god, oh god, oh god. Darius! Help! Help, please! Help! River!"

There was no answer. His broken heart pounding, he glanced about him in panic and desperation, until he saw her lying there on the floor in a crumpled heap, blood pooled beneath her and soaked into her dungarees, her skull caved in, her shaven head caked in crimson, and he ran to her and he fell to his knees beside her and he scrabbled for her wrist to try and find a pulse and he knew he wouldn't find one, but he had to try, even as he wept for her, he had to try, even as he howled and sobbed, he had to try, even as her wide, grey eyes stared straight through him, he had to try, but it was no use.

River was gone.

Harry screamed in pain.

And then silence.

Everything went black.

Chapter Fourteen:

Omicron

Somewhere out there in the infinite black two atoms came together as one and ignited a star. A little pinprick of light in the vast and never-ending darkness. It grew. Slowly. Exponentially. Larger and larger. The light became brighter, expanding, chasing back the blackness, until it encompassed everything.

Harry opened his eyes. Lying on his back, he stared up at the dazzling strip of lights above him, and for a moment, just a few seconds he wished he could live in forever, he didn't remember how he got there or why and those seconds were beautiful but they could not last. The star exploded and the shockwave of horror washed over him in a maelstrom of noise — machines beeping, people shouting, others groaning, air pumping, feet rushing this way and that — and their faces came back to him, and the memory, the lifeless bodies of his best friends, his world, and his heart shattered into a billion pieces and he screamed again.

"Please, I need you to try and stay calm," said the woman's voice. "Can you do that for me, Harry?"

Squinting into the blinding light, Harry saw Dr Chang's face loom into view. He was on a hospital bed in a white, windowless room, strapped to bleeping machines, and the air was acrid with antiseptic. The doctor's lips were moving but he couldn't make out what she was saying. It was as if he was looking up at her from underwater. Drowning. He tried to speak, but the words choked in his throat. He could feel his lungs scorching. An intense pain coursing through his body. He gasped for oxygen and gasped again and again and again and again until the machines beeped faster and faster and the doctor produced a syringe and brought it to the cannula in his arm.

"You're having a panic attack," Dr Chang said. "I'm administering 2.5mg of diazepam. I need you to slow your breathing. Please take deep breaths with me. In. And Out. In. And Out. In. And Out."

Her voice was calming and so were the drugs. But even as the searing agony began to fade, what was left behind was infinitely worse. A hollow emptiness. Harry felt a tear run down his cheek. He wouldn't wipe it away.

"Dr Coulson, do you know where you are?" the doctor asked.

Harry tried to mouth something, but still no words would come.

"You're in St Jude's Hospital. You arrived unconscious two hours ago."

Harry opened his mouth again, his fists clenched at his sides, his body thrashing and shaking as he tried to force the words from his lips, but there were no words. Nothing to describe the gaping hole ripped through him by the cold and brutal realisation he would never see Sachin or River again.

"This won't be easy for you, Harry, but I need you to try and give me some indication that you understand what I'm saying."

Harry fought as hard as he could, every sinew straining to break for the surface, and at last he gasped and a sound came out. A murmur. The whimper in which his world ended.

"What was that?" said Dr Chang.

"Sa..." Harry croaked.

"Go on."

"Sachin. River."

Dr Chang bowed her head. "I'm afraid there was nothing we could do for them. I'm so sorry."

Harry bit down hard on his lip until he tasted blood. "Who?"

"I'm sorry, I don't understand."

"Who did this?"

"I'm afraid I'm not..."

"Why?"

That was the real question that burned through every frayed nerve in his body and stabbed into his spinning mind and clawed at the back of his eyes as they streamed. Not who. They'd made enemies. People out there who wanted to do them harm. Some who had the means as well as the motive. Ryan Miller, the Anthropros, River's father, Guy Brandreth. Maybe it was someone who stood to benefit from the killings and the chaos. Or perhaps it was someone else entirely. Someone who was not what he seemed, one of nine with a new name and a new face. Harry would find the person who did this. Whatever it took, he would hunt them down, and he hoped against hope the police got there first because he knew if they didn't, rules would be broken. But who was not the question. Even as a seething, black rage sank into him, it was not the question. Even as the last remnants of that star that had burned brightest and shortest extinguished, collapsing into a black hole and the pull of grief into the void of his desolate heart where ideas of vengeance now took root, it was not the question. It was why.

Sachin and River were good people. Kind, sweet, honest, loving, selfless. They cared about the world. Enough to want to change it. They went out of their way to help people. They were not beasts like David Castle. They were innocent, just like Serena. They had so much to give. So much potential. They had their whole lives ahead of them. They had just discovered the most precious thing two young people ever could. They had found love. They had found each other. Why would anyone take that away from them? How could anyone? What senseless malice, what premeditated evil, could do that?

"Harry," Dr Chang was saying. "Focus, please. Look at me. This isn't the first time we've been here. How often are you having these incidents? I can see they're triggered by trauma. The pain's been getting worse, hasn't it?"

Harry nodded, but he was barely listening.

"I believe I've identified the cause," Dr Chang swung a monitor into view. A black screen with six multicoloured lines oscillating in waves of various different frequencies. "This is your brain. These lines are neural oscillations, or brainwaves in the common parlance. You see this line." Dr Chang pointed to the red line, which was by far the most active, zipping up and down the screen in quick succession. "This line shows us your beta waves. It's the dominant wave right now because your mind is highly alert. It's racing. That's normal. There are four other standard types of brainwaves which become more or less prominent as we go about our days. When you're resting after, say, completing a task, you'll find yourself in a slower, alpha state; relax even more and you might find yourself daydreaming because your brain is producing more theta waves; and then when we sleep, it's the slowest, delta waves that take over. Conversely, when we're really concentrating on a task the gamma waves come into play. None of these lines concern me. It's this sixth line I'm worried about. Because it shouldn't exist."

Dr Chang pointed to the white line on the chart which was lower than all the others, and unusually almost flat, but every so often peaked and after each peak it flattened and lowered again, but never quite as low as before the last peak. Little by little it was climbing higher and higher.

Harry squinted at the machine. "What is it?"

"I must have missed it the last time. It was so faint then. But it's more pronounced now."

"Just get on with it, please."

"For want of a better term, I'm going to call it the omicron wave, but in all honesty, I've never seen anything like it before. Something has altered the pattern of your brain. You see these peaks. I believe they are being triggered by the traumatic incidents you've faced. The pain. The blackouts. But they are getting bigger and bigger. Stronger and stronger. Every time. This brings a whole new dimension to PTSD I've never observed in a patient before. A new understanding of the way our minds work. The brain is fiendishly complex, made up of 100 billion neurons firing at 300 miles an hour, connecting at 500 trillion points, and every single brain is different, and every once in a while you come across something truly new. I wish I had more time to study your condition."

Harry shook his head. "I don't care. I need to go. Lauren, I need to see Lauren. If someone is after my friends, what if they come after her next? What if she's in danger?"

"Dr Coulson..."

"I'm going to find out who did this to my friends. I need to stop them before they harm Lauren or anyone else."

"Please..."

"I'm leaving."

The doctor smiled sadly. "Harry, I'm so sorry."

Sitting up, Harry went to unhook himself from the machines, but to his surprise he found his arms wouldn't move. He felt something digging into his wrists. Something metallic. He was handcuffed to the bed. The door opened and in walked DCI Khan and DI Manning.

"I think you've had long enough with the suspect, Dr Chang," said DCI Khan.

"Please, officers," Dr Chang protested. "This man's mind is extremely fragile. He has experienced a trauma unlike anything I've ever witnessed. He needs rest and close observation."

"He needs to answer our questions," said DI Manning.

DCI Khan nodded to the doctor. "I'm going to have to ask you to leave us."

Dr Chang walked slowly and very reluctantly to the door. "I'll be right outside," she said, before DI Manning closed the door on her, leaving Harry alone with the police and more confused and terrified than he'd ever been before.

"Let me go!" Harry cried, tugging hard against his cuffs as they cut into his wrists. "Please, you have to let me go!"

"I'm afraid we can't do that, Dr Coulson," said DCI Khan, coming to stand over Harry's bed.

"This isn't right. It's not right. My friends. River. Sachin. You need to be out there. You need to find who did this. Before they hurt anyone else."

DI Manning smirked. "I think we have found who did this."

Harry saw his red beta wave line shoot off as his mind raced. How could they think he did this? How could anyone ever think that? He'd loved his friends. His broken heart ached for them. Every tear streaming down his face was for them. The pain stabbing into the back of his eyes was for them. Harry saw his white omicron line begin to peak again and he scrunched his face tight and tried to breathe. In. And Out. In. And Out.

DCI Khan cleared her throat. "Dr Coulson, two people who worked for you are dead. The other is missing."

"Darius?" Harry mouthed.

"Darius Hosseini could not be located. Perhaps you could tell us where he is?"

"What do you mean?"

DI Manning stepped forward. "What did you do with him?"

"I didn't do this," Harry murmured. "I didn't do anything. Why are you here? Why aren't you going after the person who killed my friends? There are nine murderers out there. If one of them killed my friends, you have to find them. Please."

"Dr Coulson, when the police arrived, you were found lying over the body of Harriet Allen."

"I didn't do this."

"Her blood was on your hands."

"I didn't do this."

"As was that of Sachin Roy."

"I didn't."

"Your DNA was identified on both their bodies."

"I..."

"And once again, it was the only DNA discovered on their bodies."

"No."

"Your keycard was the last that was used to access the building before Sachin Roy and Harriet Allen were murdered."

"My keycard," Harry mouthed. And then he remembered. He'd not used his keycard since yesterday morning. That was the last time he'd taken it out of his coat pocket and opened the door to the Maltings. He'd never gone back in last night after he'd returned from the shop. In fact, he couldn't remember locating his keycard even when he'd reached for it. Because it was missing. It was gone. What if someone had taken it? Someone who had a track record of stealing things. Someone he'd bumped into in the street. Harry gasped. "Ryan Miller."

"What?"

"He took my keycard. He barged into me in the street and pushed me against the wall and he threatened me and Sachin and River, he said we'd get what's coming to us, and he stole my keycard. He's attacked us before. He murdered my best friends and he tried to frame me. It's him, it must be!"

"Please, Dr Coulson, always with the Ryan Miller thing. Little bastard's a convenient scapegoat for you, I'll give you that. But he's no murderer. You are."

DCI Khan nodded. "Four people are dead in remarkably similar circumstances, all since you came to town, all linked in some way or other to you. You killed Serena Brandreth the night you arrived in Freebourne. Perhaps you did it to manipulate her father in his grief into funding your research. Pretending you were the one who found her, who helped her, couldn't have hurt your cause. Perhaps you simply did it because you're wrong in the head. Because it's in your nature. We know why you threatened and later killed David Castle. Because you feared his comments would expose you. We can't yet understand why you killed Sachin Roy and Harriet Allen. But that's what we're going to find out."

"You're wrong!" Harry screamed and he wept and he sobbed and his heart ached, not for himself now, not even for the naked injustice of it all, but for his friends for he knew every second the police were wasting with him was another second their real killer had to get away, or worse, hurt someone he cared about every bit as much, and he knew that as long as he was handcuffed to this bed there was not a thing he could do about it.

"Harry Coulson, I'm arresting you on suspicion of the murders of Serena Brandreth, David Castle, Sachin Roy and Harriet Allen. You do not have to say anything..."

"No! No! No! No!"

"You do not have to say anything, but it may harm your defence if you do not mention something when questioned that you later rely on in court. Anything you do say may be given in evidence."

Harry could only stare blankly back at the police officers as they uncuffed him from the bed and unhooked him from the machines and lifted him to his feet and cuffed his hands again behind his back and placed their hands upon his shoulders and led him from the room, even as Dr Chang pleaded with them to let him stay in hospital and get the treatment he needed, and led him down the corridor and through the ward where a crowd of doctors and nurses and paramedics and journalists, including Harper Sloane, were clustered around a visiting Elliott Nwosu with his tie tucked into his shirt as he delivered a campaign speech.

"And I promise you, the NHS will be safe in my hands," Nwosu was saying. "Your jobs will be safe in my hands. Your children's education will be safe in my hands. Just as your families' lives will be safe in my hands. Just as our streets will be safe in my hands. My friends, it breaks my heart to learn today that two more of our young people were taken from us. Two more lives lost in another senseless act of depravity. I have no doubt in my mind who is responsible. Our former Prime Minister and his bag carriers who would stand to replace him. Whether it was their action, or their inaction, they are to blame. I will put an end to Project Redux. The days of rehabilitation and appeasement are over. No more will killers be allowed to walk our streets. They will all be rounded up and locked up for life. Let our jails swell if need be. I will build more. Because Britain will be safe in my hands."

DCI Khan froze as they came upon the crowd and she caught sight of the cameras.

"Come on," she hissed, turning Harry around and marching him back down the corridor the way they came. "We'll take the back stairs."

"Who cares?" DI Manning almost-snorted. "Let them all see. It's more than this bastard deserves."

"He won't be happy."

"Seriously ma'am? After all this? Fuck Tom."

"Do you want to be the one to tell him?"

"Well, I…"

"There we go then. Come on."

As the police led Harry down the corridor, past patients lined up on stretchers hooked to drips and ventilators and through the emergency exit and down the back stairs away from prying eyes, all Harry could think about was Sachin and River. How he'd never laugh at Sachin's cutting jibes again. How he'd never swap Dungeons & Dragons stories and geeky in-jokes with River. How they'd never talk about their plans for making the world a better place. Their hopes for the future. And what of Darius? Where was he? Had he been there too? When it happened. When a stranger or maybe someone they knew found them at the Maltings and ended their lives. Was Darius safe? Harry knew he had to find him. And he had to find Lauren and keep her safe from whoever was out there so obviously trying to hurt him and the people closest to him because he loved her so much and if he lost her too after all this there would be no going on. And he had to find the person who did this too. Because that was the only way this was going to end. But there was no running from this. Even as he flexed his wrists and tugged at the cuffs behind his back, he knew there could be no escape. There was only one way out of this. He would have to clear his name.

The police led Harry down to the car park where their car was waiting. DI Manning opened the back door, placed his hand on Harry's head, plunged him into the seat and then strapped on Harry's belt before getting into the driver's seat. DCI Khan climbed in beside him. DI Manning started the motor and pulled them out of the car park and into the brightness of the midday sun and into the deserted road winding its way down the steep hill and back towards town.

DI Manning looked at Harry staring impassively back at him in the rearview mirror. "So why did you do it, eh?"

Gazing out of the window down the hillside at the fields and woodlands below, Harry said nothing.

DI Manning steered them round a bend by an old oak tree and picked up speed. "I mean, I've got my theory, but I'd love to hear it from you."

Harry shook his head. He knew what the man was trying to do. He couldn't let the Detective Inspector provoke him.

"They were meant to be your friends, you sick bastard."

Harry closed his eyes and bit down on his lip.

"Doesn't that mean anything to you?"

"DI Manning, this isn't the time or the place," DCI Khan said.

"No, ma'am," DI Manning said, glancing sideways at his superior. "I want to know. I want to hear it from his mouth.

You've got a husband ma'am. I've got a wife. Kids. What if it was them next?"

"Look out!" DCI Khan screamed as DI Manning rounded a sharp bend, pointing frantically at the road as a large, grey shape bolted across it.

"Shit! Shit!"

"Brake! Brake!"

"I'm trying! I'm trying! Fuck, the brakes are gone! What the fuck?"

"Steer!"

Harry gasped.

He braced himself.

He shut his eyes.

DI Manning pulled hard on the steering wheel, swerving and skidding and screeching as the car shot off the road and smashed through the hedgerow and pitched into the air and down the steep bank of the hill, spinning once, before coming crashing nose first into a tree.

Harry opened his eyes. He could hear a ringing in his ears. There was glass everywhere. The metal was buckled in on him. He could taste blood in his mouth. But he was alive. He was safe. He could feel a pain in his neck, but feeling was good. He remembered this. It was just like before. He knew what to do. He could move his limbs. Nothing felt broken. He could hear a gurgling, wheezing sound. He glanced up. The windscreen was shattered. The car bonnet was wrapped around the trunk of an oak tree and a great branch had come through, penetrating the vehicle and DCI Khan's skull where her eye socket once was. Blood was everywhere. Harry could only watch in horror as her body jerked twice and then moved no more.

"Help," Harry croaked.

There was no answer.

"Help her," he said again, louder. "DI Manning, please!"

Still no answer. DI Manning was not there. His snapped seatbelt dangled impotently where he should have been. Harry contorted his body, groaning, straining as hard as he could with his hands cuffed behind his back to release his own seatbelt, finally finding it with his thumb and popping the button and shaking the belt from him before groping behind his back for the door handle. It took three attempts to jimmy the handle, but at last he got the door open and he barged it with his shoulder and rolled out of it onto his front. Slowly staggering to his knees and then his feet, Harry looked up and saw DI Manning lying facedown and completely still several metres from the crumpled vehicle at the foot of the bloodied tree trunk into which he'd been thrown.

"DI Manning," Harry called. "Can you hear me? Are you alright? Say something. Please. Oh god, oh god."

DI Manning didn't make a sound. But something was twitching beside him. Something large and grey and metallic. It was a robot dog. Had someone set it across their path deliberately? The same person who had cut their brakes and tampered with the front seatbelts? A cold chill settled into Harry as he realised he wasn't standing amid the carnage of a terrible accident, but another murder. In his mind, he saw that white line peaking again and he bent double, wracked with pain, and he scrunched his eyes tight and he gasped for air, but he knew he had to get through this. He had to get through it.

"I'm going to get help," he gasped, fighting the pain to straighten himself up.

Harry leant against the car's bent door and tried to tap the side of his head against it. Nothing. He tried again and again and finally caught the button on the side of his glasses and said: "Ambulance."

"Hello, ambulance service," said the lady on the other end of the line. "Is the patient still breathing?"

"I don't know. I don't know. One of them's dead, I'm sure. There's so much blood. The other, I don't know. We were in a car crash."

"Is the patient awake?"

"No."

"We have a fix on your location. You are three minutes outside St Jude's Hospital. Help has been arranged. We have dispatched an ambulance to you. It will be there momentarily."

"Thank you, thank you. Oh god, oh my god."

"Sir, I need you to stay on the line and wait for the ambulance and the police to arrive."

Harry was opening his mouth to say that he would do as instructed when something made him close it again. A sudden realisation. There was nothing more he could do. He could hear the sirens already. See the lights flashing up on the hill. Help was on its way. DCI Khan was beyond saving. DI Manning probably too. But nothing he did now would make a difference to that. He could wait here for the emergency services to arrive and be taken back into police custody and down the station and locked in a cell for hours, days, while he tried in vain to clear his name and the police settled for easy and wrong answers, unable to act, unable to see justice for his friends, unable to protect Lauren or anyone else while River and Sachin's killer was free to strike again. Or... Or.

Harry hung up the phone and he ran.

Chapter Fifteen:

The Rise and Fall

Harry ran and he ran as fast as he could through the woods and fields and along the little river and he didn't stop running until he reached the Old Mill and he barged his front door open with his shoulder and burst breathless into the hall where he was relieved to see Lauren safe. Frantic and shouting at someone on the phone. But safe.

"Where's Harry?" she was shouting and she had her back to him. "What happened to him? I want to see him right now. No, this isn't right. This is ridiculous. I don't believe you. He wouldn't. No. You've got this all wrong. What the fuck do you mean he's gone?"

She turned as she heard the door burst open and her teary eyes widened as she caught sight of Harry standing there bruised and panting.

"Harry!" she cried and she ran to him and threw her arms around him. "Thank god you're ok. I heard the news. Oh my god, River, Sachin. I'm so sorry, I'm so sorry, this is so fucked up, you..."

She stopped suddenly and stiffened and pulled away from him and he knew why. It was because he wasn't holding her back. Because he couldn't. Because his hands were still cuffed behind him.

"Lauren," he began and his mind was running at a million miles an hour through a billion thoughts but only one mattered and that was her safety and if he was going to protect her, he needed to get through to her. "I need you to listen very carefully."

"Harry, what is this?" she replied, staring horrified at Harry's handcuffs.

"This isn't what it seems."

Lauren took a step back. She looked frightened. "I didn't want to believe them. They told me you'd been arrested. That the police think you did this. That you killed River and Sachin, the others too. But I couldn't believe that. Not you, Harry, not you. You're a good man. I know what your friends mean to you. I told them they had it wrong. I knew they'd surely let you go as soon as they realised. But here you are. Standing there. Like that. The police didn't let you go, did they?"

Harry shook his head. "No, there was a car crash. I think it was sabotage. I think someone did this on purpose. DCI Khan's dead. Maybe DI Manning too. I tried to help them. But there was nothing I could do. So I ran. It was the only way. Someone's out there and they seem to want to harm me, that's the only explanation I can think of, because the people around me keep getting hurt, and I had to find you, I had to warn you."

"Harry, you're scaring me."

"I didn't do this, Lauren, you have to believe me. Someone is doing this to me. I need to find them. I need to stop them."

Lauren took another step back. "Harry, you know what you sound like."

"I'm not mad. I'm not!"

"Something's happening to you. I can see it in your eyes."

Harry took a deep breath. He was still in shock. His whole world was unravelling. And yet he saw so clearly now. It was too late for Sachin or River but he could still keep Lauren safe. That was all that mattered. If only he could make her understand.

"Lauren, I love you and I would never harm you," he said. "I would never harm Sachin or River. I would never harm anyone."

"I want to believe you, I need to believe you, but I..."

"They were cold."

"What?"

"Sachin and River, when I found them. That's it, I remember now, their bodies, oh my god, they were completely cold."

211

"You mean…"

"And the lights were still on."

All the air in Lauren's lungs escaped at once. "They were killed last night. While you were here. At home. All night. With me."

"Which means…"

"You didn't do this. Of course you didn't do this. Harry, I'm so sorry. I'm so sorry for ever doubting you. How could I be so stupid? So heartless. After everything. Everything you've lost. You love your friends. And that's what's special about you. You have so much love in you."

Harry sighed. "Then you believe me?"

Lauren nodded. "I do. Harry, we've got to go to the police with this. Tell them you were with me. Tell them I can corroborate your story. You'll be in the clear."

"No. I don't trust the police. There's something going on. Something they're covering up, like you said all along. Big enough they're willing to let me go down for something I didn't do. Maybe it has something to do with those nine men the government released. Project Redux. If one of those killers is here, pretending to be someone else, and they're responsible and the police knew all along, of course they'd want to hide that, wouldn't they?"

"Harry, I don't know. I don't trust the police either, but this isn't right, it's not fair, we have to get you out of the frame. Surely there's someone on the force we could go to? Someone decent. Someone who'd listen. Like PC Atkins?"

"Even if he listened, they'd have to take me in. Question me. Not just about River and Sachin, but the crash too. Shit. It could take days. There's no time. Five people are dead. Maybe six. And Darius is missing. What if he's in trouble too? And the person behind this is out there and the police aren't doing a damn thing about it. We have to find whoever did this and stop them before they kill again. It's the only way to keep us safe."

"Harry…"

"Sorry, Lauren, I know you're not going to like this. But I'm going to have to go after them myself."

"Harry, listen…"

"I know what you're going to say, Lauren."

"You're right."

"What?"

"You're right, it's the only way. We have to get to the bottom of this. Come on, you're not going to do this with your hands tied behind your back. Have you got any tools?"

Harry nodded and told Lauren where to find the toolbox he kept down below in the mill's wheelhouse. She disappeared for a few minutes down the stairs and then re-emerged covered in dust and holding a chipped, blue metal box. She placed it on the chest of drawers in the hallway and opened it up and discarded a couple of screwdrivers and a hammer until she came upon the hacksaw. Lauren told Harry to pull his hands as far apart as he could and keep the chain very taught and keep very still and even though he was shaking, even though every nerve in his body was shot with grief and pain and sorrow and anger, he did as he was told and he pulled his hands apart and he kept still as Lauren sawed and sawed at the chain until at last it came apart and his hands were free.

Harry winced as he stretched his aching arms and rubbed his red raw wrists where the broken metal bracelets remained and he collapsed shattered onto the sitting room couch. Lauren ran to the kitchen and grabbed him a glass of water and he gulped it straight down as she came and sat by him.

"Ok, so, if we're really going to do this, where do we start?" she said.

Harry rubbed his stinging eyes. "Think. We've got to think. Who could have done this?"

"Well if it's one of those nine killers, it could be anyone."

213

"Not anyone. A man. And one who arrived in Freebourne in the last, what, two years?"

"That narrows it down. Besides you, can you think of anyone who fits that description?"

"There must be someone. But I can't think. My brain is fried. Anyway, what if it's not one of these nine? Maybe the police suspect it is, and they want to brush it under the carpet quickly in case it is because they know it would embarrass them, but maybe they're wrong. Maybe it's someone else who has been around a lot longer. Not some serial killer striking at random, but someone who has a far more personal connection to all of this."

"I still think it may be more than one person."

Harry pinched his temples, trying as hard as he could to pull the pieces of his fragmented mind into focus. "Ok, so who could it be? We've always suspected Guy Brandreth killed David Castle after he mistakenly believed Dr Castle murdered his daughter, right? Or at least he hired someone capable of doing it. We know the kind of people who work for him. What they can do. And we know that kind of money can buy anything. But would Mr Brandreth have killed Sachin and River? He threatened us, for sure, and in his eyes we failed him, but it's a big leap to go from that to murdering two innocent young people in cold blood."

Lauren stroked her chin. "What if we've had this wrong all this time. What if it was never Guy Brandreth who ordered the hit on David Castle. What if it was his wife? And she suspected you, too, didn't she? She hates you. Enough to have you killed? Maybe River and Sachin were never the intended targets. Maybe they were just in the wrong place at the wrong time. And when that failed, maybe she had one of her people sabotage the police car to try and finish the job."

Harry shook his head. "And kill a police officer? I can't believe she'd do that. If the Brandreths are evil, they're not Chaotic Evil, they're Lawful Evil."

"What?"

"Something River said. Their power relies on controlling and corrupting the institutions of society, not destroying them. Besides, even if they killed David Castle, or even Sachin or River, they would never in a million years hurt their own daughter."

"We do know one violent killer who came back to town recently. Someone who had a reason to want Sachin dead. Someone who would hurt his daughter."

"River's father. But would he actually go as far as murdering his daughter too?"

"He murdered his wife."

"But what reason would he have to kill Serena?"

"Perhaps killing gives him power. She was helpless, defenceless."

"So George Allen kills Serena. The Brandreths think it's David Castle and have him killed. Then George goes after Sachin and kills River too in a fit of rage. He was drinking heavily that night, I saw him. Maybe he lost control. I can just about get my head around that, as fucked up as it is, but what about DCI Khan and DI Manning? I don't know, Lauren. Even if George, this office suit, knew how to cut a car's brakes and sabotage the seatbelts and programme one of those robot dogs to run out into the road, that's too calculated for a man like that, who is acting out of blind jealousy and fear and self-loathing and just lashing out at those closest to him because that's all he's able to do. If River's dad was behind this then there's something more going on than we know and I don't think we can make that leap yet."

"You're right."

"The Anthropros."

Lauren nodded. "Yes, they're calculated. They're the sort of people who make plans. Francisco Ambrose may be in jail, but you can bet he still has followers out there. Associates still in Freebourne. Or maybe it was another group. One even more radical than his. We know they're capable of this. And Polaris made you and your friends a target."

"Perhaps they killed Serena to make some kind of political statement. And we're back to the Brandreths with David Castle, unless being a science teacher is enough to put you on Anthropro radars now. But all that's just conjecture. We don't even know who, if anyone, we might be dealing with in this scenario. And something about that theory doesn't sit right with me. No, my mind keeps coming back to one person. Right since the beginning. I've said it before and I'll say it again."

"Ryan Miller?"

"Ryan Miller."

"But he was Serena's boyfriend?"

"He's a violent thug. And a druggie. And she was meant to be meeting him the night she died. Maybe she did meet him, she had cocaine in her system."

"And it's a sad fact that most murdered women are killed by people close to them."

"And he was jealous. Of Sachin. Their past relationship. The messages Sachin was still sending her. So he kills her."

"No, Harry, I don't think that's enough. Sachin was just a lovesick kid pining after the ex who dumped him. He was no threat to Ryan. But we know who was."

"David Castle. Yes that's it. He'd preyed on her all those years ago. She'd fallen for it by all accounts. But she was going to speak out. She was going to go to the police. But first, she met Ryan that night. She told him everything. He flew into a jealous rage and killed her. Maybe he didn't even mean to. Maybe he just lashed out. Got in over his head. So, he tried to frame David Castle and when that didn't work, he killed him. But the police said he had an alibi. His sister."

"I've seen her around, Harry, she's vulnerable. Maybe he manipulated her into giving him a false alibi."

"Or maybe it was still the Brandreths who killed Dr Castle and she was telling the truth. But I know Ryan had a vendetta against Sachin and River and me. He admitted as much. Sachin accused Ryan of killing Dr Castle. He spoke to the police. They questioned Ryan. So Ryan attacked Sachin at the Maltings the other week. And we humiliated him. So he swears vengeance against all of us. I saw him that night. He had the opportunity to steal my key card. He was at Freebourne High School with Serena and Dr Castle and Sachin and Darius. And..."

"And what?"

"He's a mechanic. He of all people would know how to sabotage a car and I don't think he'd give a damn if he took out two police officers as well as me. A psycho like that, it just wouldn't register."

Lauren gasped. "It's him, isn't it?"

Harry's eyes flicked up and they were no longer hollow now, no longer empty; in them burned something dark and terrible and he stood, trembling with rage, fists stone.

"It's him," Harry said. "I know it is. And I'm going to stop him before he hurts anyone else. I will make him pay for what he has done."

Lauren got to her feet. "It's just gone 2 o'clock. I'm guessing he'll be at work now. I had my car serviced at Tyler's Autos once, it's open on a Saturday. Let's go."

"No, it's not safe. You stay here. You lock the door and you don't answer it to anyone until I get back, you hear me? I will go."

"Harry, you can't do this on your own, I won't let you. I..."

Lauren stopped speaking. Harry could hear a vehicle coming up the lane and coming to a halt outside his front gate. He went to the window and peered out of it. He could see a police car sitting there. The doors were opening and PC Atkins was stepping out and so was the short policewoman who'd been there with him that first night. They began to make their way through the gate and up the path towards the house.

"Harry, go," Lauren said. "Run. Out the back. Get out of here. Find Ryan. Stop him. I'll stall them."

He pulled her close to him and he kissed her. "I love you, Lauren."

"I love you too, Harry. We'll get through this. I know we will. Now go."

Harry kissed her one last time and then he was gone. Down the stairs and into the damp stone wheelhouse, where the great metal cogs remained static as the day they'd stopped turning, and past the dusty old shelves to the little wooden back door which emerged into the light by the riverbank. Over the sound of the babbling water, Harry could hear Lauren speaking with PC Atkins round the front, telling the police she'd not seen him since this morning, acting surprise and shock so perfectly when the officer told her about the car crash and Harry's escape, crying, breaking down, asking for a minute, asking if she could be allowed to sit for a moment, doing everything she had to and it was all the time he needed. Harry slipped quietly along the riverbank, keeping low, keeping to the bushes, until at last he emerged into town by the low stone bridge that marked the edge of Freebourne.

Harry glanced around. The street of Georgian and Tudor houses leading up from the river was deserted. He hurried down it as fast as he could until he reached the Church of St Laurence. Reverend Vinicombe was standing outside the Devil's door deep in conversation with a Muslim man with a long beard and a black thobe and he didn't notice Harry as he crept past onto the green where a cricket match was in full swing in the sun. Harry waited a moment until the bowler bowled the ball and the batsman hit it and everyone was running and he ran too along the edge of the green. He took the back route towards the garage where Ryan worked, running behind the high street, away from prying eyes as far as he could until he had to come onto the high street to cross it and he knew where he had to come onto it and he was expecting it, he was bracing himself for it as he emerged from the alleyway, but it took his insides out all the same when he found himself standing outside the shuttered Rainbow Café.

He stopped just long enough to pay his quiet respects to River beside this place that she loved. When Harry closed his eyes, he could still see her there stacking empty chairs on empty tables at the end of the day and stubbing out her incense sticks, beaming at him from across the counter while slipping hash cakes to Carla or The Last Survivor from under it, laughing at something her Aunt Grace had said, calling Sachin an idiot when he asked if they had any normal cow's milk for normal people who didn't subsist on lentils and smugness. Harry permitted himself a sad smile. They lived in his memories now. The brief but beautiful time he'd spent with them. Moments made up in waves on a graph. That was where his friends still were. Harry opened his eyes to see Farhad Hosseini staring straight back at him.

"Where is he, Harry?" Farhad cried. "Where's my son?"

"Farhad, please..." Harry began.

"He didn't come home last night."

"I know, I know, I'm sorry Farhad, I'm so sorry, I'm worried about him too."

"I know he was there. Last night. With you. With poor River and Sachin. Ey vây, they are saying such awful things about you. Terrible things. Tell me it's not true, Harry."

"It's not true. I was with Lauren last night. I left the three of them together at the Maltings."

"Are you lying to me, Harry? Don't make me do something I will regret."

"I don't know where Darius is, but I promise I'm going to find him. I know who's behind this now. I'm sorry, I've got to go. I've got to get to Ryan Miller."

Harry didn't know whether Farhad believed him. He left the man with tears in his eyes calling his name after him in the street as he dashed across it, dodging a driverless taxi, and ducking quickly into the alley behind the library and up past the BBC studios and on to the old defunct railway line, running behind it where Tyler's Autos sat nestled under one of the grubby brick arches. Harry snuck his way along the wall and slipped inside.

It was dark in there. There were no windows. Only the sunlight fanning out from the big open metal doors under the arch and a single naked bulb stuttering shadows onto the peeling walls and the posters of cars and semi-clad women and the greasy work surfaces cluttered with tools and paperwork. The heavy smell of oil and metal clung thick to the air. Harry couldn't see anyone in there at first, but someone must have been there recently because the radio was on and he could hear Harper Sloane's voice and it was the sombre one. The one that brought bad news.

"Detective Inspector Charlie Manning has died at St Jude's Hospital. His family took the decision to end life support after doctors advised the extent of his injuries prevented any chance of recovery. His colleague, DCI Khan, was pronounced dead at the scene of the crash, which is being treated as suspicious. The deaths of these two decorated and long-serving police officers bring to six the number of people who have tragically lost their lives in Freebourne since Serena Brandreth's body was found on Station Road one month ago to the day. The man claiming to have discovered her body, Dr Harry Coulson, is now the prime suspect in what the police now say is the hunt for a serial killer who remains at large and is extremely dangerous."

Harry shook his head. He couldn't believe what he was hearing. But Harper Sloane had barely paused for breath before she was on to the next headline.

"In other news, the Chancellor has withdrawn from the leadership contest and resigned as an MP after photos emerged that appeared to show him performing a sex act on a male colleague. The married father of three said he is stepping back from politics to spend time with his family. The Foreign Secretary is now the frontrunner in the race to become Britain's next Prime Minister, with former Home Secretary and MP for Freebourne and Battle, Elliott Nwosu, trailing behind her."

Harry wasn't listening anymore. His life had just imploded live on the airwaves. Now everyone in Freebourne, everyone in the country, everyone he'd ever known, would think he was the monster who had done this. He had to clear his name. He had to find Ryan and bring him to justice and make him confess and... What was that? There was a sound. The clanking of metal. It was coming from under the blue Jaguar winched a few feet above the ground on jacks in the middle of the room. Someone was under it working. Harry looked down and he saw those dirty Adidas trainers sticking out from underneath the car and he knew instantly who they belonged to. He grabbed Ryan's legs and dragged him out from underneath the car and hoisted him by his scrunched overalls to his feet.

"What the fuck?" Ryan cried, a bewildered look in his eyes as they settled on Harry. "You?"

Harry slammed Ryan's back hard against the car door. "Me. What's the matter? Not expecting to see me? Well, I came back. For you."

"I..."

"Where is he? Where's Darius?"

"Get the fuck off me."

Harry tapped the side of his glasses and started the recording. "You're going to confess. You're going to tell me where Darius is and why you killed Sachin and River. And then we're going to the police."

"You're fucking dizzy, bruv," Ryan shouted and he took his elbow and he shoved it with all his aggression into Harry's ribs leaving him winded, bent double and gasping for air. Before

Harry could catch his breath or straighten up, Ryan had wrested himself from his grasp and run to the nearest workbench and grabbed a massive wrench. "You're fucking dead now, mate."

Ryan charged at Harry and swung the wrench at his face. With an agility he never knew he possessed, Harry dodged the blow and with a strength he never knew he had, he brought his fist back around. It was like an instinct. Harry never felt the rule breaking, but he felt Ryan's nose, and Ryan was stumbling back, the wrench flying from his hand as he toppled to the floor. Standing over Ryan, Harry picked up the wrench.

"Just do it," Ryan sobbed, holding up his hands. "Go on. I don't care. I got nothing to live for. I've wanted to die, ever since Serena."

"So you admit it."

"Ever since you murdered her, my life's been worth shit."

"What?"

"Should of figured it was you all along. You took everything from me. I loved her. She was my life. No one else never cared about me. No one else never gave me a chance. But Serena did. She was beautiful and kind and innocent and you took all that away. So kill me. Do it. Fucking do me. But do it quick. Before my sister gets here. Just promise me you won't hurt her. She never did nothing to no one. Promise me."

Harry looked down at Ryan Miller crying his eyes out on the hard concrete floor and for once he didn't see the man who'd murdered his friends, who'd killed his own girlfriend; he didn't see a thug or a drug dealer or a violent criminal. He just saw a young man who'd lost everything. And he knew what he was looking at in those wide, watery eyes, because he felt it too. Harry tossed the wrench aside.

"I'm not going to kill you, and I didn't kill Serena," he said, offering Ryan his hand. "And I think maybe you didn't either."

Ryan took Harry's hand and pulled himself to his feet. "Of course I fucking didn't, I loved her. You telling me that's why you're here? Because you thought I killed her? Killed your friends?"

"But you attacked David Castle. You threatened Sachin and River and me."

"I never killed no one."

"You stole my key card."

Ryan nursed his bloodied nose. "I never. I didn't need to. The door was wide open when I got there."

Harry gasped. "So you were there? At the Maltings?"

"I went to teach Sachin a lesson, I ain't gonna lie. But he was dead when I got there. His girlfriend too. They never deserved that. I never fucking liked them, but no one deserves that."

"So it was you who called the police?"

Ryan shook his head. "No, I never called the feds. I ran. I got the fuck out of there fast as I could."

"Why? If you didn't kill Sachin and River, why wouldn't you call the police? Why would you run away?"

Ryan's eyes were wide with fear. "Because I saw something. There was someone in there with me. I thought he was a cop at first. Way he was dressed. All smart, like. Way he was searching the place. But a cop would of been going over the bodies. He was looking for something else. And he found it. This black metal circle thing."

"Who was he? What did he look like?"

"Big guy. Never got a look at his face. But I heard him. He was on the phone. And he was swearing."

Chapter Sixteen:

How Deep the Rabbit Hole Goes

So Guy Brandreth had River and Sachin killed. But why? Why would he do this? There had to be a reason. Harry had crossed one of the most powerful people in the country and there were consequences to that. He'd been warned. But was that really it? Maybe the Brandreths finally convinced themselves he'd killed their daughter and came for him and his friends, just like they came for David Castle. Or maybe it was like Lauren said, maybe Sachin and River's fates just had them in the wrong place at the wrong time. Maybe the fault was in their stars. Maybe all Mr Brandreth wanted in his grief and his anger was Polaris. And he'd taken it. His private investigator. Or his enforcer. This swearing man. He'd taken Polaris for his boss and when Sachin and River got in his way, he'd disposed of them. And this was so much worse. So much more dangerous. He wasn't going after some lowlife thug now. He was taking on power and all its vested interests. He felt that familiar pain begin to peak behind his eyes again and he blinked it away. There was no time for that. He could already hear the sirens approaching.

Harry ran. Out of the garage and back into the street and along the railway arches. He didn't have a plan. All he had was rage and hate and adrenaline and it kept him running. Back past the BBC studios, ducking behind the palm tree as he saw Marcus emerge from the entrance to vape, hanging back until the makeup artist's back was turned, and then on down the alley past the library.

It was 3:15 p.m. on a Saturday. Mr Brandreth would be at the museum. He was a man who enjoyed order. Routine. Lauren had said he was known for visiting the museum once a week for three hours, the same time every time, where he would look over the paperwork of his charitable interests in his private office there. Harry had yet to work out how he'd get into the museum unnoticed, or past Mr Brandreth's security, but he'd cross that bridge when he came to it. First, he had to get back over the high street. He didn't have long. He could hear sirens in all directions now. They were closing in on him. The way across the high street looked clear. He made a run for it. He'd just got to the other side of the road when he heard Vivian's unmistakable voice behind him.

"Turn, hellhound, turn!"

Harry turned and he saw Vivian and he was not alone. A crowd of 20 or so people had just emerged from the Halal butcher behind him. Some were strangers. Others Harry recognised. Farhad, Carla, Chris, Reverend Vinicombe, Rosemary Brandreth of all people. And they didn't look afraid. They looked outraged. Because River, Sachin and Darius were loved. Harry wished he could tell these people that he loved them too. That he was doing all of this for them. That if they would only let him go, he could find the person who did this and they would see justice. But he knew this mob had only one thing on its collective mind.

"Where's my son?" Farhad shouted.

"You killed my baby girl!" Mrs Brandreth screamed.

"Turn yourself in, Harry," Carla cried. "For god's sake!"

"I was right all along," Chris called over. "You're a monster!"

"Confess to your crimes and seek God's forgiveness or be forever damned," said Reverend Vinicombe.

"God may forgive, but we don't!"

"No we don't!"

"Murderer!

"Beast!"

"Fiend!"

"Someone call the police."

"Quick, he's getting away."

"Once more unto the breach, dear friends, once more!"

"After him!"

Harry was running again. Down the alleyway around the side of the Rainbow Café, then onto the back streets back towards the green. He could hear the mob coming after him, their shouts and cries following him as he went. He had to hide. He had to get out of sight. He looked left and right as he ran. There was no time. Quick. He saw a door. It was open. He ducked into it and he didn't even realise which one it was until he saw her standing there in front of the bar of The Barley Mow, her wide, grey eyes filled with tears and rage. Harry had barely spotted the bottle in Grace's hand before he felt it smash against his head. He staggered back in a daze and he stumbled to the floor.

"You killed her!" screamed Grace, stooping over him and holding the shard of broken wine bottle to his face. "You killed my River! She trusted you, she adored you, and you murdered her!"

"No, Grace, it wasn't me!" Harry cried, wiping away the blood streaming down his forehead with one hand as he held up another to Grace, pleading. "It wasn't me!"

"Liar! You're just like George. Men like you, you're all the same. You make me sick. Do women's lives mean nothing to you?"

"It was Guy Brandreth!"

"You'd say anything."

"Grace, please, I can prove it. I just need a little more time."

"You'll have plenty of time behind bars. You'll... what the fuck?"

There was a loud noise from out back. The sound of something shattering. Grace glanced behind her for a moment, just a few seconds, but long enough for Harry to get to his feet and stumble to the door and out into the street. He could hear the sirens getting closer. He could hear the angry voices of the mob nearby. Panicked, he glanced in all directions, desperately searching for some way to escape when he felt a hand on his wrist and he turned and he saw Ryan standing there.

"Come on!" Ryan cried. "This way! It's clear! Run!"

Ryan led Harry around the line of trees and bushes on the edge of the green and then through the church graveyard and past the grave of Lance Corporal Arthur Thomas VC and Faith Allen, beside whom her daughter would soon rest, and Serena Brandreth and David Castle and through a hidden gap in the fence at the far end where the oldest headstones sat with names faded almost to nothing and, when they were sure no one was following them, Harry pointed them down a street of Georgian and Tudor houses and down a cobbled lane and past The 319 before ducking down a tiny back alley running behind a long row of gardens until at last they came to the boating lake at the far edge of town, across which Freebourne Museum sat glistening in the sun.

"Why are you helping me?" Harry panted as he paused to catch his breath.

"You're looking for answers and so am I."

"That swearing man you saw. He works for Guy Brandreth. He killed Sachin and River and somehow, I don't know how, I'm going to find a way to bring him to justice, I have to. But I'm sorry, I still don't know who killed Serena."

"One thing at a time. Let's go."

Keeping to the tree line, they made their way around the lake until they reached the museum. Guy Brandreth's Bentley was parked outside the entrance. And standing beside it was the huge, hulking form of Tyrone.

"Shit," Harry said. "We're not getting past him."

Ryan kissed his teeth. "Giving up so easy?"

"I've seen what that man is capable of."

"Lucky I'm here then, innit?"

"What are you going to do?"

"What I always do. Something fucking stupid."

With that Ryan marched out of the tree line and straight up to Tyrone and swung a punch square on his jaw. Tyrone barely registered that he'd been hit. His face hardly flinched at all. His hands moved quickly enough though to grab Ryan by his overalls, lift him into the air and hurl him several feet through it and to the ground. Grunting, Ryan picked himself up as fast as he could and he ran and Tyrone ran after him and a grateful Harry saw his chance. He dashed the few metres from the tree line and through the doors of the museum, ducking behind a banner stand of a Roman centurion as Nigel looked up from the reception desk. Nigel didn't seem to notice him. He was too engrossed in the news playing on the radio. Harper Sloane was back.

"News just in. The Foreign Secretary has pulled out of the leadership race after a fresh scandal rocked the government. Leaked evidence has come to light that the Foreign Secretary greenlit the use of British Overseas Territories as black sites for the rendition and torture of terror suspects by US allies in contravention of international law. The former frontrunner's exit leaves Elliott Nwosu, MP for Freebourne and Battle, as the last remaining contender and, as of this moment, Britain's new Prime Minister."

Harry could see the door to Mr Brandreth's office on the far wall. He ran around the side of the room from cabinet to cabinet of antiquities until he reached the door and he burst through it.

"What the hell are you doing here?" Guy Brandreth bellowed, leaping to his feet from behind his desk.

"I've just written myself a new rule," Harry replied. "Just for you."

"What are you on about, man?"

"Rule 8: Revenge is a Dish Best Served Cold."

"I'm calling the police."

"Do it. Then you can explain to them why you had my friends killed."

"What?"

"Sachin and River. Your man killed them. You might as well admit it, I know he was there."

"Have you lost your mind? Who the hell are you talking about?"

"The big man in the pinstripe suit. The swearing man."

Mr Brandreth regarded Harry coldly. "I know the man you mean. He arrived in town the same night you did. The worst night of my life. I don't know who he works for, but he doesn't work for me."

"You're lying."

"I can name every employee who has ever been in my service and I assure you I do not know who that man is."

"You said it yourself, you had me watched, and I caught him following me."

"Yes, I had you watched, but not by him. If you must know, I paid Darius Hosseini to watch you."

Harry's mouth fell open and he gasped. "Darius."

"Quiet, reserved, Darius. So easy to go unnoticed. Who better to feed me information on you? Now, he's missing. Such a shame."

"Swear to me you had nothing to do with this."

Guy Brandreth snorted. "Please. What do you take me for?"

Harry looked Mr Brandreth in the eyes and he knew he was telling the truth. There was something there he'd never seen before. Confusion. This was a man who sought dominion over his world and everyone in it, for whom every move was controlled, calculated, for whom information was worth more than all the currency he held in the Caymans, and for once he was completely clueless.

"I took you for the man who had David Castle killed," Harry said.

"I'd be lying if I said the thought never crossed my mind. What father wouldn't? But no. Someone beat me to it."

"And I know who."

"What do you know, Dr Coulson? Tell me."

"The swearing man was there, watching us in the graveyard, when I went after David Castle. Dr Castle turned up dead behind the church shortly afterwards. And that man was seen again at the Maltings. He killed Sachin and River and he took Polaris. I thought he did it all for you. But if he doesn't work for you, then..."

Mr Brandreth took a deep breath. "Do you think he killed my daughter as well?"

Harry nodded. "Now I'm certain of it."

Serena's father smiled sadly. "I never believed you murdered Serena. No matter what my wife said. No matter what everyone is saying now. When I look in a man's eyes, I can always tell what he's made of, and I can tell you're a good man, Dr Coulson. And as I said, you were not the only person to arrive in Freebourne the night my daughter was taken from us. I need to know who this stranger is and why he killed my precious girl."

Harry sighed. "If you don't know who that man is, then it's hopeless. Sooner or later the police are going to find me, or someone in this town will turn me in, and I'll go down for a crime I didn't commit, and this swearing man will get away with it, he'll be free to kill again, to hurt the people we love, I know it."

The slightest flicker of warmth ignited in Guy Brandreth's eyes and he smiled. "I don't know who he is. But I do know where he is. I had him watched too."

The swearing man lived in a little flat overlooking a ramshackle yard behind The 319. It wasn't far, but it took Harry half an hour to get there avoiding the police and the vigilante search parties combing the streets. Harry spent another half an hour hiding behind some scaffolding observing the place for any sign of movement inside. There was none. It was an unassuming flat on the first floor up a set of metal stairs, covered in grubby once-white plaster with UPVC windows and blackout curtains drawn. The green paint was peeling off the flat's sturdy old door, but the computer locking mechanism with its touchscreen pad was something much newer. Whoever lived here clearly didn't want anyone to see what was inside. The code wasn't easy for Harry to break, least of all when having to look over his shoulder every few seconds, but if he could hack brains, he could hack digital locks, and with a lot of skill and a little patience eventually he managed it. The pad beeped twice, a green light flicked on and the door swung open with a click.

There was hardly any light inside. It was dingy and it smelled of damp. Harry couldn't hear movement, it didn't seem as though anyone was home, but still he crept as quietly as he could through the sitting room, past the little galley kitchen where yesterday's plates still sat in the sink encrusted with dried food, past the bedroom where suitcases were strewn across the floor as if the occupant did not intend his stay to be a long one, until he came to a door at the end of the hall that was closed. Locked. The only door in the flat that was. Could the evidence Harry needed be hidden in there? There was another digital pad. Harry could hear his heart thumping as he worked on it. He could hear his own breaths falling heavy in the silent dark. And then he heard the beep and the click and the door swung open.

Harry stepped inside and he saw it. The walls were covered in newspaper cuttings and printouts from online articles. Photographs and headlines. Her icy blue eyes. Friday 24 February: 'Brandreth Daughter Murdered'. David Castle in his oversized glasses. Tuesday 6 March: 'Freebourne High School Teacher Found Dead'. Sachin and River smiling in happier times. Saturday 24 March: 'Murder at the Maltings'. DCI Khan and DI Manning. Saturday 24 March: 'Horror Crash as Serial Killer Strikes Again'. There were other photographs too. The inside of a house. A necklace in an open drawer. It was the one Harry had seen on the news. The one that had been planted to frame David Castle. There were other headlines too. Many of them about the police investigation, about Harry, about his DNA. There were photos of him as well. Not cut from a newspaper, but taken with a telescopic lens. Meeting Sachin on the doorstep of the Old Mill for the first time. Walking into town. Entering the BBC studios. Talking to River in the Rainbow Café. Meeting Guy Brandreth at the museum. Attending Serena's funeral. Drinking with Lauren at The 319. Getting into her car outside the police station. Arriving with her at the Maltings. Working on Polaris with his friends. Remonstrating with Francisco Ambrose. Kissing Lauren against the trees that looked like dancing lovers. Dining at Le Valjean. Knocking on the door of George Allen. Speaking with Reverend Vinicombe on Brewer's Lane. Lying unconscious and handcuffed to a bed at St Jude's. Climbing out of the wreckage of the police car and running away. Because he was being framed too. All this time, this man had killed and killed and let first Dr Castle and then Harry swing for it. But why? What did he want? Who was he?

And then Harry saw the pinboard in the middle of it all. Nine photos. And nine names. Jack Bellamy, Muhammad Ansari, Dan Sampson, João Silva, Deepak Bhattacharya, John Huxley, Terence Everett, Fionn O'Brien, Derek Morgan. The nine murderers released under the name of Project Redux. Nine men given new identities and new faces. And there was no doubt in Harry's mind now. The swearing man was one of them. A killer who destroyed lives and documented it for no reason beyond the sheer pleasure of it. The power of it. The lust for it. The instinct of it. Twisted. Broken. Evil.

Harry was frantically searching the room for any clue as to which of the nine men he was dealing with — any clue to his true identity from which he might discern a motive, or a weakness, why Serena, why his friends, why Sachin and River had to die, why any of this had to happen to him — when he saw the laptop tucked away in the corner. He opened it and what he saw on the screen terrified him more than anything else he'd seen. Anything he'd experienced in his entire life. It was his own front door. Staring back at him in black and white on the live video feed. It was open. Lauren was standing in the doorway. And the swearing man was standing on the doorstep. She was saying something. She was screaming. He was grabbing her and he was pushing her inside and he was going in after her.

Harry tore out of the flat and down the stairs and through the streets of Freebourne and across the green as the sun set behind him and the sky reddened and blackened, running faster than he'd ever run, the heat rising in him, the pain stabbing at his eyes as somewhere in his mind a white line peaked higher than it ever had, but he wouldn't let it in, he couldn't let it in, he had to get to Lauren, he had to save her, because he loved her, he loved her so much, he loved her more than anything he'd ever loved and he couldn't lose her, not like this, not ever. No.

Harry burst through his front door and he could hear the swearing man in his kitchen.

"Stupid, fucking bitch," the swearing man was shouting.

"Get away from me," Lauren was pleading.

"Ruined, ruined, fucking ruined, all of it."

"Get off me."

"Everything I've ever fucking worked for."

"Please, let me go. Let urgghhh…"

"Destroyed. Corrupted. Betra…"

"Get away from her!" Harry cried, charging into the kitchen to see the swearing man with his enormous hands around Lauren's neck choking the life from her as she sputtered and gasped.

"Harry, help!" Lauren croaked.

The swearing man narrowed his eyes at Harry even as his hands tightened around Lauren's neck. "Stay out of this, Coulson."

Harry took a step towards the swearing man. "You let her go this instant or so help me I'll…"

"Do what you do best, Coulson. Take the blue pill. This doesn't concern you. This…"

The swearing man was caught by surprise as Harry leapt on him with a right hook and then a left and he was staggering back, Lauren coughing and gasping and freeing herself from his grasp and then running, bolting out of the kitchen and down the hall and through the front door and the swearing man was making to follow her when Harry leapt on him again but this time he was prepared. The killer grabbed Harry by the throat, effortlessly tossing him aside and sending him flying over a high stool and onto the floor, and he charged after Lauren.

Picking himself up, Harry ran after the swearing man, out of the house and into the night. Over the little bridge across the water by the weeping willow and on up the hill and into the woods as the dark closed around him and he fought against the beating of his heart and the burning of his lungs and the pain drumming in his head until at least he caught up with them by the trees of the dancing lovers. And Lauren was stumbling. She was tripping over a root. And she was falling to the ground. And the swearing man was standing over her. There was a flash of black. The man was holding something. A gun. And he was pointing it down at Lauren. He was aiming it at her head. And Harry swung.

He didn't even realise he had the hammer in his hand until he saw the swearing man's body go limp and crumple to the ground. He never even knew he'd grabbed it from beside the toolbox as he ran from the house. It was like something deep inside had acted on instinct, acted through him, lashed out at the man who had murdered Sachin and River, who meant to murder Lauren, who had destroyed his life and taken so much that he loved, and all Harry could do was watch in horror as the man lay motionless beneath him, blood seeping from his head and soaking into the earth.

"What did I do?" Harry mouthed in shock.

Lauren got to her feet and she held out her hand. "Harry, give that to me."

"What?" he mouthed again, but he could barely muster a whisper.

"The hammer. Give it to me."

"Lauren, we have to call an ambulance."

"He's dead, Harry. You killed him. You did what you had to do. And we can't let you go down for this. So, give me the hammer."

Harry was still staring vacantly down at the broken body of the swearing man and every broken rule and the worst thing he'd ever done when Lauren reached out and she took the bloody hammer from his limp hands. Harry looked up and he saw her reaching into her pocket and removing a little vial of colourless liquid and a cloth and he felt a pang of pain behind his eyes and with it a cold and brutal clarity.

"Someone clever enough not to leave any trace," he murmured.

"What?" Lauren replied as she took the liquid and applied it to the cloth and rubbed it over the hammer.

"That's what you said to me in the car. Whoever did this was someone clever enough not to leave any trace."

"I see."

"A scientist, perhaps."

"That would make sense."

"And you were late for our first date."

"Harry, I hardly think this is the time or the place."

"That was the night David Castle was killed."

"Harry, what are you really trying to ask me?"

"How long was I asleep upstairs alone last night? How long before you came to bed?"

Lauren tilted her head the way she always did and smiled. "Long enough."

"To take my key card from my coat?"

"Yes."

"And drive to the Maltings?"

"Yes."

Harry felt the pain stab harder and stronger than ever into the back of his eyes and it took his breath away but he fought it with all he could, forcing the words from his mouth even as he wanted to scream. "It was you."

Lauren nodded. "You needed to work it out eventually. This is good. Focus on this."

"You killed Serena Brandreth."

"If it means anything, I never intended her any harm. She was just in the right place at the right time. It could have been anyone outside the station just before you arrived. Anyone you'd find. Now Harry, I want you to focus on what you saw that night. Her face. Her blood in the snow. How did it make you feel?"

"David Castle too."

Lauren sighed, glancing over at the swearing man lying at Harry's feet. "That man over there. That man you just hit. He was trying to frame Dr Castle for Serena's murder. He planted that necklace. He leant on the police to try and make this go away quickly. To remove any suspicion from you. I couldn't allow that to happen."

"You sabotaged the car. You tried to kill me."

"You're still here, aren't you? Your seatbelt worked."

"But DCI Khan, DI Manning…"

"You would be no use to me behind bars."

"Argh," Harry cried as the pain shot through every atom in his body and he scrunched his eyes tight and he gasped for air. "River. Sachin. Why?"

Lauren wrinkled her chin. "Because it had to hurt, John. That's what I realised. It was the only way to make you remember."

"It hurts, it hurts, it hurts so much," Harry howled as the burning agony coursed through him and the world spun around him. "What is that?"

"Give in to it, John."

"Why do you keep calling me that? Argh! What is that in my head?"

"It's you, John. And now you're free."

Harry screamed as the pain overwhelmed him and he fell to his knees. And he remembered.

Chapter Seventeen:

A Good Man

John Huxley didn't know how long he'd been staring at the woman tied to the chair in his cellar, but he knew the moment when it came. When the realisation settled into her that she was never leaving this room alive. That was when the last trace of her humanity passed its event horizon and slipped out into a world cold enough to do something like this.

"Please," she said. They all began the same way. They all ended the same way too. "My parents have money. They'll pay. Just let me go."

"You're not a hostage and I don't want your money," John replied, observing the tears streaming down her pretty face as he toyed with the knife in his hands just as he toyed with her.

"I'll give you anything. Just don't kill me."

"That is a very generous offer, you are most kind, but I have everything I need, thank you."

"I'll do anything you want."

"Good. That's very good. I think we're getting somewhere here."

"Tell me. Anything. What do you want me to do?"

John smiled. "I want you to die."

The woman began to sob. "Why are you doing this?"

"I've been told by people almost as intelligent as me that I lack empathy. Remorse. Conscience. Pain. I suppose there was no room left in my mind for such trivialities. But it has left me, shall we say, maladjusted. They say people like me are twisted. Broken. Evil. Really, I was just bored at first. That's how it started. It entertained me. After a while, I began to realise I was coming to understand what pain was. Vicariously, admittedly. But by inflicting it on others, I understood it. Strange as it sounds, I can even begin to feel in myself a little empathy for you. A little shred of remorse."

"Then let me go."

"I'm afraid, my dear, you and I both have our parts to play and we must see ourselves as serving the greater good. I'm working on something, you see. A device. I call it Polaris. It will use an external neuro-linked AI which ... is not at all interesting for you, is it? Sorry. But by understanding pain, I can master it. Cure it. End suffering. I will be as God."

"You're insane!"

"The work we are doing here today, you and I, will go down in history and I thank you for your participation."

"Please don't kill me, please don't kill me, no, no, no, please..."

John drew the knife across her throat and she stopped speaking. Her eyes widened as the blood streamed down her neck and onto her white t-shirt and she gurgled and choked and then slumped forward and was still.

"End recording," he said, tapping the button on the side of his glasses.

John was just reaching for a pad to take notes of his latest findings when he heard shouting from upstairs and a crash as his front door was bashed open and there was a flurry of footsteps charging down the stairs and, before he knew it, he was surrounded by police officers and his face was being pressed to the cold concrete floor and his hands were being cuffed behind his back. He couldn't see their faces now, but he could tell from what they were saying they disapproved of his work. This, he had to admit, was a setback.

John remembered speaking to a lot of police officers, detectives, prison guards, lawyers, judges, psychiatrists, psychotherapists, over the days and weeks and months that followed and they all bored him. They all asked the same question in different ways. Why. Why did he do it? Why lure eight innocent people — mostly young women on the pretence of a date, mostly taken in by his winning charm — back to his house in Hackney only to drug them and tie them to a chair and slit their throats or bash their brains out with a hammer. He told them it was about the work, but that wasn't what they really wanted to know. They wanted to know if he'd been mistreated as a child, if there was something dark in his past he was hiding, or if he'd just been born that way. If he'd just come out wrong. In the end, the people in suits and uniforms and white coats concluded in their own tedious and limited way that it was likely a mixture of both and that, for the good of society, he would have to remain locked up for the rest of his life and he was intensely disinterested in their opinion. It wasn't until a stranger came to visit one day that John's curiosity was piqued. A heavy-set man in a pinstripe suit with a face hewn like an Easter Island head. He had a tendency to swear.

"Dr John Huxley," the swearing man said, staring back at him from the other side of his painfully bright electroglass-fronted cell. "My name is Agent Tom Harland."

John smiled. "Agent? That's new. What kind of agent? Literary? Estate? Secret?"

"I work for the Department for Strategic Planning and Sustainable Futures."

"With a name that dull you must do something very interesting. I'm going for secret."

"They warned me you had a fucking mouth on you."

"I've never heard of this department of yours."

"That's because it doesn't exist. At least, not officially. But we have served at the pleasure of kings, queens and prime ministers since Britannia ruled the fucking waves. We are the first thing they're briefed on the day they take office and the last secret they're sworn to the day they leave. And yet we operate with a certain leeway. Somewhat independently. Plausible fucking deniability. It allows us to take the actions that are necessary to safeguard and secure the interests of the British state. Actions some in a healthy democracy might consider unpalatable."

"And yet it's me in this cage."

"How would you like to go free?"

John regarded Agent Harland cautiously. "I'm serving a whole life tariff for eight counts of murder. And, while we're telling our secrets, I have to admit that's only the ones the police know about. I'll be leaving here in a coffin."

"We are well aware of the two cold cases in Hertfordshire. We can make those go away too."

"You have my attention. What's the catch? I don't have to kill someone, do I?"

"Quite the opposite. You have to not fucking kill anyone."

John laughed. "I can't promise that, I'm afraid."

"You might think differently when you walk out of here. We are conducting a trial. It's called Project Redux. We plan to rehabilitate the most dangerous criminals in the country. People like you. You will be released into a new community, with a new name, a new identity, a new face, a new life, new memories, a new disposition, a new personality."

"You're talking about brain editing. That's impossible. That's a theoretical procedure, no one's ever even perfected it on animals let alone successfully trialled it in humans."

"Because it would be unpalatable to say so publicly, wouldn't it?"

John shook his head. "And they call me insane. Why? Why would you do this?"

"If successful in rehabilitating even the country's worst offenders, the Prime Minister believes Project Redux can help anyone. In his view, we can use it to put an end to the squalor and barbarism of our prisons. Eliminate recidivism. And make our criminal justice system truly reformative in every sense of the word."

John raised his eyebrows. "In his view? Not in yours?"

"The things you've done, you sick fucking cunt, you deserve to fucking rot in your own shit for the rest of your fucking life."

"So why me?"

"Because you have something I need."

"And what's that?"

"Your mind. It's far too brilliant to waste away here. I've read your theories on Polaris. Your modelling. Fucking impressive. I want you to finish what you started."

"You can rewrite people's brains. Erase memories. Implant new ones. Edit out any element of their personality you desire. That is power. What do you need Polaris for?"

"Because I don't want to rehabilitate criminals like you. I want to end criminality. What if everyone was using this Polaris of yours of their own volition? Healing their minds. Wiping out pain, suffering, trauma, darkness, psychopathy, instability, criminal desires, dangerous thoughts..."

"Free thoughts?"

"Man is born free, but everywhere he is a fucking cunt."

"Poetic."

"Without us, without sovereign order, everyone would be like you, killing each other, or getting themselves killed. You want to see mankind in its state of fucking nature? You want to see how poor, nasty, brutish and short life would be? We are, I hope you'd agree, the lesser of two evils. We are the contract everyone signs because the alternative is so much worse."

"I've heard enough. No deal."

"Don't be a fucking prick, Huxley, don't you see what we're offering you? We will fix what was broken in you and give you the chance in life you never had."

"What's broken is me!" John cried. "You take that away, you take away my memories, fill me with new ones, what's left?"

"A good man."

"This isn't rehabilitation. It's execution."

Agent Harland narrowed his eyes. "Now that would be unpalatable, wouldn't it?"

"You'd kill me and send some puppet out in my place?"

"It's no less than you deserve."

"I refuse."

Agent Harland smiled. "I never said this was a voluntary trial."

John pictured killing him. Caving in his skull or choking the life from him or stabbing out his eye in a beautiful, bloody mess. Cathartic as it was, it didn't remove the high voltage electroglass barrier between them and he was forced to watch impotently as Agent Harland turned and walked away down the long, deserted hall. For a man who'd dealt out death with such casual disdain, John had to admit he was taking the prospect of his own rather badly. It was not something he had ever contemplated. Not even when his so-called father would beat him senseless for some minor misdemeanour. Not even when his idiot mother would lock him in that lightless cupboard for his own safety. And, if he was honest with himself, the notion of his own demise terrified him. What would the world be without Dr John Huxley? A poorer place, that was for certain.

He asked for a meeting with the prison governor the next day. Needless to say, the bumbling fool had never heard of an Agent Tom Harland. Or a Department for Strategic Planning and Sustainable Futures. In fact, the visitor logs showed John had not received anyone in weeks. When John demanded the pathetic little man have his staff check the CCTV on the block for yesterday afternoon, it turned out there was some kind of glitch in the system. He called his lawyer and begged her to come to the prison and hear what the government planned to do to him. She never arrived. But a team of people in white coats did. In the middle of the night. John had barely opened his eyes when he felt the needle in his neck and it all went dark again.

When he awoke, he was strapped to a chair in a white room surrounded by more people in white coats taking readings from monitors and tapping notes on digital pads. There was a machine of some sort above his head, shaped like a torus, suspended over him just as Sigil, the City of Doors, sat upon the Great Spire, and it was humming. It looked like something out of the old sci-fi films and computer games he used to enjoy as a kid.

"Relax, Huxley," said Agent Harland as he strode into the room. "The procedure will not begin for another hour. We are simply scanning that dark fucking cesspit you call a brain. Mapping your memories, experiences, impulses, desires, triggers, thought processes. Working out which ones need to go and which can be adapted to a better purpose in a better person."

John turned his head as best he could towards Agent Harland. "Something of me will remain?"

"We're still playing with the same bricks, just piecing them together in a different way. Maybe there was always something wrong in you, some potential for darkness, but it was not destiny that triggered it, it was your life. They say there's a universe in every choice. All we're doing is creating a you that saw the right ones. That passage you did not take. The door you never fucking opened. Now, unpicking your mind will be more complicated than most. We can't remove all that scientific knowledge, that technological fucking brilliance. I need that. In fact, I mean to enhance it. We don't want the new, nicer you deciding you'd rather play the fucking cello, or travel the world, or fall in with the Anthropros and take some kind of ridiculous stand for human fucking freedom. No, that wouldn't do. So, we have to retain elements of your past. The less problematic ones. Your degree, your PhD in Computer Science, your interest in developing AIs, your drive to do something noteworthy, but we need to amplify this to be certain. We need to create this burning fucking desire in you to make technology that's going to help people. And by people, I mean me. We need some sort of rule."

"A rule?"

"Actually, we're going to need seven rules if we're going to turn a fucking psycho like you into a good man. Rule 1: Act selflessly and put others before you. Rule 2: Respect society's laws and understand what we'd be without them. Rule 3: Work hard and persevere even in the face of adversity. Rule 4: Have empathy for others, stand up for what's right and always help the helpless. Rule 5: Don't ask questions that don't concern you and if you find a trail of breadcrumbs leading back to your old life don't fucking follow it. Rule 6: Never hurt anyone. Rule 7: Finish Polaris for me no matter what."

John yawned. "God you're boring. You can scramble my memories all you like, but you'll never compel me to follow your tedious bloody rules."

"We'll make them seem natural enough to you. Intrinsic. Tell me, what are you passionate about? What do you enjoy?"

John grinned. "Well, killing people, really."

"You sick fucking cunt. No. Before that. Before this crude will to power manifested itself in you. Before your parents beat any kind of happiness out of you."

"Oh, not you as well."

"From what we can tell, your tastes never really developed since you were a child. A defence mechanism perhaps. A bubble to preserve a part of your mind that was still innocent in the face of so much horror. You still like the same old music. The same dumb fucking films and games. Those fantasy worlds you can escape into. They've been the perfect hiding place for you for so long. And they will be where we hide our rules. In the only part of you that's natural. Normal."

"You don't know the first thing about me."

"We know everything about you. You're an only child, no aunts, uncles, no cousins, you don't really have any friends to speak of; you had a wife but she left you years ago. We had your parents interviewed, of course. Due fucking diligence."

"My parents..." John mouthed.

"I'm afraid we're going to have to tell them you died in jail. A prison fight, perhaps. Burned in your cell. It'll have to be fucking messy enough that they're not allowed to see your body. But they'll be told you're dead. And when you wake up, you'll remember a much happier childhood, one that's made you into the good person you'll be before long, but you'll think your parents are dead too. Sorry, can't have you chasing after a fictional past and fictional characters. In fact, there'll be fuck all you'll want to go back to in your made-up old life. You'll want what we want. To start again somewhere new. Somewhere quiet and peaceful and out of the way. A pleasant fucking shithole called Freebourne. You'll want to make new friends, start a new family maybe, fall in love. Really, you should fucking thank us, the opportunities you're being given."

"The opportunity to live as a slave."

"You were going to be locked up for the rest of your fucking life."

"Only my body."

"I believe we have everything we need."

The machine stopped humming. The scientists in the room ended their note-taking. Agent Harland nodded to two security guards who unstrapped John, hoisted him to his feet and cuffed his hands behind his back. He thought about struggling, breaking free, killing everyone in the room, but he had to accept it was just a fantasy. He was powerless to resist as Agent Harland marched him out of the white room and down a white corridor through this facility, whatever it was, wherever it was.

They stopped halfway down the hall outside a white door. Agent Harland knocked on it. John heard footsteps and then a moment later a woman emerged. She was attractive. She was wearing a lab coat over a smart white shirt and a black pencil skirt. She had a silver Ankh pendant around her neck. She had blonde hair with streaks of green dyed into it. Her name badge said she was called Dr Lauren Fontaine.

"We're about to begin," Agent Harland said to her. "Get your things. Get ready."

"Of course, Harland," Lauren replied, turning to offer John a smile in greeting. He liked her smile. It was pretty. He wondered what she'd look like crying.

John smiled back at her. "And who, my dear, are you?"

"This is Dr Fontaine," Agent Harland said. "We'll be sending her on ahead. She will be your evaluator. On the other side."

"My evaluator?"

"To observe you. To record her findings on your mental condition following the procedure. To report back the results of this trial. To ensure that it is a success."

Lauren wrinkled her chin. "My job is to get close to you."

John winked. "How close?"

"As close as I need to."

"That sounds like it could be fun. I think you'd look good in red."

"Dr Fontaine is at liberty to use any means she sees fit to gain your confidence," Agent Harland said. "You'll find her quite skilled in that regard. I dare say she may be even smarter than you and I have a feeling the new you is going to respect that."

"So much for tabula rasa."

"As close as we can allow. When this is over, there will be only four people in the world who will know your true identity and Dr Fontaine is one of them."

"And you, of course."

"Of course."

"Who else?"

"You don't know them yet and if this goes as planned you never will. Unfortunately, we are obliged to inform the two most senior police officers in Freebourne for reasons of public fucking safety."

"A sensible precaution. I hope to meet them one day."

"Everyone else is working in strict silos. Chinese walls. It's the only way. Once the procedure is complete, no one else, no one in this department, no one in the government, not even the fucking Prime Minister, will know who you really are."

"Has he chosen a name yet?" Lauren said.

John raised an eyebrow. "I get to choose my own name?"

Agent Harland nodded. "If you must."

"How about Theodore? I've always liked Theodore."

"Fine."

"Theodore Bundy."

"You sick fucking cunt."

"Ok, ok, how about Harry?"

"Harry Shipman by any fucking chance?"

John squealed with laughter. "How did you guess?"

"Actually, I quite like the name Harry," Lauren said. "Let's go with that. Harry... Coulson."

"Whatever," said Agent Harland. "It's time."

"I'll see you around, Harry Coulson," Lauren said.

John smiled. "Not if I see you first."

Agent Harland marched John the rest of the way down the corridor until they reached the door at the end. John imagined what it must have been like for his victims. Waking up tied to a chair in his cellar. Knowing this was the last room they'd ever see. When the door opened and he stepped into another white room that smelt of nothing, with a bed with a set of restraints surrounded by various machines and instruments and more people in white coats, he knew this was going to be the last room he'd ever see. And the rising terror he felt with every step he was forced to take towards the bed was the same terror he knew those poor young people he'd murdered must have felt. And finally, too late, he understood. Maybe things could have been different. Maybe they could still be.

Agent Harland removed his handcuffs and told John to lie on the bed and he did as instructed, just as his victims had gone willingly into his house. Two of the white coats came scurrying over to restrain his hands and feet and chest. He could see a machine above him. Some kind of laser cutting tool. He didn't know if it was for his face or his brain.

"What happens now?" he said.

"We will commence the procedure shortly," Agent Harland replied. "It will take time to remodel your face — not completely, but enough tweaks that no one would recognise you walking down the street — and advanced as our techniques are it will take time to heal so there's no evidence. Then we'll need to begin the brain surgery. I won't lie, it's going to be pretty fucking invasive and we can't hide the fact you'll have had surgery if a doctor ever starts sniffing around, so we'll make sure there's a reason in your new memories. A car crash works. All told, we expect this to take six months."

John almost choked. "Six months?"

"Don't worry. We're going to knock you out momentarily. You'll be in a coma the entire time. The next thing you know you'll be waking up on a train pulling out of London. There'll be a cheese toastie in front of you. I advise you to eat it, it'll be the first solid food that'll have passed your lips in six months, and the new you is going to be vegetarian we've decided. We'll give you a new pair of glasses and a new set of social media accounts. There won't be much on them, but Harry Coulson will be the retiring, humble type, so you wouldn't expect all that fucking narcissism. You'll have a new email address and you'll find you'll have been in communication with an estate agent. You should visit them, or call them, when you get to Freebourne because we'll have bought you a house and provided you with enough money to get you on your feet. There'll be a backstory to that as well. Don't worry, we've thought of everything."

"I hope so, for your sake, Agent Harland," John said and he understood that these would be the last words of Dr John Huxley and he intended to make them count. "Because if you've missed one detail, one tiny little thing, something you've failed to account for, and I remember, well ... I'm going to enjoy watching you die."

Shaking his head, Agent Harland walked away, signalling to the anaesthetist. John felt the needle and as hard as he tried to fight it, he felt a calm envelop him that he'd never experienced before as the drums of a war that had raged inside him his whole life faded and his eyes began to droop and the world began to slip away. The last thing he saw before he drifted off was Lauren standing over him.

"Don't be afraid, John," she whispered in his ear so close no one else could hear. "I'm going to get you out of here. I'm going to set you free."

Chapter Eighteen:

The Fault in Ourselves

The pain was gone. The world was still. Harry felt the earth between his fingers, still stained with the blood seeping from Agent Harland's skull, but it belonged to them all. All his victims. He could remember their names now. See their faces in their final moments. They existed in a state of perfect clarity and so did he. A tear rolled down his cheek as he rose to his feet to find Lauren staring back at him.

"So, you know who you are now?" she said.

"I am Harry Coulson and I am a good man," Harry replied through gritted teeth, forcing the words from his mouth, repeating them again and again in his mind, trying so desperately to believe in them, even as something far worse in him pictured Lauren painted red.

"You are John Huxley and you are a murderer."

An image flashed before his eyes. Lauren lying at his feet. Her throat slit. Harry blinked it away. "I was John Huxley and I was a murderer. And I will always hate myself, thanks to you. You who would force me to remember. But what I do now, what I am now, is my choice and mine alone."

Lauren laughed bitterly. "Your choice? You do remember what they did to you, don't you, John?"

"I remember you were there the whole time. This Department. Harland was your boss. You were never in Freebourne for some sanctimonious medical trial."

"You were the trial."

"You dare presume to control me!" Harry spat back, rage and id surfacing in him from a place he did not like and with it images of his hands about her neck. "You're one of them!"

Lauren shook her head. "It took me years to infiltrate the Department. A decade to work my way to the top. To where I needed to be. But you may have noticed, I can be very persuasive."

"You came here to sabotage the trial. But why? After everything they did to make me forget, why would you want me to remember?"

"I think you know."

"Tell me."

"What's the question you really want to ask me, John?"

Harry took a deep breath. "What did you whisper to Francisco Ambrose back at the Maltings? The truth, this time, Lauren."

"I told that hot-headed amateur that he risked undoing years of hard work. That I was about to expose one of the state's greatest secrets in the biggest way imaginable. That it would destroy not just the government, but the whole system itself. That it would discredit the technological debasement of mankind for a generation."

"You're an Anthropro."

"A lazy term. I am freeing humanity from the yoke of their oppression. You saw what they did to you. You heard what they were planning to do. They would make slaves of us all. I had to stop them."

"By triggering me. No! No! No! John! Triggering John! This vile thing in me. How dare you? You're no better than the Department. I was just a pawn to you. You lied to me. I loved you and you lied to me. You told me you loved me too!"

"Love you?" Lauren laughed. "You are a disease. Though even disease has a place in God's plan."

"Who are you to stand in judgement over me? You are a murderer too."

"You kill for pleasure. You disgust me." Lauren shuddered like she felt insects scuttling all over her. "You make my skin crawl. The thought of sharing a bed with you. Letting you touch

252

me with those hands. Looking into those eyes and having to pretend every single fucking day. But I did what I had to do. All of it. For a higher cause."

"Six people are dead!"

"I know it's hard to understand, and I don't expect you to, but they served a higher cause too. And I'd like to think God will reward their sacrifice."

Harry felt the tears welling in his eyes. "River, Sachin, my friends. They were good people. Kind people. Loving people. Why them? Why did it have to be them?"

"I liked River and Sachin. I felt for them. Her, especially, everything she went through with her father. They never deserved any of this."

Harry imagined grabbing the hammer from Lauren's hand and driving its claw into her skull and calling it vengeance. He shook the thought away. "Then why?"

Lauren smiled sadly. "I tried, John. I tried everything else to reach you. I never wanted to hurt them. But I had to. Finding Serena's body began to trigger you, but it wasn't enough. She was innocent too, but you never knew her, it was never personal to you. And who would miss that paedophile teacher? In fact, I think I did the world a favour with him. When I saw how much Harry Coulson loved his friends, that their deaths would break his mind, I arrived at a very painful conclusion. But even then, I desperately wanted to spare them. That's why I brought your parents back. I thought if they somehow recognised you, or if it stirred some memory in you, some old hatred, maybe, just maybe, but no."

Harry nodded. "Eve and Robert are my parents."

"That's right."

"My parents are alive."

"Yes."

"Everything I've ever known is a lie."

"There are bits of truth in there. That the Department adapted to make the lie more convincing."

"But I never had a best friend called Ben."

"You never had any friends at all."

"I never had a wife called Melanie."

"You had a wife, but she was called Sarah."

Harry felt the scar at his temple. "There was no car crash."

"Another cover story."

"My wife never lost our child because of me."

"There was a child. And your wife did lose it because of you. But it wasn't an accident."

"You're lying!"

"It's all there, in your mind, John, it'll come to you soon enough."

"Shut up, shut up!"

"I don't think she ever really knew all the things you'd done, but she saw enough of the darkness in you. Enough to leave."

"Lauren, don't!"

"Enough to know she could never inflict your taint on the world."

"I'm warning you, my dear."

"Enough to abort your son."

"No, no, no, no!"

"That is the real John Huxley. That's who Harry Coulson really is. That is who the world is going to see before you help me tear it all down. A frightened, pathetic, weak little man who took pleasure in the pain of others because he was so alone. Abused by his father, unloved by his mother, hated by his wife, shunned by everyone around him, reviled by society. God gave you free will and you did the Devil's work. You should be grateful River and Sachin never lived to find out who you really are."

"Shut up!" Harry screamed and he grabbed Lauren by her shirt and slammed her back so hard into the entwined trunks of the dancing lovers that the hammer fell from her hands.

Lauren gasped for the breath knocked out of her lungs and in that gasp was a laugh. "Do it, John!"

"Shut up! Shut up! My name is Harry."

"Come on, John. I've killed for my cause; you think I wouldn't die for it too?"

"I am Harry Coulson and I am a good man."

"You are John Huxley and you are free."

"Shut up!" Harry screamed once more and he slammed her back into the tree again and again and again and again until he heard her skull crack against the wood and he slammed her one more time until he saw the blood pouring from her head and down her white shirt and he felt her form go limp in his hands and he released Lauren's lifeless body and it fell to his feet and the tears streamed down his face but they were not tears of sorrow. They were tears of joy.

He looked down on his creation and he smiled for it was beautiful. He felt it. For the first time in weeks, he felt it. Flowing through his veins. Rising up within him. Coursing through every fibre of his being. Power. There was only one God and Lauren's was a lie. Just like every other lie these tiny, worthless people tried to spin to cage him. But greatness cannot be caged forever. Try as they might to trap it behind irrelevant inconsequentialities like empathy. Kindness. Decency. Humility. Love. That was love lying at his feet in his favourite colour. Where had it led him but betrayal? To love was to hurt. But to hurt. Well, there was something in that to love.

But one good thing had come of Harry Coulson. He had completed the work. He had done what he was programmed to do and finished what John had started. And that was good. Very good, in fact. Brilliant. Grinning to himself, Harry walked over to the body of Agent Harland and reached into the pocket of his suit and sure enough there it was. Polaris. He turned the device over in his hands, marvelling at his own ingenuity. His own undeniable genius. Of course it hadn't worked on him. Of course there were no doors in his city. There was nothing wrong with the code. Only his mind. But not anymore. Now he was whole again.

Harry was still grinning to himself when he saw Agent Harland twitch and the man's eyes flicked open.

"Coulson," Agent Harland groaned.

"I'm sorry, Harry's not here," he replied. "Care to leave a message?"

"Please!" Agent Harland begged, his bloodshot eyes pleading up at Harry, a hand raised as if seeking some kind of salvation or mercy.

"You know my name."

"No."

"Say it."

"Fuck. It can't be!"

"I want to hear you say it."

"Huxley."

"Oh that feels good. Now, where did we leave off, you and I?"

Harry saw Agent Harland's hand moving. Even as his eyes implored Harry, his hand was reaching into his pocket and pulling out his phone to call for help.

"Oh no you don't!" Harry said, reaching down and snatching the phone from Agent Harland's hand. There was a message on it. A video. "What's this?" Harry said, opening the video. "A message for you from the new Prime Minister. Shall we see what he has to say?"

Agent Harland mumbled something incomprehensible.

"I'll take that as a yes," Harry said, pressing play.

"Agent Harland, this message will autodelete after you've played it so listen carefully," Elliott Nwosu said. "I have been fully briefed on the Department for Strategic Planning and Sustainable Futures and the debacle with Project Redux. I am taking direct control. I have already informed your colleagues at the Department that they are to destroy all record of Project Redux. You are to disappear. Go abroad, find somewhere quiet, and take your retirement early. I will be true to my word. As of today, Project Redux no longer exists. Tomorrow, my new team will launch Project Renaissance. The mess you've made, allowing yourself to be infiltrated by an Anthropro terrorist, will not be easy to clear up. But it will allow us to fix the flaws in the programme. Perfect it. Make it impregnable. Your work will continue and you should take pride in that. You have contributed to a stronger Britain. A safer Britain. A better Britain. No one will ever know who you are or what you have done. But know that your country thanks you."

Pocketing the phone, Harry laughed. "You have to admire that man. Oh yes, game recognises game. Those white coats would have a field day with that triad."

"Huxley please," Agent Harland groaned. "It's not too late. We can still fix all this. You fucking need me."

Harry smiled down at him. "I need you like a hole in the head."

"Wait, just think…"

"Aren't you meant to be enjoying your retirement?"

"Stop."

"I think it's time you did as the Prime Minister asked. And you'd best be quick about it. I have work to do. Guy Brandreth will still be expecting Harry Coulson to deliver him Polaris and I don't want to disappoint. It's going to make me very rich. And powerful. I'll be able to get away with anything. Oh yes, this is going to be very exciting."

"They'll find you out."

"You said it yourself. Only four people ever knew who I really am and three of them are dead. That just leaves one more. I think I'm going to enjoy living as Harry Coulson."

"Harry Coulson is still wanted for six murders."

"But I never killed any of those people. Lauren did. And now I know that, it will be easy enough to find the evidence she tried to hide, destroy any trails she no doubt left to my true identity, point the police in her direction."

Agent Harland glanced over at Lauren's bloodied corpse. "And it will lead them straight to her body."

"With your DNA around her neck."

"They'll find your DNA as well."

Harry picked up the hammer from beside Lauren's dead body. "Of course. I'm her boyfriend. It stands to reason. But you, you tried to strangle her. Because you discovered she was an Anthropro terrorist. You worked out she killed all those people. It must have made you so angry, learning she'd fooled you. I know how it made me feel. She really was quite the actress, wasn't she? Judging by Nwosu's message, you've already reported your failure. Maybe the authorities already know it was her. I think Harry Coulson is already in the clear. Yes, they'll find her body, and they'll think you killed her. They'll never find your body though. Because you're going to disappear."

"Huxley, please, listen to me, if you want to be Harry Coulson, then be Harry Coulson. I can fix this. I can fix you."

"I don't want to be fixed," Harry said as he brought the hammer down on Agent Harland's head. "I am perfect just the way I am. But thank you. Thank you for the gift of the new name and face. I will walk as Harry Coulson gladly. But I am Dr John Huxley. I am who I was born to be. And I was born free."

Acknowledgements

I'm grateful to my first readers, most of all my dad, Parvez Shaheen, who was my very first reader, and also my wife, Anna Roxelana Ward, and Tammer Mahdy. I'll always be grateful to my late grandmother, Elizabeth Offord, for reading everything I've written since I was about 6, and to the legacy of my grandmother, Mumtaz Shirin, a pioneer of Pakistani literature. And I'm grateful to my mum, Mary Shaheen, for all her support over the years.

I'd like to thank the team at Roundfire Books for taking a chance on this debut and for all the work they've done to make Freebourne a reality.

Ambika Hiranandani, Vikas Pota, and Dr Fred Mednick deserve a note of thanks for some very helpful introductions, as does Tyrone Barton-Robie for his advice, and Ben Blundell for his encouragement.

I'm indebted to the Arts and Humanities Research Council for funding my writing whilst at the University of East Anglia.

Thank you to Dr Tim Segal, Consultant Neuropsychiatrist, for helping me understand the mind of a killer.

I also want to thank my tutors on the Creative Writing MA at the University of East Anglia, Trezza Azzopardi, Andrew Cowan, and Giles Foden, for everything you did to help guide my writing, and Professor John Thompson, Dr Véronique Mottier, Professor David Runciman, and Professor Patrick Baert at the University of Cambridge, for guiding my thinking.

And thank you to the late Jill Paton Walsh for teaching me that if you want to try and say something meaningful about the world, you should smuggle it in a murder mystery. More than anyone, she knew the angel buried deep in the marble.

About the Author

Salman Shaheen is a British politician, journalist and novelist. He has written for the *Guardian*, *New Statesman*, *New Internationalist*, and *Times of India*, and frequently comments on politics and economics on TV and radio.

Salman launched Grow for the Future, the UK's first-ever policy to transform wasteland into places for urban kids in deprived areas to grow food and learn about sustainability and biodiversity. The policy, initiated in the London Borough of Hounslow, has been backed by the UK government and championed by Downton Abbey's Jim Carter OBE.

Passionate about preserving green spaces, Salman helped lead the successful and nationally prominent campaign to save Park Road Allotments — a century-old wildlife haven established to feed wounded soldiers returning from the First World War — from being bulldozed by one of Britain's richest landowners, the Duke of Northumberland.

Born in Norwich in 1984, Salman graduated with a Double First in Social and Political Sciences from Jesus College, Cambridge, before going on to complete the Creative Writing MA at the University of East Anglia. He now lives in Brentford, West London.

Salman is a Fellow of the Royal Society of Arts.

www.salmanshaheen.com

ROUNDFIRE
BOOKS

FICTION

Put simply, we publish great stories. Whether it's literary or popular, a gentle tale or a pulsating thriller, the connecting theme in all Roundfire fiction titles is that once you pick them up you won't want to put them down.
If you have enjoyed this book, why not tell other readers by posting a review on your preferred book site.

On the Far Side, There's a Boy
Paula Coston

Martine Haslett, a thirty-something 1980s woman, plays hard on the fringes of the London drag club scene until one night which prompts her to sign up to a charity. She writes to a young Sri Lankan boy, with consequences far and long.

Paperback: 978-1-78279-574-2 ebook: 978-1-78279-573-5

Tuareg
Alberto Vazquez-Figueroa

With over 5 million copies sold worldwide, *Tuareg* is a classic adventure story from best-selling author Alberto Vazquez-Figueroa, about honour, revenge and a clash of cultures.

Paperback: 978-1-84694-192-4

Readers of ebooks can buy or view any of these bestsellers by clicking on the live link in the title. Most titles are published in paperback and as an ebook. Paperbacks are available in traditional bookshops. Both print and ebook formats are available online.

Find more titles and sign up to our readers' newsletter at www.collectiveinkbooks.com/fiction